"This mission is not a setup."

"It's not a trap for you and your men," the KGB agent assured Yakov Katzenelenbogen.

A voice over the intercom interrupted the conversation as the TU-144's pilot announced the plane's descent into Moscow.

From the air, Moscow could have been any European city. Office buildings towered over the downtown core, and apartment complexes spread to the outskirts. Not even Red Square suggested the politics of the nation at that height.

But the ZIL-151 trucks lining the runway did.

The tires of the TU-144 squealed as the plane touched down and braked to a stop.

"Shit," Calvin James muttered. "That's some reception committee."

Phoenix Force watched as Soviet troops armed with Kalashnikov rifles surrounded their plane.

D1173592

Mack Bolan's
PHOENIX FORCE

PHOENIX FORCE

Weep, Moscow, Weep

Gar Wilson

A GOLD EAGLE BOOK FROM

W◉RLDWIDE

TORONTO • NEW YORK • LONDON • PARIS
AMSTERDAM • STOCKHOLM • HAMBURG
ATHENS • MILAN • TOKYO • SYDNEY

First edition January 1987

ISBN 0-373-61327-X

Special thanks and acknowledgment to
William Fieldhouse for his contribution to this work.

Printed in Canada

1

Professor Aleksandr Mikhalivich Stolyarov removed a cigarette case from his coat pocket as he gazed up at the night sky. The Mongolian sky was different from the Russian sky, Stolyarov decided. At least it didn't look like the night sky he was accustomed to in Moscow and Leningrad. There were no streetlights, airport searchlights or pollution from factories and automobiles to distort its blackness.

The stars were magnificent. Stolyarov wished he knew more about astronomy. The state education department had recognized his aptitude for chemistry when Stolyarov was a teenager, and his studies in science had concentrated in this area. Chemistry was practical, but astronomy had a romantic appeal. Space was the last great challenge for mankind, the last uncharted region for exploration.

Stolyarov recognized the North Star, and Ursa Minor and Ursa Major—the Little Bear and the Great Bear. Every Russian knew these constellations. Stolyarov had no idea what the other star formations might be, but still, he appreciated the beauty of the celestial display. The full moon dominated the velvet sky. Its round pockmarked surface reminded Stolyarov of his late father's face. His father had been a hero during the Second World War. Stolyarov recalled how he had spoken about the battles against the Germans. The Nazis had been better armed than the Russians, with far more tanks and heavy artillery than the Red Army. Stolyarov's father had seen thousands of Russian soldiers fall in battle. It had seemed the Germans would never be stopped, but the Russian front had held firm and had eventually begun to wear down the Nazis.

Stolyarov's father had also marched into Berlin. He had spoken fondly of the American soldiers. They had sung and danced with the Russian troops. The Americans had had wonderful cigarettes, which they had traded for good Russian vodka. He had said the Americans were generous and brave.

"They are very much like we Russians," his father had claimed. "Don't believe everything the Communist Party tells you about Americans. Politicians are always telling lies. That is their nature."

Stolyarov's father had only said these things when he was certain his words would not reach the ears of the NKVD, the secret police under Stalin. There was much fear in the Soviet Union during Stalin's reign. When he died, many Russians, including Stolyarov's father, had hoped to see great changes in the Soviet Union. Some changes had occurred, but they were mostly cosmetic.

During the Khrushchev years, it became clear that the Politburo was one of the true powers that ruled the Soviet Union. The Politburo and the Komitet Gosudarstvennoi Bezopasnosti—the Committee of State Security—ruled together. The KGB was simply another version of the NKVD. The state controlled everything and decided the future of the citizens. Stolyarov's ability in mathematics and his aptitude for formulas had gotten him a fine education in a university in Leningrad where he had later become a state research chemist.

The system had not treated Stolyarov badly. He had enjoyed privileges beyond those granted to most Soviet citizens. He had a car and a television set, and he did not have to stand in line to get coffee, chicken or cheese. His wife could afford new clothes every spring, and his children never went hungry. This was the good life in the Soviet Union. Stolyarov doubted that it was any better anywhere else, so he was fairly satisfied with his life. His work was interesting, even if he had to accept the restrictions and directives placed upon him by the state.

However, Stolyarov did not like his new assignment, a posting to a tiny installation in a remote area of the Mongolian People's Republic. There were jokes about being sent to "outer Mongolia." It was not as bad as being sent to Siberia. Russians do not joke about being sent to Siberia.

Stolyarov missed his family. He lit a cigarette and stared up at the moon. His father had been dead for more than a decade. Stolyarov had loved his father, and he knew that, while the old man would not have approved of the sort of work he was doing at the installation, he would have understood why he was doing it. The government made the rules, and men like Stolyarov had to follow them.

"Aleksandr," Professor Voroshilov called as he passed the guards at the entrance of the building. "I have found you at last. You know Captain Zagorsky doesn't like us leaving the building without telling him. He thinks the bandits in the hills are religious fanatics who sacrifice Russian captives to Buddha and indulge in cannibalistic feasts afterward."

"Zagorsky is a pig," Stolyarov muttered as he finished his cigarette and tossed the butt to the ground.

"Of course," Voroshilov agreed with a grin. "He's KGB. What do you expect? But he's still in charge of security. The captain wants to talk to us about the VL-800 formula."

"Vacpalenee Lagkech 800." Stolyarov shook his head. "Remember how it started? We were supposed to develop a new antibiotic and instead we produced a monster."

"Nasty business," Voroshilov said with a shrug. "Chemical-biological weapons are just another evil of the twentieth century. If the Americans didn't make such things, we wouldn't have to either. Just as we wouldn't have to aim thousands of nuclear missiles at New York and Washington. It's all part of state defense.''

"That's what I've been told," Stolyarov sighed.

"Politics doesn't make much sense, my friend," Voroshilov admitted. "But I suppose the world couldn't get along without it."

"It might not be able to get along much longer *with* it," Stolyarov commented. "Nuclear missiles, killer lasers, chemical-biological weapons and God knows what else, all in the hands of the politicians. How long before they wind up destroying the entire planet? Why are we doing this? How did it all start?"

"Like you said," Voroshilov said, grinning. "God knows. Don't use that expression around Zagorsky, though. He doesn't believe in God. Just in the Kremlin. His prayers must be very simple: 'Please, Kremlin, don't have my friends from the KGB put bullets in my head.'"

Stolyarov laughed. He liked Voroshilov, and he wished he could share the older man's nonchalant attitude about world politics and the morality of devising weapons that would kill millions of people. Voroshilov placed a hand on Stolyarov's shoulder.

"Let's go see what the captain wants," he urged. "Maybe Zagorsky had a religious vision last night. Perhaps Karl Marx came to him in a dream or something like that."

The chemists returned to the building. The two guards snapped to attention. They were Soviet soldiers, officially assigned to protect the research personnel from the Mongolian bandits who supposedly lurked in the mountain range to the west. Of course, the soldiers were also there to help Zagorsky keep a careful watch on the chemists. Stolyarov thought this was a bit silly. Did the KGB think any Russian citizen would defect to Mongolia? The Mongolian government was owned and operated by the Kremlin. Why defect to an underdeveloped country that was virtually an extension of the USSR? It would be like defecting to the Ukraine.

Of course, as the installation was less than a hundred kilometers from the Chinese border, Stolyarov could understand why the KGB might worry about Chinese agents spying on them, but it was absurd to think a Russian citizen would willingly defect to the People's Republic of China. The Chinese could not even decide what sort of government they really wanted. Mao had been a treacherous, ruthless bastard, but at least he had been devoutly Communist and had not tried to pretend to be anything else. The current leaders in China were also Communists, but they were making changes that smelled of capitalism. Stolyarov did not understand this. Like most Russians, he distrusted the Chinese. The USSR and China had been close allies immediately after the Second World War, but the relationship had decayed into bitter distrust and resentment. Historians suggested several reasons for this, but Stolyarov accepted the Russian explanation: the Chinese were to blame.

Stolyarov and Voroshilov entered the building. The bored sergeant sitting at the front desk glanced up at the chemists and nodded. The sergeant knew they were civilians and that neither man was part of the power structure of the Communist Party, so he did not have to jump up and stiffen his body like a board every time they approached.

The chemists walked to Captain Zagorsky's office. Lieutenant Pasternak, Zagorsky's second-in-command, stood by the door. A hard-faced young KGB junior officer, Pasternak always wore a twisted smile as if he was enjoying some sadist's private joke. Stolyarov had always suspected that Pasternak had been selected as Zagorsky's aide because he was a psychotic and would have no qualms about murdering the chemists in cold blood if they refused to obey orders.

"They're here, Captain," Pasternak announced, turning toward Zagorsky, who sat at his desk inside the office.

"Show them in, Lieutenant," Zagorsky replied. "And close the door."

Captain Zagorsky looked up from his desk and smiled. Stolyarov considered the KGB captain to be one of the most repellent men he had ever met. Zagorsky's small eyes were lost behind squinted lids, and he had a wide mouth like that of a toad. Zagorsky rested his elbows on the desktop and interlaced his fingers.

"I trust you gentlemen had a productive day," the captain remarked. "How is the VL-800 project coming along?"

"We have more than fifty liters at this time," Voroshilov answered.

"Very good," Zagorsky said with a nod. "We will transport twenty-five liters to Ulan Bator. Please prepare it for shipping."

"Where is the VL-800 going?" Stolyarov inquired.

"That is none of your concern, Professor," Zagorsky replied in a hard voice.

"I disagree, Comrade Captain."

"Aleksandr," Voroshilov began, his tone urgent. "The captain is in charge of these matters—"

"Captain Zagorsky is with the Committee for State Security," Stolyarov stated. "The security of the Soviet people is of vital interest to us all, but I understand the last shipment of VL-800 was sent to Siberia."

"Who told you this, Professor?" Zagorsky asked, pursing his rubbery lips.

"I overheard one of your people talking about it, Captain," Stolyarov answered. "The individual also mentioned that tests would be conducted on dissidents at a labor camp."

"Captain?" Lieutenant Pasternak, his hand resting on the butt of the pistol on his hip, waited for a command.

"Relax, Lieutenant," Zagorsky said. "Professor Stolyarov has heard an unfortunate rumor."

"Then the VL-800 isn't being used on dissidents?" the chemist inquired.

"Where the formula goes and what it is used for is none of my concern, Professor," the KGB officer insisted. "Nor is it yours. Personally, I have no sympathy with dissidents. They are traitors attempting to disrupt our way of life in the Soviet Union. They are puppets of capitalist troublemakers and enemies of the state."

"Everyone is supposed to work equally and receive equal treatment and an equal share of the nation's wealth. That's how communism works, isn't it, Captain? But that doesn't always happen here," Stolyarov argued.

"The State has treated you well, Professor," Zagorsky said. "I suggest you be glad that you're not treated 'equally.' I'm certain your wife and children are delighted."

"Perhaps," Stolyarov agreed. "But there is no need to test the VL-800 formula."

"Then the rumor you heard is probably false," Zagorsky said with a shrug.

"Of course, if a dissident died from exposure to VL-800," Stolyarov continued, "an autopsy would diagnose the cause of death as pneumonia. Hardly remarkable for prisoners in a Siberian labor camp to die of pneumonia. The victims could be given medication, which wouldn't save them, but it would give the impression that everything possible had been done to try and save them."

"Then the bodies of the dissidents could be handed over to the United Nations, where doctors from Western democracies could examine them," Zagorsky said, smiling. "And we could get away with murder, eh? You ought to write mystery stories, Professor. What an active imagination you have for a scientist."

"Imagination is an asset to a scientist, Captain," Stolyarov replied. "It is our substitute for a conscience, but some of us have that, too."

"Rein in your...imagination, Professor," the KGB officer warned, his eyes cold behind hard slits. "And don't worry about what the State does with VL-800. Perhaps it is going to Siberia. Perhaps not. That isn't your problem...unless you decide to make a problem for yourself. I'm sure you'd prefer that VL-800 be sent to Siberia rather than *you*."

"We'll start packing the twenty-five liters, Captain," Voroshilov interceded quickly.

"Do that," Zagorsky said with a nod. "And talk to your friend about the realities of life. Warn him that careless talk can cause problems with the State, and I'm sure he doesn't want to do that. It is improper behavior for a citizen of the Soviet Socialist Republics."

"I'll talk to him, Comrade Captain," Voroshilov assured the KGB officer. "And I ask that you please consider that we have been under considerable stress here. I know you have also, Captain Zagorsky, but you're a soldier, trained to deal with assignments that take you far from home. Aleksandr has never been outside the Soviet Union before. He has never been separated from his family for any length of time. He is a fine scientist and a loyal citizen of the USSR. He's simply feeling isolated, and his imagination is becoming overactive."

"I see," Zagorsky said, smiling. "Do you see this as an accurate explanation for your behavior, Professor Stolyarov?"

"Yes, comrade," Stolyarov answered, aware he was inviting danger by questioning the activities of the Soviet government or the KGB. "I apologize for my outburst."

"Apology accepted," Captain Zagorsky assured him. "Now get to work. I'll send some soldiers along to help you with the task."

THE GUARDS DID NOT SEE or hear anything until it was too late. Black shapes suddenly materialized from the shadows. The soldiers fumbled with their Kalashnikov assault rifles, desperately trying to unsling straps from their shoulders. A long steel blade flashed. The sharp edge struck one guard in the side of the neck. Metal cut deep and severed the carotid artery and jugular. Blood splashed from the terrible wound as the soldier fell.

The other guard lived a few seconds longer. He had nearly unslung his weapon when a hand seized the barrel and shoved it back against the soldier's throat. He saw a face—impassive features, almond-shaped eyes above a flat nose. A knife blade plunged into the guard's solar plexus. He opened his mouth to scream, but a gloved hand muffled his voice. The knife thrust upward and pierced his heart. He lost consciousness as the assassin shoved him to the ground. The soldier died quickly, an expression of helplessness and terror frozen on his face.

A puttylike substance was placed against the doorjamb above the knob. More figures in black appeared. Some had crimson stains on their clothing. There had been two other sentries on duty.

One of the men inserted a blasting cap in the putty. The others stood clear of the door. The explosives expert merely turned his face away from the door when he pressed the plunger on an electrical squib that was attached to the blasting cap by copper wires. He was accustomed to handling plastique and knew the blast would be sufficient to blow the door's lock but would not extend beyond that to threaten the assault team.

The explosion burned off the lock and threw open the door. The sergeant stationed at the desk cried out with surprise. He yanked open a desk drawer and reached for a Makarov pistol. His boot slid under the desk, searching for the button mounted on the floor.

An Asian appeared in the doorway. He was dressed in black. Gloved hands were fisted around the butt of a pistol with a nine-inch sound suppressor attached to the barrel. The gunman aimed his weapon at the sergeant's face. The soldier desperately clawed at the Makarov in the desk drawer and tried to duck at the same time. The silenced pistol coughed twice. The sergeant's head recoiled from the impact of slugs through the forehead. As he slid from the chair, his boot found the button.

Sirens wailed a frantic warning to the personnel within the installation. Three soldiers quickly charged to the front entrance. Two carried AK-47 assault rifles. The third man, a lieutenant in the Soviet infantry, unsheathed his Makarov from its holster as they approached the door. The desk sergeant's corpse was draped over the desk. His brains still oozed from his shattered skull.

"Check on the sentries," the lieutenant instructed one of his men. The door was closed, but the damage to the lock was obvious. "Be careful."

"Yes, sir," the soldier replied.

"Cover him," the officer told the other trooper. "I'll watch the corridor. The bastards must still be in the building—whoever they are."

The first soldier carefully eased open the door. Peering inside, he saw nothing but darkness. He glanced down and gasped. The bloody bodies of the two guards lay inches from the tip of his boot. The trooper opened the door wider.

A long blade whistled through the gap. Sharp steel caught the soldier under the chin. He dropped his rifle and staggered away from the door. Both hands clutched at his throat, and blood streamed between his fingers. He collapsed on the floor, life draining out of the gruesome grin beneath his chin.

The other trooper swung his Kalashnikov toward the door. The lieutenant also turned in the same direction. Neither man saw the black shape emerge from beneath the desk. The assassin shoved the dead sergeant aside, rose quickly and fired his silenced pistol twice. Both bullets tore into the soldier's back, drilling him between the shoulder blades. The trooper screamed and fell forward, his spine severed.

The infantry lieutenant whirled and fired his Makarov. A 9 mm slug punched into the Asian gunman's chest. The assassin fell back, but he triggered his silenced weapon. A bullet burned through the lieutenant's stomach. The Russian officer fired his pistol again and pumped a round into the heart of his opponent.

As the Asian fell, another black-clad figure burst through the door. The lieutenant glimpsed the sword in the man's fist. The blade flashed and chopped through the officer's wrist with a single stroke. The Makarov hit the floor, still clutched in the lieutenant's fist. Blood jetted from the stump at the end of his arm.

The lieutenant wailed in agony, but his pain was brief. The swordsman raised his weapon and swung it once more. The blade struck the nape of the wounded officer's neck. Steel sliced through muscle and bone, and the lieutenant's head dropped to the floor. The decapitated body twitched briefly as the black-clad invaders hurried inside.

Two Soviet soldiers met the intruders in the corridor. Their AK-47 assault rifles were difficult to maneuver in the narrow area, and they spent a second or two fumbling with the long-barreled weapons. That time cost them their lives. The Asians shot them down with pistol fire. One invader slit their throats to be certain both soldiers were dead while the others continued to swarm through the installation.

Captain Zagorsky and Lieutenant Pasternak emerged from the KGB officers' quarters. They held Makarov pistols in their fists, but neither man was experienced in combat. Pasternak's eyes glowed, and his smile was a grimace plastered across his youthful features. He had hoped for an opportunity to kill someone, anyone. When he was sixteen, Pasternak had settled an argument with his father by stabbing him to death. They had locked him in a cell until the KGB decided to recruit him for their Morkrie Dela assassination section. Pasternak had eagerly awaited a chance to kill again, and it seemed that chance had finally arrived.

Zagorsky had two concerns: personal survival and keeping the VL-800 formula from falling into the hands of the invaders. He had never fired a weapon except at a target range. He did not have the desire to kill anyone, but he wanted to live, and he would use the gun if he had to. The captain found little comfort in the fact he held a gun in his fist. He had never done well at the firing range.

Damn it, he though angrily. I'm a captain with the Administrative and Supply Directorate, not Spetsburo or Morkrie Dela. Shooting people and being shot at is not part of the job.

"There they are!" Pasternak cried with delight when he saw a black-clad figure dart from a corner at the end of the corridor.

The lieutenant fired his pistol. The shape had already dropped to the floor, and the bullets passed harmlessly above him. The lead missiles burrowed into a wall as another invader in black peered around the corner. He removed two star-shaped objects from a pouch on his belt and hurled them at the lieutenant.

One metal disc whirled past Pasternak, narrowly missing Captain Zagorsky as the senior officer dashed for the laboratory. If the lieutenant wanted to stay and fight, Zagorsky was willing to let him. He heard Pasternak scream when the second star struck his chest. Pasternak's pistol roared as he fired at the man who had wounded him with the thrown weapon. The bullet smashed a chunk of plaster from the corner of the wall where the assassin lurked but missed its intended target.

The man who had thrown himself to the floor aimed a pistol at Pasternak and squeezed off two shots. Both bullets struck the lieutenant in the lower abdomen. As hot metal tore into the officer's intestines, he doubled up with a groan of agony. A third steel star hurtled from the end of the corridor. Sharp points struck the top of Pasternak's head. The star pierced bone. The KGB lieutenant slumped to the floor, blood oozing from his skull.

Zagorsky charged into the laboratory. A soldier jerked his rifle toward the ceiling and sighed with relief. He had almost opened fire on the KGB commander but had recognized him before pulling the trigger. Stolyarov and Voroshilov had heard the shooting. They had no idea what had happened or what to do about it. The two soldiers who had been assigned to help them load the VL-800 in crates were nearly as confused as the chemists. They decided to simply stay put and wait for an officer to tell them what to do.

"What's going on, Captain?" Stolyarov asked. "Has someone attacked the installation?"

"Yes," Zagorsky replied, gasping for breath. "They got past the guards and they're fighting with soldiers in the building. I think they may have killed Lieutenant Pasternak. Six or seven of them attacked us. When the lieutenant went down, I knew I couldn't hold them off any longer. At least I got three, maybe four of them. But there are many more to deal with."

"Who are they?" Voroshilov asked. "Bandits?"

"I don't think so," Zagorsky stated. "Right now, that doesn't matter. The mission comes first. That means we have to concentrate on protecting the VL-800 formula. How much of it has been packed in the crates?''

"Thirteen liters," Voroshilov answered.

"That'll have to do," the KGB officer declared. "You can make more later when we get relocated at another site. Wherever we set up next, it won't be in Mongolia. Damn those idiots at the Kremlin! Why they insisted on sending us here is beyond me.''

"They probably thought that there would be less of a chance of the Soviet public learning about our work with chemical-biological weapons if we conducted our activities outside the USSR," Stolyarov commented. "So what do we do?''

"The VL-800 in the crates has been safely sealed in lead containers, correct?" Zagorsky asked. He was almost as frightened of the killer chemicals as he was of the armed attackers.

"Of course," Stolyarov assured him. "We handle this stuff all the time, and we're very careful with it. If we weren't, we probably wouldn't be alive to talk about it. For that matter, none of us would be. VL-800 is tasteless, odorless and very lethal. All you need to do is—''

"I know," Zagorsky said sharply. "I know all about it. Now let's carry the crates outside and load them on the truck.''

"What about the lab?" Voroshilov asked.

"There's a destruct system built into the lab for just such an emergency," Zagorsky explained. "An incendiary device will be ignited and everything in this room will burn, including the VL-800 left here. We'll switch on the timer as we leave. That'll give us three minutes to get out of here before the place goes up. If we're lucky, all those bastards who broke in here will go up with it.''

Each crate contained four liters. Two crates were already packed and sealed. A third contained three lead-lined jars with sealed metal lids. There was room for one more. Zagorsky gestured at the two soldiers.

"One of you guard the door to the corridor," he instructed. "Keep it locked and bolted. You!" The KGB officer pointed at the closest trooper. He recalled that giving orders in vague terms was sloppy and ineffective. It was best to give direct orders to a specific individual. "I want you to finish sealing the last crate."

"You don't expect us to take time to prepare a last liter for shipping?" Stolyarov asked in astonishment.

"No," Zagorsky assured him. "I just want the crate sealed. We'll take the...what is it? Eleven liters actually crated? You told me it was thirteen."

"Two canisters are ready, but the formula isn't in them yet," Voroshilov explained. "I'm sorry. I'm not thinking straight—"

"You damn well better start!" Zagorsky snapped. "You scientists are such smug intellectuals. You think you know everything. You criticize your government, the military and the KGB, but, you come apart in a crisis like rotted fruit!"

Zagorsky realized he was wasting precious time shouting at the chemists. He suddenly moved to a fuse box at the corner of the room, opened the metal lid and inserted a key in a compartment beneath the fuses.

"What are you doing, Zagorsky?" Stolyarov demanded. He was sick and tired of the KGB officer.

"Just canceling the security override for the timer for the incendiary destruct mechanism," Zagorsky replied.

Zagorsky had lied. He had, in fact, activated the incendiary destruct device. They had three minutes to escape, but only Zagorsky knew this. The enemy could burst into the lab at any moment. Someone had to remain to slow them down.

Zagorsky believed he had decided who would be saved and who would be sacrificed in a fair and coldly logical manner. The soldiers were enlisted men. Their worth to the state was minimal, in Zagorsky's opinion. They were more expendable than Voroshilov and Stolyarov. The chemists had vital skills. They were not trained to handle weapons and therefore would be useless in holding off the enemy. Naturally Zagorsky himself had to survive: he was a trained KGB agent, an official of the state, and he would have to report the incident in detail. A trained observer, he could do this better than a pair of panic-stricken chemists. Zagorsky had to protect the scientists until they reached safety. He had to guard the VL-800 with his life. It was all perfectly logical: Zagorsky would accompany the scientists and sacrifice the soldiers.

"Bring the first crate," Zagorsky told Voroshilov and Stolyarov as he unbolted the thick steel fire door that led to the ZIL-151 truck outside.

The chemists grabbed the rope handles of the nearest crate. The box containing the lead-lined canisters was heavy. Zagorsky opened the fire door and stepped outside, pistol in hand. Voroshilov and Stolyarov carried the crate to the big ZIL-151. The KGB man slammed the fire door and hastily locked it.

"What the hell do you think you're doing, Zagorsky?" Stolyarov demanded.

"Shut up and get that crate in the truck," the KGB agent replied, pointing his Makarov at the chemist's chest.

"The soldiers—" Stolyarov began.

"They're expendable," Zagorsky replied. "So are *you*. Now get that crate in—"

Voroshilov had already removed a section from the gate at the rear of the truck. He barely glimpsed the boot that swung from the opening before it delivered a hard kick to the side of his skull. Voroshilov fell, stunned by the vicious blow. A figure in black pointed his pistol at Zagorsky.

The KGB officer gasped and swung his Makarov toward the gunman. A bullet struck Zagorsky in the belly. He heard the shot, but did not see the muzzle flash of the pistol fired by another gunman positioned beneath the truck. Zagorsky cried out and staggered backward. The gunman at the tailgate fired two more rounds into the KGB man's torso. Zagorsky collapsed, his body trembling as life seeped away.

Stolyarov was dumbfounded. He raised his hands in surrender. The chemist did not know what else to do. Asian hit men emerged from under the truck and jumped down from the rear of the vehicle. One of them calmly shot Professor Voroshilov in the head while two others loaded the crate into the ZIL-151.

No one seemed to pay any attention to Stolyarov. The chemist wondered if it was all a dream. Perhaps he would awake from the nightmare to discover he was at home in Leningrad, lying in bed with Anna by his side. Stolyarov would have been glad to simply wake up in his cot outside the installation. He closed his eyes and prayed that none of what he had seen was real.

Four Asian killers jogged around the corner from the front of the building. One man drew his sword and charged toward Aleksandr Mikhalivich Stolyarov. The Russian chemist heard a furious battle cry. He felt air rush against his skin as something slashed at his neck. Stolyarov still kept his eyes shut. If it was just a dream, he would wake unharmed. If it was real . . .

A flash of terrible pain jolted through his neck. The shock was so great his brain seized. Stolyarov's head hit the ground and rolled more than a meter before coming to rest near the rear of the truck. A foot kicked it aside as the black-garbed killers scrambled into the back of the ZIL-151. There was plenty of room in the vehicle since it was designed to haul three tons.

The incendiary explosion ripped through the lab, releasing a chemical similar to napalm, which the Soviets had been rumored to use against rebel forces in Afghanistan. The fireball instantly consumed the laboratory and the two un-suspecting soldiers still stationed there. The Asian behind the wheel of the ZIL-151 stomped on the gas. The truck bolted from the area. A few members of the hit team had missed the rendezvous at the truck. There was no leeway for waiting now. The stragglers were on their own.

The truck raced from the installation as the building burned. Windows burst from heat, and flames danced throughout the structure. The hit squad watched the fire from the back of the fleeing ZIL-151 until the blaze resembled a distant campfire. Several men smiled with grim satisfaction. A few laughed and punched their comrades on the arms, but most remained quiet and thoughtful. The first phase of their mission was complete, but there was much left to do.

It was only the beginning....

2

"How do you feel?" Colonel Yakov Katzenelenbogen inquired as he approached the hospital bed.

"Like I should have packed a white flag with my gear," John Trent replied with a thin smile.

"Yeah," Calvin James commented. "The cavalry arrived after we took care of all the bad guys, and one of them mistakes you for a terrorist and you get shot by somebody on your own side. Ain't that a bitch?"

"I don't blame the soldier who shot me," Trent assured his companions. "They knew there were enemy ninja in the Vatican, and I was dressed in ninja clothing."

"Nonetheless," Katzenelenbogen began, "you were very lucky, John. The bullet struck a couple of steel throwing stars in your breast pocket. Must have impacted at an awkward angle, because it glanced off your chest. I'm sure it felt like you'd been kicked by a mule. The doctor tells us all you suffered was a bruised rib."

"Is everyone else all right?" Trent asked.

"Calvin and Rafael were worked over pretty bad," Katz answered. "But they weren't seriously injured."

"Wanna see my Purple Heart?" James asked. He held up his left hand. The tip of his little finger was bandaged. "Rafael got a dandy scar in his right palm. It's a perfect circle. Looks like somebody put a red-hot coin in his hand."

"What happened to him?" Trent inquired.

"Somebody put a red-hot coin in his hand."

Calvin James spoke of the incident in a casual manner, but Yakov Katzenelenbogen realized that both the tough black hardass from Chicago and Rafael Encizo, a Cuban warrior and a veteran of the Bay of Pigs invasion, carried emotional scars far worse than the relatively minor physical wounds they had brought home from the mission. To be injured in battle is bad enough, but the torture chamber inflicts a special kind of wound. Katz knew this from experience.

Few men could match Katzenelenbogen's exceptional background as a soldier, espionage agent, freedom fighter, antiterrorist and special operations commander. His remarkable career had started during his teenage years in Europe. His family were Russian Jews who had fled to France after the Bolshevik Revolution. Yakov's father had been a noted translator and linguist. The Bolsheviks had declared open season on intellectuals who had failed to embrace communism, so the Katzenelenbogens had decided to move to a safer residence.

The rise of Adolf Hitler brought a new nightmare to Yakov's family. Most of the Katzenelenbogen clan died in the Nazi death camps, but young Yakov joined the resistance and fought the invaders. Already fluent in French, German, Russian and English, Yakov infiltrated enemy lines on his bicycle and quietly gathered information for the underground. He came to the attention of the American OSS, which enlisted his talents for several missions during the war.

After Berlin fell, Katz moved to Palestine and joined the Israeli war for independence. Constant battles and miniwars followed. Katz married and raised a son, but his wife was killed in a car accident—at least, it was officially listed as an accident—and his son was killed during the Six-Day War. The explosion that killed his son also claimed Katz's right arm. Damaged beyond repair, the limb had to be amputated at the elbow.

Despite this disability, Katz continued to pursue his career as a top-notch espionage agent. He rose quickly in the ranks of Mossad, Israel's main intelligence organization. He had added Hebrew and Arabic to his battery of languages and had amassed a smattering of several other tongues as well. To gain needed cooperation from the Western powers, the Israelis traded Katz for favors. He was possibly the only man in history to serve with the American CIA, the British SIS, the West German BND and the French Sûreté.

Yet Katz's greatest challenge, and the zenith of his career, was to be chosen to act as the unit commander of Phoenix Force. A five-man team of the best antiterrorists and commando specialists in the free world, Phoenix Force had been created by Mack Bolan, better known as the Executioner, and Bolan's longtime ally, Hal Brognola.

The other members of Phoenix Force were younger than Katz, but they had crammed as much experience and expertise into their lives as their years permitted. Rafael Encizo, the former Cuban freedom fighter, had been captured by the Communists after the Bay of Pigs had failed. Encizo was sent to El Principe, Castro's infamous political prison. He had been starved, beaten and tortured, but he had not broken. Encizo had eventually killed a guard and had escaped from Cuba, fleeing to the United States.

Encizo had worked at many professions. He had once been a scuba instructor, a professional bodyguard and an insurance investigator, and he had searched for sunken treasure off the coast of Bermuda. He had found his true calling when he had joined Phoenix Force.

Gary Manning was a muscular Canadian combat expert. A superb rifle marksman and one of the best demolitions men in the world, Manning had acquired his battlefield experience as a "special observer" in Vietnam. He had been attached to the Fifth Special Forces and had participated in numerous missions behind enemy lines. Manning was one of the few Canadian citizens to receive the Silver Star for courage during the Vietnam conflict.

Manning had been recruited into the intelligence section of the Royal Canadian Mounted Police. He had then been sent to West Germany to train with the elite GSG-9 antiterrorist squad. The GSG-9 was one of the finest antiterrorist commando units in the world, and as a member, Manning had received firsthand experience in urban warfare against the Baader-Meinhof gang, Black September and the Second June Movement.

The RCMP had retired from the espionage business after scandals concerning illegal wiretaps and other abuses of power. The newly formed Canadian Security Intelligence Service had offered Manning a desk job, but he had decided that, if he was going to be deskbound, it would be in the business sector.

He had risen quickly in the executive world. Manning was being groomed to become president of North America International when Phoenix Force had given him an opportunity to return to the field. The Canadian could not refuse the offer and had eagerly become part of the team.

David McCarter was a veteran of the British SAS. The tall fox-faced Briton had participated in military operations in Oman and Northern Ireland and had served as a "special observer" in Nam. He had also been part of a covert "police action" in Hong Kong and had been among the SAS commandos involved in Operation Nimrod, the spectacular raid on the Iranian embassy in London in 1980.

McCarter was an excellent pilot, an Olympic-level pistol champion and an expert in virtually every form of combat. He lived for action and thrived on excitement. The Briton was an ideal choice for Phoenix Force. McCarter tended to be sharp-tongued and a bit short-tempered before he went into action, but when the shooting started he was magnificent.

Calvin James had not been one of the original five members of Phoenix Force. The tall, lanky black dude had been recruited for a mission against a terrorist outfit known as the Black Alchemists. James had been a SEAL team member when he was in the navy and had been a corpsman in Vietnam. After Nam he had pursued his study of medicine and chemistry at UCLA on the GI bill, then fate had thrown him a curve.

James's mother in Chicago had been murdered by muggers, and his younger sister had died from a drug overdose. Aching for justice, he had not returned to college. He had decided the best cure for his own pain was to combat crime, and the best way to get this medicine was within the system. He had joined the San Francisco Police Department. He knew he could not join the Chicago PD; he would see every hoodlum as a suspect in the murder of his mother or sister.

Calvin James had been with the SFPD's SWAT, Special Weapons and Tactics, squad when Phoenix Force had enlisted him for the Black Alchemist mission, supposedly a one-time shot. However, when Keio Ohara, the Japanese martial artist and electronics expert who had been one of the original members of the five-man Phoenix Force team, had been killed in action during the assignment, James had stepped in to fill the ranks.

Phoenix Force had a one-hundred-percent success rate in the field. Their missions had included assignments within the United States and more than twenty foreign countries. They had been on every continent except Antarctica... and not one of them would be surprised to find that their next assignment was at the South Pole.

The nature of their work had changed over the years. Originally Phoenix Force had dealt exclusively with terrorists, and they had specialized in hitting one particular band of fanatics at a time.

However, terrorism has international connections. The KGB, the governments of Iran, Libya, Cuba and Syria had all been linked to terrorism. While some groups were totally independent, others were connected to one or more governments or shadow organizations.

The most recent mission had been an example of the grand scale that modern terrorism was reaching. A group of terrorists had held an entire nation—the Vatican—hostage. The episode had also been an example of how different terrorist groups could join forces for a common goal. Iranian and Syrian fanatics had enlisted Basque separatists and a group of ninja for their mission.

Phoenix Force had recruited John Trent for the mission. Trent had been born and raised in Japan. He was half Japanese. His father was an American, and his mother was Reko Nakezuri, a descendent of a long line of ninja who had served the Kaiju Clan for more than five centuries. John's uncle, Inoshiro, a ninja, was virtually a second father to the boy and had trained John Trent in the traditional skills and knowledge of the Nakezuri family.

However, Inoshiro had given John Trent something even more important than skill in the practices of the ninja. He had instilled in his nephew a code of honor and principles. While fiction has been more than kind to the shogun and the samurai, painting them as romantic figures, most popular depictions of the ninja have sketched them as sneaky killers in black. In fact, the shogun were military dictators and the samurai were soldiers serving daimyo warlords, many of whom were vicious and cruel. Most ninja were not assassins, but freedom fighters pitted against the oppressive tyrants of their day. To John Trent, the history of the ninja was a proud family tradition.

Trent had worked with Phoenix Force once before in San Francisco, where the ninja ran a dojo, a school of martial arts. When the commandos had learned that the terrorists at the Vatican had ninja among their members, Phoenix Force had decided to enlist Trent to join them once again. The American ninja had accepted the assignment.

The Vatican mission had been one of the toughest that Phoenix Force had taken on. James and Encizo would carry the physical and mental scars of their ordeal in the torture chamber for the rest of their lives, and Trent's survival was owed to a freak accident.

"Well," Katz began as he stood at the foot of Trent's hospital bed. "I think we've all earned a brief vacation. Do you think you can afford to spend a week in Italy before you return to your business in San Francisco?"

"You fellows told me I'd be well paid for this," Trent said with a smile. "So I guess I can afford to goof off for a few days."

"Great," James commented. "We can all act like tourists. Be nice to spend some time in an exotic setting without getting shot at for a change. I'd also like to see the sights up close instead of bolting past them on the way to the next firefight."

"We got to see plenty of the Vatican," Trent remarked.

"Yeah," James muttered, glancing down at the bandaged tip of his abbreviated little finger. "I don't think I'll ever forget it, either."

"We'll see the sights in Rome and perhaps take a train to Venice," Katz suggested. "The trains are rarely on time, of course, but then again that's a small price to be rid of Mussolini. We deserve a holiday, and Italy is a wonderful country for it."

"Damned if you didn't talk me into it, Yakov," James replied with a grin. "Let's soak up culture by day and the famed Italian nightlife when the sun goes down."

The door opened, and Rafael Encizo entered. Gauze covered the palm and the back of his right hand, leaving the fingers unbound. The Cuban smiled when he saw Trent was sitting up in bed.

"I heard you were lying around," Encizo remarked. "You know you don't have any excuse to stay here unless you've got a pretty nurse taking care of you."

"I plan to leave soon," Trent replied. "How's your hand?"

"No damage to muscles or nerves," the Cuban answered. "I've got a new conversation piece branded into my palm, but otherwise I'm fine. Sorry to say, I didn't come here for a friendly visit."

"What's wrong?" Katz inquired.

"Coded message came for us through the embassy," Encizo explained. "Our boss is here."

Phoenix Force had only one "boss"—Hal Brognola, the head of operations for Stony Man. The Fed got his orders from the President, but Brognola still called the shots.

"You mean *here*?" James asked. "In Rome?"

"He's at the American embassy," Encizo confirmed. "And he wants to meet with you, Yakov. Apparently the rest of us are supposed to wait for you to tell us what he says."

"There goes the weekend," James groaned.

"Yeah," Katz sighed. He turned to Trent. "I'll remind our boss that you'll need proper authorization to get your weapons through customs and a flight back to the U.S. I'm sure it won't be any problem."

"Don't suppose I can meet this mystery man or learn any details about who you guys are exactly." Trent was not expecting an answer. He had worked with Phoenix Force twice, but he still knew virtually nothing about the organization, including its name.

"Sorry," Katz replied. "Security. You understand?"

"I'm a ninja, remember?" Trent smiled. "Of course I understand. If I don't see you again, good luck."

3

Hal Brognola was seated at a conference table in a sound-proofed room in the basement of the U.S. embassy at 119 Via Vittorio Veneto, Rome. Two other men were seated across from the Fed. Yakov Katzenelenbogen did not recognize either man, but he guessed their nationality the moment he saw them. The pair wore black suits with white shirts and thin black neckties. Their faces were grim, and they smelled of rose-scented cologne.

"Hello, Mr. Gray," Brognola greeted, calling Katz by one of his most common cover names. "Have a seat."

"Thank you." The Israeli colonel moved to a chair next to Brognola.

"Guess I'd better introduce you guys," the Fed began, chewing an unlit cigar as he spoke. "Mr. Gray, meet Mr. Fektistov and Mr. Batyuk. Fektistov is from the Soviet embassy here in Rome, and Batyuk is the city's friendly neighborhood KGB case officer. This is going to be hard to believe, Mr. Gray," Brognola continued, "but the Soviet Union has come to us for help."

"The Soviets want *us* to help *them*?" Katz shook his head. "It's finally happened. The world has truly gone mad."

"Will you listen before passing judgment?" the Russian with the long face asked. "It is true the Soviet Union needs help, but the United States will also benefit."

"Last month somebody raided a supposedly secret installation in Mongolia," Brognola began. "It was a remote laboratory where Soviet scientists, under the watchful eye of the KGB, were experimenting with germ-warfare chemicals. What's it called? VL-800?"

"That is correct," Batyuk said with a nod. "A self-destruct device was used to burn the installation to the ground. The chemicals were destroyed, although we believe the invaders stole at least one liter of the VL-800 formula."

"One liter?" Katz said, frowning. "How powerful is this chemical?"

"One liter is enough to kill everyone in a small city," the KGB official answered. "It needs only to be released into air. It is colorless, tasteless, odorless and fatal if it is absorbed by the body through the nose, mouth or pores of the skin."

"Is there an antidote?" Katz asked.

"Antidote?" Batyuk was unfamiliar with the word. "A cure, yes?"

"Means about the same," Katz answered.

"No," the Russian said, shaking his head. "There is no cure yet. Both Soviet and American chemists are working on one now."

"*Our* chemists?" Katz turned to Brognola.

"That's right," the Fed confirmed. "The Soviet Union has given the United States government the VL-800 formula as a gesture of goodwill and to prove that they don't want to threaten us with it."

"Now that it's fallen into the hands of someone else," Katz remarked. "So you fellows don't think the capitalist imperialist warmongers of the CIA were behind the theft?"

"No," Batyuk admitted. "We think the Chinese stole VL-800. Whoever did it killed everyone at the installation in the Mongolian People's Republic. We have tried to find out who has VL-800 and where they took it. The KGB is the

argest intelligence network in the world, but we haven't a
lue where the chemical might be.''

"They want us to help them locate it," Brognola stated.

"Us?" Katz said, frowning. "I think I see a hole in our
ecurity, and I don't like it.''

"We know you are part of a team that is very good at
inding enemies of your country and stopping them from
loing things your government sees as threats," Batyuk said
wkwardly. "You have ruined some KGB operations in the
ast, yes?''

"That's right," Katz confirmed. "We've done so well at
t that last year the KGB sent a small army of Morkrie Dela
ssassins, Soviet paratroopers, GRU military intelligence
ersonnel and assorted KGB specialists to hunt us down and
ill us.''

"I know nothing of this," Batyuk declared.

"It happened whether you know about it or not," Katz
old him. "And for all I know, this is a scheme to lure my
eam into a trap so the KGB can murder us.''

"That possibility has occurred to me," Brognola sighed.

"Then why are we talking to these two?" Katz de-
nanded. He had rarely had cause to doubt Hal Brognola's
udgment, but this situation smelled too much like a setup.

"Moscow is offering a deal," Brognola began. "The
resident wants to go for it.''

"Maybe the President trusts the Kremlin," Katz de-
lared. "I don't.''

"Damn it, Gray," Brognola snapped. "I'm not crazy
bout this shit either, but the President thinks the deal's for
eal and he doesn't trust Moscow a hell of a lot either.''

"What's the deal, or don't you know?''

"Moscow gave us the VL-800 formula, okay?" Brog-
1ola began. "It's a genuine CBW weapon. We didn't know
bout it before, and they could have given us something
ve'd already found out about, claiming they didn't know we

were wise to them. And—this stuff's wicked. The President figures they wouldn't just hand something like that to us unless they had a good reason. Hell, we could make this VL-800 formula an international incident and drag Moscow through the mud.''

"The Kremlin doesn't worry about bad publicity," Katz groaned. "They didn't worry about it when they drove tanks into Hungary or Czechoslovakia. Or when they had Andrei Sakharov or Lech Walesa thrown into prison. And they don't worry about it when they slaughter freedom fighters in Afghanistan—"

"That is distorted CIA propaganda," Fektistov declared.

"Look, Gray," Brognola said, getting frustrated, "everything you've said is true, but have you ever heard of the Soviet Union simply handing us a secret formula to a CBW weapon? For that matter, have you ever heard of *any* world power simply giving something like that to a hostile government?"

"I can recall a few incidents that came close," Katz answered. "But none that were so direct."

"That's why the President thinks Moscow might play this pretty straight," the Fed explained. "The Kremlin might even keep its word about the missile silos."

"Missiles?" Katz raised his eyebrows.

"The Soviet government is worried about the VL-800 formula," Brognola explained. "Whoever stole it might use it against the Soviet Union. This VL-800 stuff is fairly easy to make. I'm not a chemist, but I understand that it would be extremely easy for somebody to get competent chemists to produce gallons of this VL-800 junk. Because nobody is sure who has this killer chemical, they might use it anywhere. Maybe the bad guys will use it on the Soviet Union. Maybe they'll use it someplace else. Either way, Moscow loses.''

"Because even if the formula is used in a country other than the Soviet Union," Batyuk explained, "the Kremlin will suffer when people learn that my government made the VL-800 in the first place."

"How do missiles come into this?" Katz wanted to know.

"You're familiar with our attempts to come to mutual arms agreements with the Soviet Union?" the Fed asked.

"I haven't noticed that anyone tells the truth," Katz said with a shrug.

"Moscow claims that, if we'll help with the VL-800 crisis, they'll give us the locations of one hundred missile silos in the Soviet Union and Bulgaria," Brognola explained. "A hundred silos that aren't visible to our surveillance satellites."

"According to the Kremlin," Katz said suspiciously.

"I know, I know," Brognola sighed. "They might be blowing smoke up our asses, but the President thinks it's worth a try. Hell, you've been involved in covert and clandestine operations longer than I have. You know that governments are more apt to keep their word in a secret agreement than when everything is public."

"Will Americans be allowed to check these silos?" Katz asked.

"That's part of the agreement," Brognola confirmed.

"It is also to be understood that the United States must respond to this by granting permission to the Soviet Union to inspect American missile silos as well," Batyuk added. "If this is not done within a year, we will relocate our missiles."

"I don't see any reason to object to that," Katz said, smiling. "It would be one less hurdle in the arms race and both sides would have reduced their number of nuclear weapons."

"Then you agree to the mission?" Batyuk inquired.

"I'll have to talk that over with my teammates," the Phoenix Force unit commander replied. "They'll have to decide if they're all willing to work with the KGB. I know none of them is going to be thrilled about the idea."

"You will be working with a very good field-grade officer," Batyuk stated. "Major Alekseyev, Special Operations Section."

"That's great," Katz muttered. "We'll have to come to some agreement about operational procedures. It might be awkward, but the KGB has to agree to certain conditions if we're to maintain security."

"Of course, Mr. Gray," the KGB case officer assured him.

"You might feel different after you've heard the conditions," the Israeli colonel warned. "Now I'd like to talk to my boss privately."

"You want us to leave?" Batyuk inquired.

"No," Katz replied. "I want you both to stay in this room. My boss and I will step outside. We'll tell you when we've finished."

"Keeping secrets, eh?" Fektistov sneered.

"You'd better believe it," Katz answered.

Katz and Brognola left the conference room and walked upstairs from the basement. Neither man spoke until they had stepped outside of the embassy.

"Are you certain neither of them got a chance to slip a wireless microphone into one of your pockets or clip one to your clothing?" Katz inquired.

"Fektistov pinned one on my jacket," the Fed replied with a grin. "I left it on the floor under the table. Tried to crunch it under my foot. Think I mashed it pretty good."

"Nothing like mutual distrust," Katz commented. "Anything you want to say without our two friends from the Soviet Union listening in?"

"Not really," Brognola said as he fired the cigar and puffed deeply. "I was pretty straight back there. The big question is: How straight is the Kremlin being with us?"

"They're never straight with their own people," Katz remarked. "Why should we believe them now?"

"If this is a setup," the Fed said with a shrug, "they're sure going to a lot of trouble. If the Kremlin hadn't just handed over a sample of the VL-800 to our government, I wouldn't even consider that this might be for real."

"It's a big risk," Katz commented, taking a pack of Camels from his pocket. The Israeli wore a prosthesis attached to the stump of his right arm. The device was largely cosmetic, with a metal "hand" complete with five fingers. Inside a pearl-gray glove, the prosthesis looked very lifelike, but functionally it was of little use. Katz shook his left hand to loosen a cigarette from the pack.

"Yeah," Brognola agreed. "But there's a lot to gain if this works."

"We'll all get killed if it doesn't," Katz said, gripping the cigarette with his lips and pulling it out of the pack. "Even if it isn't a KGB trap, we might not be able to find the bastards who ripped off the Russians. After all, the KGB has been working on this for over a month."

"You've never let us down, Yakov," Brognola stated. "Maybe we've gotten used to expecting miracles from Phoenix Force."

"Ask God for miracles," the Israeli replied as he snapped his lighter and lit the cigarette. "We're professionals, and we're very good at what we do, but teaming us up with the KGB is changing the rules pretty drastically. Damn it, Hal. The KGB is our worst enemy."

"I know," Brognola nodded. "But we might have a mutual interest that puts us on the same side this time."

"I'll talk to the others," Katz sighed. "But I don't know if they'll agree to it. Frankly, this is a bad time for another mission to hit us so soon. We haven't had a chance to report the details of the Vatican mission, Hal.''

"I understand it was a total success," Brognola replied.

"Calvin and Rafael were captured and tortured by the enemy," Katz explained.

"My God." The Fed shook his head with dismay. "How bad was it?"

"Physically the damage was minor," the Israeli said. "Encizo's hand was burned, and James lost the tip of the little finger of his left hand. Neither injury is enough to put them out of action, even for a day, but I'm worried about the psychological damage. They've survived a nightmare, Hal. After a man has been tortured, he's never quite the same afterward."

"Encizo was tortured before, in Cuba," Brognola stated.

"Twenty-five years ago," Katz replied. "Time may not heal all wounds, but it can certainly reduce the sting. His most recent experience is bound to revive the horrors of those days in Castro's prison."

"You think they're unfit for duty?" the Fed asked.

"No," Katz answered. "They're both tough, and they've got sound minds. But I've seen men who'd been tortured freeze under stress, and not necessarily in a combat situation. A threatening gesture, a careless remark, a sound that reminds them of the ordeal or a wall that reminds them of the room they were tortured in...anything that would bring the terror and pain rushing back to them could make them a liability to themselves and to the mission."

"Christ, Yakov," the Fed said, biting down on his cigar. "What do you think we should do?"

"I wish we had time to let them rest for at least two weeks and then go through some simulated combat exercises," Katz answered. "But there isn't time for that if we take this mission."

"Maybe they should sit this one out."

"That would leave only three of us for the mission."

"Four," Brognola corrected. "I think you'd better take Trent."

"Trent's a civilian, Hal," Katz reminded the Fed. "He's very good, and his survival instincts are excellent, but he isn't a professional."

"Shit," Brognola said, laughing. "He's been through two missions with you lunatics. That makes him a professional."

"I'll ask him," Katz sighed. "But if Trent wants to go back to San Francisco, that's up to him."

"Trent might be useful if it turns out the KGB are right about the Chinese being involved in this," Brognola stated. "According to his file, Trent speaks Japanese and Chinese—Mandarin and some Cantonese."

"I didn't know you had a file on Trent."

"We do now." Brognola explained. "What do you want to do about Encizo and James?"

"They're smart enough to understand the situation if I hit them with it point-blank," Katz answered. "If they don't want to go into the field right away, nobody will blame them. God knows, they don't have to prove their courage. If they agree to go on the mission, then I'm going to respect their decision. But I'll also watch them for any sign that they're having trouble dealing with stress. If that happens, we're pulling out as soon as possible, and the KGB can clean up their mess on their own."

"You know even the President doesn't always get what he wants," Brognola commented. "Nobody can blame you guys if you decide to pass on this one. Maybe the others will turn thumbs-down on the assignment after you tell them about it."

"Are you serious?" Katz laughed, more in irony than in amusement. "I know those four men as if they were parts of my own mind and body. They're not going to pass up a mission. You know that as well as I do."

"Yeah," Brognola agreed. "But take extra care on this one, Yakov. We don't know who stole the VL-800 formula, but we know who you guys will be traveling with. Like you said: The KGB is your worst enemy."

4

"I can't believe we're really doing this," Calvin James muttered as he sunk into the cushioned seat and leaned against the backrest. "And I feel like I'm going to a Halloween party."

All five members of Phoenix Force and John Trent wore transparent plastic masks that covered their faces from forehead to upper lip. The clear plastic distorted their features, yet the masks were virtually invisible from a distance. The commandos also wore black knit hats and tight-fitting gray gloves.

"Trick or treat," Rafael Encizo remarked as he sat beside the black commando. "I just hope the trick isn't being played on us by the KGB."

"I never thought I'd enter a Soviet airliner with a Russian pilot unless my hands were cuffed behind my back and somebody was holding a gun to my head," David McCarter commented. He glanced up at the Cyrillic letters that lit up on a sign overhead. The Briton did not understand Russian, but he assumed it meant he was supposed to buckle his seat belt.

The plane was a Soviet TU-144. It belonged to Aeroflot, the state-owned commercial airline. Soviet aircraft were a rare sight at the international airport in Rome. Brognola's sources and the Soviet embassy had helped cut a lot of red tape with the Italian officials. Of course, Soviet embassy personnel had the advantage of diplomatic immunity that allowed them to avoid customs under most circumstances. Phoenix Force had entered the airport with the Russians and so had passed through customs without any trouble.

"Those masks look ridiculous," Major Vikor Ivanovich Alekseyev remarked as he buckled himself into a seat across the aisle from Phoenix Force. "Do you seriously intend to wear them throughout the entire mission?"

"For now," Yakov Katzenelenbogen replied.

"We've got to consider our security," Gary Manning added. The muscular Canadian placed a backpack on his lap. He opened it and slid a gloved hand inside.

Alekseyev shook his head. The KGB case officer was a tall, athletic man with a long face. His features were strong; lantern jaw, high cheekbones and bushy blond eyebrows beneath a high forehead. Forty-two years old, Alekseyev had been recruited into the KGB when he was a student officer in the Red Army. He had been in the Special Operations Section for the last eight years.

His performance in the field had been exceptional. Alekseyev had been promoted from captain to senior captain to major. Alekseyev had been up for promotion to lieutenant colonel when he had been ordered to Rome to team up with a mysterious group of commandos working for the Americans. The idea was outrageous, but Moscow had told Alekseyev that if the mission succeeded he would be promoted to full colonel with a guarantee of making senior colonel— the equivalent of a brigadier general in the American army—within two years.

The Kremlin was clearly desperate. The VL-800 formula had become a threat and an embarrassment. The latter worried Moscow as much as the former. The fact that Alekseyev had been chosen to handle the assignment proved that his superiors thought highly of his ability. Of course, Alekseyev realized that if he failed Moscow would be less than sympathetic. His superiors would use Alekseyev as their scapegoat. He would be lucky if they assigned him to permanent duty in some godforsaken post in Siberia.

Alekseyev wondered which senile Bolshevik dinosaur in the Politburo had decided to bring these demented Americans into the mission. Alekseyev was extremely suspicious of the six strangers, but he and his fellow KGB personnel did not insist on wearing masks to prevent anyone from getting a good look at them.

"We're not hiding our faces," the major remarked.

"You're not on board an American aircraft either," Katz replied as he felt the plane race along the runway. The Israeli squirmed uncomfortably in his seat. Katz disliked flying under any conditions, and he decided he liked traveling in a Soviet aircraft least of all.

"I thought we all understood that this was to be a cooperative venture between your group and our people," Professor Sudoplatov commented, polishing the lenses of his wire-rimmed glasses with a silk cloth. "After all, we share a common concern here. *Da*?"

"Trust isn't part of our agreement, Professor," Manning replied. "Expecting us to trust the KGB is expecting too much."

"Too bad for you, American," Boris Abakumov, a wiry, grim-faced KGB operative, sneered. "You're playing this game in our court, so to speak."

"But that doesn't mean you blokes will be making all the rules," McCarter stated.

"Is that so?" Abakumov smiled. "Do you know where we're going? We're flying to Moscow. How many rules do you think you can force on us there?"

"Moscow?" Encizo asked, his hand sliding inside his jacket, toward the Walther PPK in shoulder leather under his left arm.

"We're just going to Moscow to get fuel," Alekseyev explained quickly. "Then we'll fly to Mongolia as we agreed before."

"I fail to see what this will accomplish," Abakumov complained. "What's the point in going to the installation in Mongolia? Our best specialists have already thoroughly investigated the remains of the building. They didn't find a single clue to help us track down the thieves."

"One starts at the beginning," John Trent told him. "This business started in Mongolia, so we must start there as well."

"Might help if we knew more about this VL-800 chemical weapon," Calvin James remarked. "What can you tell us about it, Professor?"

"VL-800," Sudoplatov began, "is the official abbreviation for Vacpalenee Lagkech: Experiment 800. Actually, it was Experiment 816, but the science department decided to clip off the sixteen."

"What does *vaspal*...that Russian word mean?" James asked.

"Vacpalenee Lagkech," the professor said with a nod. "I believe the English translation is 'pneumonia.' As I'm sure you know, it is very simple for a person to catch the common cold, and a cold can easily lead to pneumonia under certain conditions. Pneumonia can be lethal."

"There's more than one kind of pneumonia," James stated. "The most common is lobar pneumonia, which can be treated with penicillin and can usually be cured within four days. Bronchopneumonia and most atypical pneumonias can be effectively treated with broad-spectrum antibiotics. In the United States about five thousand people die every year from pneumococcal pneumonia. Most victims are elderly or suffer from chronic lung or heart disease. Is this VL-800 sort of a super strain of pneumonia, maybe similar to the pneumococcal form?"

"I didn't know you were a medical man, Mr....?" Sudoplatov said with surprise.

"Just call me Johnson," Calvin James said with a shrug. "And I've studied medicine a little."

"VL-800 is not a form of pneumonia or a super strain, as you suggested," the Russian professor continued. "The formula is inhaled by a subject, and it breaks down the person's natural immunity to pneumonia. The individual soon develops a severe case of pneumonia, usually involving two or more strains. However, penicillin and broad-spectrum antibiotics don't help because there is no natural immunity system to build on. So the person dies within five to ten days."

"So the victim appears to die from natural causes," Katz remarked. "Thousands could die from a mysterious pneumonia before anyone knew a CBW weapon was involved."

"Wait a minute," Gary Manning said angrily. "This VL-800 breaks down the body's immunities to pneumonia when it's inhaled. Did your wonderful CBW research-and-development teams create anything similar to this in the past?"

"It should be mentioned that VL-800 was developed by accident," Alekseyev declared. "Originally, the staff was trying to make a more effective antibiotic—"

"Did somebody 'accidentally' make a similar virus that causes the body to lose its immunity to disease?" Manning demanded. "Maybe one that's transmitted by sexual intercourse or through the blood?"

"AIDS," Encizo said grimly.

"That's what I was thinking," Manning confirmed. "Acquired Immune Deficiency Syndrome. Thousands of people have died from AIDS in the United States alone. There's no cure for it. Not yet."

"That's a paranoid notion," Abakumov snorted. "You think the Soviet Union made this disease that kills homosexuals? It is a bit absurd to suspect that AIDS is a Soviet CBW virus even if it is similar to VL-800. If you're going to raise this theory, don't forget that *your* country runs experiments in CBW weapons as well. Perhaps your CIA or the Defense Department created the AIDS virus and it got out of control."

"Cute theory," Manning replied. "But it occurs in other countries besides the United States. A lot of people think it may have first occurred in central Africa. There have certainly been a large number of cases in that part of the world. Neither the United States nor any other Western democracy has been very active in that area for more than a decade. But the Soviets and Cubans sure as hell have been."

"Bloody right," McCarter agreed. "There are tens of thousands of Russian and Cuban troops and 'advisors' in Angola. The Soviets also have people in the other African Marxist countries, such as the Republic of the Congo and Ethiopia."

"The Kremlin has used dissidents at Siberian labor camps to test CBW stuff on in the past," Encizo commented. "Maybe some of your comrades in Africa decided to use a few villages as group guinea pigs in some experiments."

"That's a ridiculous accusation!" Alekseyev snapped.

"Gentlemen," Katz urged. "Let's stop this conversation right now. Major Alekseyev doesn't have any more to do with his country's research in CBW than we have in whatever our countries are doing in the field, yet you're putting him in a position where he feels obligated to defend his country's activities. We'd do the same if the situation was reversed."

"Since this is a Russian airliner," Trent added, "the major is, in a sense, our host right now. This argument is becoming unfriendly, which means it's rude."

Trent shook his head sadly. His Japanese upbringing had made him regard bad manners as a major sin.

"I guess I was out of line," Manning said with a sigh. "Sorry, Major. If we've got to work together on this mission, we'd better start by trying to get along."

"Even if we can't manage trust," Alekseyev said with a shrug.

"No wonder our countries are always bitchin' at each other," James commented. "*We* can't even work together without butting heads."

"But we've got good reason to be suspicious of the KGB," Encizo reminded the black warrior. "They might be planning to capture or kill us when we arrive in Moscow. Major Alekseyev might not know what they have planned. They could lie to him as easily as they can to us."

"Well," Manning began. "They won't take us alive. I have four kilos of C-4 plastique explosives in this backpack. If they try to raid this plane or come aboard with any sort of hostile intent, I'll blow this craft to bits and all of us with it."

"You really are lunatics," Abakumov rasped.

"Like you said, mate," McCarter told the KGB agent, "this game is being played in your court, so we have to be ready to deal with any trick plays you blokes might serve us." McCarter smiled. "You put us in a position where we can't win and we'll settle for checkmate...even if it kills us."

"Is this the way we're going to cooperate?" Alekseyev asked. "By threatening to blow each other up?"

"That's how your country and the United States have cooperated with each other the last thirty-five years," Katz said simply. "Don't worry about it. Let's just hope the Kremlin doesn't force us to use drastic methods when we reach Moscow."

"Drastic methods seem to be the only type you people know," Alekseyev said sharply.

No one spoke for almost a full minute until Calvin James asked, "Hey, man. Do we get to watch a movie on this flight?"

"A movie?" Major Alekseyev chuckled. "As a matter of fact, the regular Aeroflot flight usually includes a fifteen-minute documentary about the Soviet Union. It shows people driving tractors and working in steel mills and some Ukrainians folk dancing. I've seen this movie maybe fifteen times. Got to tell you, it's really boring."

Laughter relieved some of the tension.

"After you saw it fifteen times—" James began.

"It was pretty boring the first time," Alekseyev insisted.

The mood within the plane lightened until the pilot announced that they were approaching the Soviet Union.

5

Major Alekseyev was curious about the man who called himself "Mr. Gray." The unit commander of the mysterious group was obviously the oldest of the six men. Despite the mask, hat and gloves, Alekseyev could still make a rough estimate of the age and general physical characteristics of the strangers. Gray was probably in his late forties or early fifties. He was slightly overweight, showing the beginnings of a paunch, yet he seemed to be in good physical condition otherwise.

The group leader had a strange accent. Alekseyev was not certain if the man spoke with an unfamiliar American accent or if he had spent his youth in England and his accent was somehow "mixed." Perhaps he was a Canadian. Alekseyev was not sure what sort of accent Canadians had. He knew most of them spoke English, but he did not know if Canadian English sounded British or American.

Of course, Alekseyev had noticed that Gray's right arm was a prosthesis. The limb moved in a rather natural manner, but the right hand was too rigid. The fingers were stiff like those on the hand of a statue. Alekseyev had an idea who the man calling himself Gray might be; not his real name of course, but he had heard stories about an elite five-man fighting unit that worked for the Americans. The stories varied a bit in their descriptions of the commando team. Some mentioned a tall Oriental, probably Japanese. Others claimed one of the men was black. One member was allegedly Hispanic, probably Mexican-American. Two were supposedly Caucasians, mid-thirties, and one of them might be British or even Australian.

The only detail about the group that seemed consistent was the description of the group leader. He was supposed to be a middle-aged man with one hand or possibly one arm.

"How long have you been involved in this cloak-and-dagger business?" Major Alekseyev inquired.

"A few years," Katz replied with a shrug. "Long enough to know better than to give details to someone on the other side."

"We're on the same side for now," Alekseyev remarked.

"For now," the Phoenix Force commander replied. "But not forever. Nothing personal, Major. Governments create these conflicts between nations. Men like us get mixed up in intrigue due to the cold war. Yet if it wasn't for people like us, spying on each other and tripping each other up, the cold war might have turned hot by now. Since 'hot' could mean nuclear weapons, I'd say the cold war isn't so bad."

"The nuclear threat might diminish if this mission is successful," Alekseyev commented. "They told you about that."

"They told me," Katz confirmed. "Governments make all sorts of promises, but it seldom means much. Last year, Gorbachev claimed he had a plan for total nuclear disarmament. That's not going to happen. He knows that as well as you and I do."

"Why not?" the KGB officer inquired. He actually agreed with Katz, but he wanted to hear the other man's reason for his opinion.

"If we could somehow get rid of all nuclear weaponry in the world tomorrow," Katz began, "the next day, someone would start making replacements. Even if the Americans and the Soviets didn't do it, other countries would. The other nations might not be able to put together ultrasophisticated firing systems with pinpoint accuracy, but they could still make crude missiles and bombs with nuclear warheads. As long as there are still nuclear reactors, there will be plutonium. That's enough for trained personnel to put together a nuclear weapon. There are people all over the world who know how to do it. You don't even need plutonium. Uranium can be used for smaller, less destructive weapons.''

"And uranium is a natural element," the Russian added, "so it can't be legislated out of existence."

"Exactly," the Israeli colonel said, nodding. "And as long as it's possible for anyone to create a nuclear weapon, your government and my government are going to make certain they still have nuclear weapons, too. It would be damn foolish if they didn't."

"Then you think the arms talks are a total waste of time and the Kremlin is making false promises about giving the locations of Soviet missile silos?" Alekseyev asked.

"I think the idea of total disarmament is unrealistic," Katz answered. "But increasing the number of nuclear weapons is dangerous. The arms talks will be valuable if they lead to a reduction of missiles and bombs. The Kremlin might be telling the truth about giving the U.S. the location of a hundred missile silos if this mission is successful. I doubt it, but it might be true."

"You and your men are taking quite a chance," the KGB officer commented. "Risking your lives for something you don't think will even work."

"There's still a chance," Katz said with a shrug. "Reduction of nuclear weapons would be advantageous for everybody—the United States, the Soviet Union, the world in general. It would also give people of both sides hope that we aren't going to destroy each other, hope that there might be a chance people of different ideologies can cooperate."

"Isn't that what we're doing with this mission?" Alekseyev said with a smile.

"This isn't a covert detente operation," the Israeli replied. "We're supposed to find out who stole the VL-800 formula. At least, that's what I'm told we're supposed to be doing."

"You still think this might be a setup." The KGB man sighed.

"I guess we'll find out," Katz said. "But if this goes badly for us, it'll be just as bad for you and your men."

"Attention all passengers," the pilot's voice announced in thickly accented English through the intercom speakers. "We are preparing to land. Please extinguish all cigarettes and fasten your seat belts."

The TU-144 broke through the cloud barrier, exposing Moscow. Tall buildings and steeples rose from the city. The plane passed over Red Square. Tiny dots clustered around a terraced structure that resembled a ziggurat—Soviet citizens paying homage at Lenin's mausoleum. The great wall of the Kremlin stood behind the tomb. Curved domes and towers jutted beyond the famous monuments to Soviet communism.

The plane continued to descend. Modern skyscrapers towered over Kalinin Prospect, a center of office buildings and huge pedestrian shopping malls. Moscow resembled Rome or Athens from the air. It was a city that blended magnificent landmarks of the past with structural achievements of the present.

At last the TU-144 swooped down on the Moscow airport. The buildings and observation towers surrounding the runway seemed to grow larger as the plane's landing gear touched down. Blurred images appeared at the windows as the plane passed the vehicles that lined both sides of the runway.

"Oh, shit," Calvin James rasped as he peered outside. "We're surrounded by soldiers."

Several ZIL-151 trucks were parked near the runway. Soviet troops armed with Kalashnikov rifles were stationed by the vehicles. Two T-55 tanks stood guard; the gaping muzzles of the 100 mm D-10T cannons seemed like black tunnels of doom. Gary Manning gripped the electrical squib wired to the special blasting caps inserted in the C-4 bomb on his lap.

"Quite a reception committee," Katz told Alekseyev. As he turned from a window, the Israeli smoothly drew a SIG Sauer P-226 9 mm pistol from shoulder leather. "Maybe they just happened to be driving by and decided to visit the airport."

"Some blokes just love to watch planes take off and land," David McCarter added. The Briton had taken an M-10 Ingram machine pistol from his briefcase. He worked the bolt to chamber the first of thirty-two nine-millimeter rounds from the magazine.

"What do you intend to do with those guns?" Alekseyev asked stiffly. He raised his hands to shoulder level to assure them he was no threat.

Boris Abakumov was less passive. His hand plunged into his jacket, reaching for a Makarov in shoulder leather. Suddenly an object flashed past his eyes. Steel links encircled his neck. The chain tightened. Abakumov uttered a feeble groan as he pawed at the chain with one hand and tried to draw the pistol.

"I can snap your neck before you can get that gun clear of the holster," John Trent whispered near the KGB's agent's ear.

The American ninja had silently slipped behind the backrest of Abakumov's seat and had adroitly wound a *manrikigusari* around the Russian's throat. The Japanese weighted chain was a traditional weapon of both the samurai and the ninja. Trent was an expert with this centuries-old instrument. He slid one weighted end into the loop at the nape of Abakumov's neck to form a noose, then he pulled the other end with one hand to demonstrate that he could easily throttle the Russian using only one hand.

"Extend your arms and interlace your fingers," Trent ordered.

Abakumov followed instructions. Trent held the *manrikigusari* taut with one fist while his other hand slid into the Russian's jacket and pulled the Makarov from shoulder leather. Trent stuffed the pistol in a hip pocket and unwound the chain from Abakumov's throat.

"Thank you," he said politely. "Now just sit quietly and I won't have to kill you."

"*V'nebrachnee...*" the Russian rasped. "Bastard. Son of a bitch."

"Sticks and stones, Mr. Abakumov," Trent said calmly.

"Just relax," Katz urged, raising the barrel of his SIG Sauer toward the ceiling. "Nobody gets hurt unless one of you presents a threat. Pull a weapon, allow soldiers into the plane, and you'll start a bloodbath."

"If anybody has any clever ideas about releasing nerve gas or a tranquilizer through the air vents," James added, a .45 caliber Colt Commander in his fist, "they'd better cancel that plan right now. If we start getting sleepy or ill, we'll start wasting you dudes."

"Nobody has any plans of that sort," Alekseyev assured Phoenix Force. "No one is threatening you—"

"That's why the May Day Parade is parked outside?" McCarter sneered. "I feel a bit sorry for you chaps. I really don't think you knew this would turn out to be a trap."

"They won't take us alive," Rafael Encizo announced, his voice strained. The knuckles of his fist were white as he clenched the butt of his Walther pistol, but Katz noticed the Cuban's hands were steady.

"Major Alekseyev," Katz began. "I suggest you go to the cockpit and ask the captain to get in touch with someone in command out there. He can tell them you've got some nervous passengers in this plane."

"Ochen korosho," the KGB officer replied. "Very good, Mr. Gray. Let's not do anything hasty, or none of us will live to regret it."

"Remember that when you talk to the pilot," Manning told him.

The men of Phoenix Force and John Trent closed the shutters of most of the windows to discourage Soviet sharpshooters from trying to pick them off one by one. James was about to slide a shutter into place when he noticed a large tanker truck roll toward the plane. The black commando sighed with relief.

"Looks like they're gonna pump fuel into this sucker," he announced. "Maybe this isn't a trap after all."

"And maybe the fuel truck is a trick to get us to drop our guard," Encizo replied through clenched teeth. "Do you know what it's like to be a political prisoner in a Communist installation? In the late sixties the United States and a number of Western European countries made a proposal at the United Nations that torture be outlawed by all nations. It was defeated. The Soviet Union and its allies voted against it."

"So did South Korea, the Philippines and a number of other non-Communist countries," Katz reminded Encizo. "Let's not make any rash decisions until we know what's happening."

"Yeah," Manning added, the detonator to the plastic explosives still in his hand. "If we blow ourselves up, it'll be a permanent decision. We won't be able to change our minds about it afterward."

"I spoke with the commander of the battalion outside," Major Alekseyev declared as he returned from the cockpit.

"We're getting fuel now. There's nothing to worry about. We'll be leaving in an hour or so."

"Why the tanks and soldiers?" James asked.

"All I was told was that it is a 'security precaution,'" the KGB officer answered. "I'm not sure what they mean by that."

"Probably similar to the C-4 'security precaution' that I've got in my lap," Manning commented dryly.

"Nice to see we're not the only people who feel a little paranoid," John Trent remarked. The ninja removed the magazine from the pistol he had taken from Abakumov and pumped the slide to eject the last cartridge from the Makarov.

"We all have reason to be a little paranoid," Katz stated. "That comes with the job."

"Good," Trent commented. "I must be getting used to this work then."

The men inside the TU-144 remained alert, and their nerves were taut with tension as they waited for the plane to be refueled. However, time crawled by without incident. Forty-five minutes later, the pilot announced that they were about to depart. Their next destination would be the People's Republic of Mongolia.

As the plane rolled along the runway, Katz gazed out the window at the Soviet troops and the surrounding buildings. He almost wished he could visit Moscow. Katz had ancestral roots in Russia. His father had been born in Moscow. But he knew the KGB had a file on Colonel Yakov Katzenelenbogen from his days with the Israeli intelligence service. Their information on him was outdated, of course, and Katz suspected they did not have a recent photograph, or he would have been recognized by the KGB on past missions when Phoenix Force had crossed swords with Soviet agents. Whatever the risk, it was too great for Katz to set foot in the city even as a tourist.

The TU-144 increased momentum and rose from the ground. The plane soared into the sky, and Katz stared down at Moscow one last time. Trent handed the empty Makarov pistol to Abakumov and stuck the magazine in the breast pocket of the Russian's suit.

"Well," Major Alekseyev commented. "We managed to survive our first crisis on this mission. Think anyone gained any trust in the process?"

"Paranoia is part of this business," Katz replied. "Trust isn't. There's still a possibility this is a trap, but it might not be sprung until we reach Mongolia. After all, there will be fewer witnesses there than at an airport in Moscow."

"You mean we have to go through this again and again?" the Russian sighed, shaking his head with dismay.

"Cheer up, Major," Gary Manning said with a grin. "A little inconvenience beats the hell out of a big boom."

6

In the thirteenth and fourteenth centuries, the Mongol Empire had been the greatest power on earth. The Mongol khans once ruled most of Asia, holding power in China, India, Persia, Turkey, Armenia, Manchuria, Korea, Georgia, Afghanistan, Iraq, Russia and most of Tibet. The Mongols were never really overthrown; the empire fell apart for other reasons. The rulers were influenced by the cultures, politics and religions of their subjects. The khans in China converted to Buddhism and embraced the teachings of Confucianism. In the western Asian countries, other khans adopted Islam. As they became more concerned with the domestic problems of the lands they ruled, gradually the empire faded.

All that remains is the Mongolian People's Republic, a Communist state under the thumb of the Soviet Union. Although twice the size of the state of Texas, Mongolia has a population of approximately two million.

Phoenix Force and their companions arrived at the capital city of Ulan Bator during the night. The emptiness of the streets was startling for men accustomed to the hectic crowds of modern city life. An occasional truck rolled across the poorly paved streets. The only car they saw was the black Russian Zim that had been waiting for them at the airport.

A Mongolian army officer, a captain, met the group on the runway. He wore three silver stars on the shoulder boards of his uniform, in the U.S. Army, the insignia of a lieutenant general.

"Dobri V'echihr," the Mongol greeted them, with a salute to Major Alekseyev. *"Yah Kapetan Tsedenbal."*

"Ochen preyahtno," Yakov Katzenelenbogen replied.

"I did not know you spoke Russian, Mr. Gray," Alekseyev remarked with surprise.

"A little bit," Katz said modestly. "It's fortunate that Captain Tsedenbal speaks Russian. That'll make communication a bit easier."

"Every school in Mongolia teaches courses in Russian," Captain Tsedenbal declared proudly. He was a small man with a wide face. The corners of his mouth turned up, suggesting he smiled more often than he frowned. "We have almost 580 schools in Mongolia."

"Captain," Alekseyev began. "You can see we have almost a dozen people in our group. We can't put them all in one car."

"Of course not," Tsedenbal agreed. "I have a truck for you as well. However, you must be tired after a long flight from Moscow. Perhaps you'll want to sleep before setting forth on a long road journey in the morning."

"We got some sleep on the plane, Captain," Katz assured him. "And we're eager to see the installation site to evaluate the evidence."

"I understand there is not much to see, Comrade," Tsedenbal said with a sigh. "The fire destroyed everything."

"We'll look at it anyway," Alekseyev stated. "I want to contact Captain Zhdanov, the Soviet officer who has headed the investigation team there. He's been sifting through the ashes and examining everything under a microscope. Zhdanov probably knows more about the remains of the installation than anyone else. He's staying at Bayandalay. Do you have his phone number?"

"Da, tovarishch," the Mongol said with a nod. "I have a telephone in my office. You know, we have almost forty thousand telephones in Mongolia. Of course, there are five times as many radio receivers, but we're getting more and more telephones every year."

"That's very good news," the KGB officer said with a nod. "I'm glad your country is advancing so quickly."

"Thanks to our great friend and benefactor, the Soviet Union," Tsedenbal said, smiling. "I shall take you to my telephone and you may contact Captain Zhdanov. Then we'll get a truck ready and prepare for our..."

He stared at Katz and the other members of Phoenix Force. In the dim light he had not noticed they wore masks until that moment. The startled Mongol decided it was healthier not to express too much interest about matters concerning the all-powerful KGB.

"Let's go to your office and get all the details taken care of before we start our trip," Alekseyev urged. "Would you care to join us, Tovarishch Cerbee?"

Katz smiled. Alekseyev had called him "Comrade Gray" in Russian. *"Da, spacibo."*

Major Alekseyev spoke briefly with Captain Zhdanov on the telephone. He told the junior officer to meet him at the ruins of the VL-800 installation and instructed Zhdanov to bring the files concerning the investigation. Zhdanov agreed. Junior officers do not argue with their superiors, especially members of the KGB.

True to his word, Captain Tsedenbal soon had a truck ready. It was a big ZIL-150, a husky vehicle with a four-ton capacity. The driver's name was Dzhambin. He was built like a fireplug and seemed about as talkative as one. Captain Tsedenbal said Dzhambin was a Kazakh and rolled his eyes as if to suggest Kazakhs were beyond the comprehension of mortal man.

Katz, Alekseyev and Professor Sudoplatov joined Tsedenbal in the Zim. The others climbed into the back of the big ZIL-150 truck. The two vehicles rolled into the street, headlights slicing through the darkness.

Captain Tsedenbal's most endearing quality was his enthusiasm for the alleged leaps and bounds his country was making in education, technology and industry. As the captain drove the Zim through the streets of Ulan Bator, he cheerfully pointed out national landmarks.

The Mongolian State Archives and State Public Library looked like any large city library, but Tsedenbal claimed it contained more than three million books. They passed a building that vaguely resembled the Jefferson Monument, with block-shaped six-story houses at each end. The Mongol captain announced that this was the parliament, where the 354 members of the People's Great Khural—the legislative branch of the Mongol government—assembled.

Surprisingly, the Mongolian government, like that of the United States, has legislative, executive and judicial branches. The Council of Ministers is comprised of the executive, but those offices are filled by those appointed by the Great Khural; they are not elected offices. The judicial system consists of a supreme court, eighteen provincial courts and district courts. Their members are also appointed by the khurals on each level. Members of the khurals are elected to office, but there is only one legal party in Mongolia to choose from—the Mongolian Revolutionary Party, which is the colorful title for the nation's brand of Soviet-inspired communism.

The supreme power in Mongolia is the Presidium, also appointed by the Great Khural. The chairman of this nine-member elite group is also the head of state. Captain Tsedenbal did not seem to mind that only members of the Communist MRP could elect someone to the Khural, or that those who were elected then decided who would run the whole government. Of course, if he did mind, he would never say so in front of a KGB major.

The two vehicles left the city limits of Ulan Bator behind and headed for the open country. The streets had seemed lonely and deserted, but the vast emptiness beyond struck Katz even more. Mongolia reminded Katz of Alaska, the largest state in the U.S. Alaska was only slightly smaller than Mongolia, with perhaps one-quarter of Mongolia's population.

Although it was summer, the night was cold. The temperature in Mongolia seldom reaches eighty degrees in summer, and in the winter it often plunges to minus twenty. There is little rainfall, and animal life is far scarcer than one might expect in such a vast and sparsely populated country.

The car and truck continued across the rugged dirt roads as the sun rose. The dawn revealed mountains in the distance, adorned with forests of pine and larch trees. However, Mongolia has never developed much of a lumber or paper industry. Livestock, wool and fur comprise Mongolia's chief exports.

"Our wonderful allies in the Soviet Union are helping us with our newest five-year plan," Tsedenbal declared, chatting about his country as he continued to drive. "We're concentrating on mining operations, you know. It is believed we have great untapped reserves of valuable minerals. Coal, copper, silver, gold and uranium are waiting to be dug out of the mountains and perhaps from the grounds of the desert."

They soon saw the desert for themselves. The great Gobi Desert extends across central and southeast Mongolia and stretches into the Sinkiang province of China. Five hundred square miles, the Gobi is the largest desert in Asia and is second in the world only to the Sahara Desert.

Yet they saw no sand dunes or nomads traveling the Gobi. Miles of arid land surrounded them. The earth was dry and cracked. A few dead shrubs jutted from the rugged tiles of hard mud. Only a handful of sturdy weeds seemed able to survive in the hostile environment.

"I hope you've got enough petrol," Alekseyev remarked. "I'd hate to get stranded out here."

"There are extra petrol tanks loaded on the truck," Tsedenbal assured the KGB major. "And extra tanks of water. That's the biggest danger when you travel through the Gobi. The desert gets only about 120 millimeters of rainfall a year."

The engine of the Zim began to overheat before they passed through the wide strip of desert. Tsedenbal and Dzhambin did not seem concerned about this. They assured the others that vehicles often overheated in the Gobi. The Mongols opened the hood, poured water into the radiator and splashed some over the hot manifold. The car needed to sit for a while, so the pair took advantage of the time to fill the gas tanks of both vehicles. They decided to put water in the truck's radiator as well. Steam hissed and spat when liquid splashed hot metal.

"We can all use a break, eh?" Tsedenbal suggested. "I packed some food. Plenty of dried beef, cheese and bread, with some bottled water and beer."

Phoenix Force, Trent and the three Russians would rather have waited until they were out of the desert, but the Mongols were doing most of the work, so it seemed fair that they decided when to take a lunch break. The afternoon sun burned brightly overhead. The temperature was only about seventy-eight degrees, but the air was leaden. The lack of a breeze, the dry hot air and the psychological effect of being in the middle of the Gobi Desert had most of the men of Phoenix Force sweating cold beads of perspiration and gulping bottled water to relieve the unnatural dryness in their throats.

Only Katz and McCarter took the desert in their stride. Both men had spent extensive time in desert environments in the past. The Israeli had traveled and fought in many deserts throughout the Middle East, and McCarter had been in Oman with the SAS and had spent part of that time in the harsh Muscat region. They realized the situation was not as bad as the others feared.

The three Russians were particularly uncomfortable. They were accustomed to harsh winters, but deserts were alien to the Soviet-bred trio. They were visibly relieved when the Mongol captain announced that the vehicles were ready and they could move on.

The travelers continued on their journey through the strip of desert without further incident. The terrain became steadily less hostile. First they saw only thistles and thorn-bushes, then plants with full leaves and small yellow flowers. Finally they encountered a prairie with grass and a few young larch trees. From a burrow at the base of a rock formation, a marmot watched the vehicles approach. The large rodents, similar to the American groundhog, were hunted and bred in Mongolia as part of the fur industry. This marmot may have sensed that man was a potential enemy and retreated, or it may simply have been frightened by the noise and size of the car and truck. Either way, the marmot had escaped capture or death, at least for now.

At last, the Zim and the ZIL-150 approached the site of the remnants of the VL-800 installation. The reports had been correct; there was not much to see. A large charred imprint marked the spot. Most of the ashes had been scattered by the wind. A few burnt rafters stood among the debris. It seemed unlikely Phoenix Force would find anything of importance among the ruins.

Another big black Zim was parked near the burnt rubble. Two flags were mounted on the hood above the headlights. The blue and red bars, with the scepter-shaped *soyombo* national emblem, capped by a gold star, was mounted on one side. Across from the Mongolian banner was the familiar red flag with a hammer-and-sickle symbol in the left-hand corner. Two men waited by the car, patiently watching the other two vehicles draw closer.

"Priveht, tovarishch," a weary, balding man greeted them with a halfhearted salute. "Welcome to Mongolia, Major Alekseyev. How do you like it so far?"

"I've been to worse places," Alekseyev replied as he emerged from the Zim. "Are you Captain Zhdanov?"

"Da," the bald man confirmed. *"Ohchen preyahtno puznakom'ettsu svami, Maeer Alekseyev."*

"Spacibo," the KGB major replied with a nod. "These gentlemen will be assisting us. You are to give them full cooperation."

"Of course," Zhdanov agreed. He turned to the muscular young man who stood rigidly at attention near his Soviet liaison car. "This is my aide, Lieutenant Vladimir Yurivich Savchenko. He is also with Special Operations. Vladimir was a sambo champion in Kiev before the KGB realized he had the potential to learn languages. He speaks Chinese, Mongolian and English. I couldn't get along without him here because he can communicate with some of the Mongols who don't speak Russian."

"Sambo champion?" Alekseyev stared at Savchenko and frowned. Sambo is a Russian form of wrestling, similar to jujitsu. "Tovarishch Savchenko, did you participate in a judo tournament in 1981 at Leningrad? It was to determine the athlete who would represent the Soviet Union in the Olympics in 1984."

"Da," the lieutenant said with a nod. "I participated in such a contest, Comrade Major."

"I saw that tournament," Alekseyev declared. "You fought very well, Lieutenant."

"Some might say *too* well, Major," Savchenko replied.

"I remember," Alekseyev remarked. "You were disqualified from judo because you killed an opponent. Broke his neck."

"It was an accident," Savchenko stated. "But after it happened, the KGB took an interest in me as a possible recruit."

"Well, the Soviet Union boycotted the Olympics in 1984, so you couldn't have won a gold or even a bronze medal that year anyway," Alekseyev commented. "Glad to have you on our team now, Lieutenant."

"Spacibo, tovarishch," Savchenko replied dryly.

"Shoto eto?" Zhdanov asked, staring with surprise at the six figures with clear plastic masks covering their faces. "What is this? Who are these people?"

Savchenko quickly unslung a PPSh-41 submachine gun from his shoulder. Alekseyev gestured for the lieutenant to put down his weapon. The junior KGB officer dropped his weapon and raised his hands. The men of Phoenix Force had pointed half a dozen weapons at Savchenko before he could work the bolt to his PPSh-41.

"Whoever they are," Savchenko remarked, "they're good."

"Don't worry about the masks," Alekseyev urged. "They're on our side. They're not Russians, but they're on our side."

"We need to see your files, Captain Zhdanov," Katzenelenbogen stated. "Descriptions of the site before it was disturbed by your investigation team, photographs, physical evidence, whatever."

"Major Alekseyev," Zhdanov said, turning to the KGB case officer, "are you certain about this, sir?"

"Check with Moscow if you want," Alekseyev invited. "But leave your records and Lieutenant Savchenko here while you head for a transceiver to contact the Kremlin. These men have to get to work immediately."

"I can't leave those records unprotected," the captain said.

"That's why you'll leave Savchenko with us," the major answered.

"I'd better stay, too," Zhdanov said, shaking his head with an air of defeat. "But I am going to contact Moscow as soon as we finish here, Comrade Major. If these men aren't authorized, you'll never get out of Mongolia alive."

"Captain Tsedenbal can verify that we arrived on a Soviet plane from Moscow," Alekseyev told Zhdanov. "Did you bring your files on the investigation?"

"They're in the car," Zhdanov replied.

Katz, Alekseyev, Gary Manning and Professor Sudoplatov followed Zhdanov to the captain's Zim. Calvin James and Rafael Encizo walked to the burnt ruins of the installation. The black man shook his head as he stared down at the ashes and charred pieces of metal and wood.

"We're not going to find anything here unless we use a microscope and chemical tests," James told Encizo in a quiet voice. "That would take months, and even then we might not find anything that will help."

"Zhdanov's team must have chemists who've already exhausted the debris," Encizo replied, keeping his voice low. There was no need to rattle the cages of Zhdanov or the Mongols by allowing them to hear the masked strangers speak English. "Maybe you should look at the files, Calvin. You're our chemist."

"Yeah," James said. "But I don't understand Russian. Professor Sudoplatov can probably handle the files better than I can. The guy's obviously a biochemist, and he's familiar with the VL-800 formula. Probably worked on it back in Moscow."

"I hope somebody comes up with something," Encizo sighed.

Gary Manning did not understand Russian either, so he examined photographs from the files while Katz and Alekseyev read parts of the records. Captain Zhdanov pointed to a sheet from one of the folders.

"You'll notice the bodies of Voroshilov, Stolyarov and Captain Zagorsky, the KGB case officer in charge of the installation security. The other two men were chemists, working on the VL-800 project. They were killed outside, near the tire tracks of the truck. This is why we believe the VL-800 was stolen. Apparently, Zagorsky and the others had set the self-destruct for the lab and tried to flee in the truck with some of the VL-800. The enemy was waiting for them."

"What happened to the truck?" Alekseyev asked.

"It was abandoned in the Gobi," Zhdanov answered. "Apparently, there was another vehicle waiting for them. They left in it and headed for the coast. We believe the thieves fled the country—"

"It says here Zagorsky was shot to death," Katz said, glancing over an autopsy report. "But Voroshilov was stabbed and Stolyarov was decapitated. Chopping a man's head off isn't standard tactics for most military commandos. The Gurkha mercenaries still use a kukri knife with a long, heavy curved blade that can decapitate an opponent with a single stroke. But it seems very unlikely the Gurkha would be involved in this."

"Herr Gray," Manning said, turning toward Katz.

"Was ist das?" the Israeli replied, easily switching from Russian to German. *"Was haben sie?"*

"Die Photographie," Manning stated, handing a photo to Katz. *"Eine Schwert."*

"Ja," Katz agreed as he examined the picture of a pile of burnt wreckage. A long, curved blade jutted from the ashes; the steel blackened with smoke and soot.

"What are you talking about?" Zhdanov demanded.

"My friend found a photo of a sword," Katz answered.

"Da," Zhdanov said, nodding. "I was about to explain that. It was apparently a weapon used by the invaders, one of them used a sword like that to decapitate Professor Stolyarov."

"It looks like a Japanese sword," Katz commented, handing the photo to Manning. "We happen to have an expert on Oriental swords in our group."

Manning carried the picture to John Trent. The American ninja studied the photo and returned it to Manning.

"It's a *wakazashi*," Trent declared. "A samurai short sword."

"That's what I thought it was," Manning said. "We've seen blades like these before. Just thought I'd check with you to make sure."

"Was this found here?" Trent asked, tilting his head toward the remnants of the installation.

"That's right," Manning confirmed. "And this gives us a pretty good idea who hit the place and stole the VL-800."

The Canadian returned to Katz and told him what Trent had said. The Phoenix Force commander nodded.

"Gentlemen," Katz told Alekseyev and Zhdanov. "We have a very strong suspicion about who raided the installation and stole the VL-800 formula. We could be wrong, of course, but we don't think the Chinese did it. In fact, we don't think this involved any government organization or the military."

"What?" Zhdanov glared at Katz. "What are you talking about? If a government didn't send agents to do this, then who did it?"

"A criminal organization," Katz replied. "A worldwide network of Asian criminals. Very clever, very ambitious, very dangerous. We know it's real because we've encountered them twice before. It calls itself TRIO."

7

Temujin peered through the lenses of his binoculars, his mouth pressed into a firm line. The young Mongol had been watching the site of what remained of the Russian installation since the first Zim had arrived with Captain Zhdanov and Lieutenant Savchenko. The Russians had been there before, and it had not seemed very important until Temujin realized the two men were waiting for someone. Then the second car and the Soviet truck arrived.

Six men were among the newcomers. Six strange individuals who wore masks and gloves as if trying to hide their identity from the Soviets. Temujin decided he should watch and learn more about these bizarre strangers. He had heard his father speak of five men, five special enemies who had caused two great operations to fail.

"Lord Temujin," Yumjaagiyin began. "Are these men a threat to us?"

"Anyone who is not a member of the brotherhood of TRIO is a threat," Temujin declared as he lowered the binoculars.

He was a serious man with a slender rock-hard body and a sleek head with fierce features. His eyes resembled black almonds, and a long mustache drooped from the corners of his mouth. Temujin was only twenty-six years old, but he was accustomed to command. He was used to giving orders and to being obeyed.

Temujin was the eldest son of Tosha Khan. He believed his father was a great man, a man of destiny. Tosha Khan believed he was descended from the great Genghis Khan, who had united the Mongol and Tartar tribes and had conquered Northern China, Korea, Iraq, Iran and most of Russia. A family legend led Tosha Khan to believe that a distant ancestor had been a concubine of Genghis Khan. Thus, he believed it was his birthright to rule an empire.

But Tosha Khan's inheritance was only stories of the past greatness of the Mongol Empire. The Mongols had not been a world power for six hundred years. Tosha Khan believed the Mongol nation would have risen to its former greatness if the Soviet Union had not thrust communism upon his country, making it a puppet of the USSR. Yet Genghis Khan had also been born into a world full of enemies and oppressors. Now, the man who claimed to be his descendant was determined to triumph over the Soviets.

Tosha Khan had realized he could not have a military or political empire... not yet. So he had built a shadow empire, a criminal network that extended across Asia and had branches in Europe and the South Pacific. He called this crime network the New Horde, his own modern version of the Golden Horde. Led by Batu Khan, grandson of Genghis, the Golden Horde had invaded Eastern Europe and had forced the Russian princes to surrender. One day, Tosha Khan vowed, the New Horde would repeat this historical victory and crush the Soviet Union.

Although Tosha Khan's dreams of conquest were unrealistic, the Mongol was not stupid. He realized that nothing could be accomplished without hard work and discipline, and he also knew that power consisted of more than mere wealth. While most people mistakenly saw money as the root of all power, Tosha Khan understood that real power was found in people. The man who influences and controls the most people has the most power. The path to that influence and control lay in connections.

Every successful politician and world leader had understood this fact. Presidents and prime ministers formed symbiotic relationships with the heads of major corporations, business tycoons, union leaders and the chairmen of international banking conglomerates. Tyrants and terrorists might casually butcher women and children, but they seldom harmed television newsmen who provided them with the opportunity to reach a wider audience. Any audience. In turn, television networks presented any news story—right wing, left wing or simply insane—if it attracted more viewers.

Tosha Khan had helped create TRIO because it increased his power over others. It was a consortium of crime. His partners—Wang Tse-tu, the head of the Black Serpent Tong, and Shimo Goro, the chief of the Snake Clan yakuza, a Chinese and a Japanese—were traditional enemies and former rivals in the shadowy world of crime. And both had been competing with Tosha Khan's New Horde. However, the three mighty Asian crime networks had formed a merger for their own mutual gain.

None of the three heads of TRIO cared much for the other two. Yet their combined forces gave them more influence and power than they could have hoped to achieve separately. Tosha Khan was willing to continue the partnership as long as it suited his needs, but he fully intended to seize control of the entire organization.

Tosha Khan had named his son "Temujin" because this had been the original name of Genghis Khan himself. Temujin shared his father's ambitions and lust for power. He too believed that dominating nations, if not the entire planet, was his destiny. The son of Tosha Khan had been mamed Temujin in hope that one day he too would become "Genghis"—"Precious Warrior Lord."

As Temujin watched the figures move about near the charred carcass of the Soviet VL-800 installation, he considered a plan of action. Temujin was his father's eyes and ears in his native land. His father had told him to command the New Horde in Mongolia. The young man had been told to supervise the surveillance of the burnt installation and to gather intelligence about the Russians' activities. Temujin had not been ordered to take any direct action against the enemy.

However, Tosha Khan had not anticipated the special devil team. Temujin could not be certain that these masked strangers were the same warriors who had caused TRIO so much grief in the past, but their presence at the installation suggested they might be. They must be important, he reasoned, and separate from the Russian pigs who accompanied them.

How did one deal with an enemy? Temujin knew the answer. In the year 1219, several Mongol traders and merchants had been murdered in the Khoresm, a huge Turkish empire that had once included Iraq and Iran. Genghis Khan had responded to this outrage by launching his armies into battle. They had massacred the Khoresm forces and had charged across Turkestan to seize control of the empire.

If Temujin was to be truly worthy of his honored name, could he allow a handful of opponents to escape unscathed? The young Mongol leader had not brought an army to the cedar forest at the base of the mountain, where he observed the enemy from a densely camouflaged position. Yumjaagiyin and two other New Horde members were his only companions. Since they were disguised as common peasants, the group had not armed themselves with automatic weapons. To attack the enemy would be suicide, but there was another way that might allow Temujin to report the incident to his father and claim blood vengeance as well.

"Go to the radio," Temujin told Yumjaagiyin. "Contact Balor and tell him to get his band of cutthroats together. We will pay well for their services."

THE ZIM DRIVEN by Captain Tsedenbal and the the ZIL-150 truck driven by Dzhambin headed north, back to Ulan Bator. Phoenix Force, John Trent and their three Soviet companions rode in the vehicles as before. Major Alekseyev and Boris Abakumov were still questioning Katz about TRIO. Professor Sudoplatov wisely decided to let them discuss the matter without getting involved in the conversation.

"A giant secret Asian crime syndicate," Abakumov scoffed. "It is absurd. Who is the leader, Gray? Is his name Fu Manchu?"

"Have you ever heard of the Triad?" Katz inquired. "Or don't they bother to teach you fellows that sort of trivial stuff when you're training for the KGB?"

"I've heard of the Triad," Alekseyev stated. "It's a Chinese criminal outfit. They're supposed to be involved in the opium trade in the Golden Triangle. They're probably involved in white slavery operations in Taiwan. Similar to the Mafia in your country."

"We have the Triad in my country," Katz told him. "Probably in your country, too, and almost every place else. The Triad isn't just operating in the Far East, Major. The organization is global and has been for a long time. Triad operations have occurred in Holland, England, Australia, Canada, West Germany, the United States...the list goes on. The Triad is probably connected to seventy-five percent of the heroin traffic in the entire world."

"Then why don't more people know about it?" Abakumov asked. "Everyone has heard of the Mafia, but Triad certainly isn't a familiar term to most people."

"No, it isn't," Katz admitted. "I don't really know why. Interpol has been trying to alert police forces throughout

Europe and America about the Triad since 1965, but nobody seems to listen. A lot of top police officials refuse to admit the Triad even exists. Others say the Triad is only a bunch of teenage thugs in gangs. Maybe most people still think of the Chinese tong as a bunch of opium addicts running around with hatchets. But the Triad is real. So is TRIO.''

"You say this TRIO combines Chinese, Japanese and Mongolians?" Alekseyev shook his head. "I thought they didn't get along with each other."

"Neither do the British and the French," Katz replied. "But they joined forces to fight the Nazis during the Second World War. The Black Serpent Tong and the Snake Clan yakuza—"

"Japanese gangsters, right?" Abakumov snorted. "And these yakuza carry samurai swords, and when they make a mistake they have to cut off a finger—"

"You wouldn't find the yakuza amusing if you'd gone a few rounds with them," the Phoenix Force commander told him.

"But I don't understand why—" Alekseyev began.

His sentence ended suddenly when he saw a line of two dozen figures mounted on horseback block the path of the Zim. The horsemen had simply appeared at the horizon, dark shapes set against the dark blue-gray twilight sky. Hooves hammered the hard dry ground of the Gobi as the horsemen charged straight for the vehicles.

"They don't play night polo in the fuckin' desert here, do they?" Calvin James remarked as he drew his .45 Colt.

"Looks like a good old-fashioned ambush to me," McCarter replied as he grabbed his briefcase.

The men in the back of the ZIL-150 truck had seen the riders a moment before Alekseyev had spotted the horsemen. Manning had already yanked open his duffel bag and had removed an FAL assault rifle with a folding stock. The

Canadian shoved an extended forty-round magazine into the well and chambered the first cartridge. Encizo also managed to draw his Heckler and Koch MP-5 machine pistol from another duffel bag. Trent pulled a .45 caliber Colt Commander from shoulder leather. His left hand tugged the silk case from the long lollipop-shaped object that jutted from the mouth of his bag.

The American ninja seized the sharkskin-and-silk-covered handle of his sword and pulled the blade from its black scabbard. His *ninja-do* had a thirty-inch long straight steel blade unlike the samurai sword, which had a curved blade. Samurai swords were noted for ornate handguards that collectors cherished as works of art. Trent's sword, with its large, square black handguard, was not meant for display on the wall of his den. Everything about it, from the razor tip of the blade to the steel-capped pommel, was designed for only one purpose—combat.

Captain Tsedenbal brought the Zim to a halt. Dzhambin followed his example and stomped on the truck's brakes. Phoenix Force leaped from the vehicles, aware that the car and truck could easily become coffins if the advancing horsemen were to blast them. Alekseyev and Abakumov were a bit slower to react. Tsedenbal reached under the front seat of the Zim to remove a Stechin machine pistol from a hidden compartment. Professor Sudoplatov stayed in the back seat, kept his head down and prayed for survival. An atheist and a devout Communist since age twelve, Sudoplatov had little experience with prayer, but he was doing a remarkably thorough job of it under the circumstances.

Several rifle shots snarled from the advancing horsemen. Orange flames streaked through the night. Bullets whined against metal and ricocheted from the steel frames of the Zim and the ZIL-150. Any thoughts that the horsemen might be harmless nomads were now eliminated.

Tsedenbal and Abakumov returned fire. The Mongol captain's Stechin blazed a dramatic burst of rapid fire as he triggered a long volley on full-auto. Abakumov's Makarov was less impressive to watch, but just as effective as Tsedenbal's machine pistol…that is, not at all. The enemy was not within handgun range.

The others held their fire and waited. Manning unfolded the stock to his FAL. It locked in place, and the Canadian raised the butt stock to his shoulder as he aimed around the rear of the truck. The front sight bisected the upper torso of a horseman. Manning squeezed the trigger. A 7.62 mm slug smashed into the attacker and sent him tumbling from the back of his mount.

Enemy bullets sizzled through the air near the defenders. Some rounds sang on metal when they struck the vehicles. Other slugs kicked clouds of dirt from the ground. Most of the bullets did not come within a foot of hitting any of the members of Phoenix Force or their allies. The attackers were firing at full gallop and had no chance for accuracy.

Katz heard Abakumov mutter something about "stupid Mongol apes." The Phoenix Force commander had formed no conclusions about the attackers. First rule of combat: never underestimate the enemy. The horsemen appeared to be armed with a variety of weapons: a few Kalashnikovs, but mostly old semiautomatic Tokarev rifles and Simonov semiauto carbines—Soviet army surplus weapons, leftovers from the Second World War.

The horses and outdated firearms suggested that the attackers were bandits. Katz frowned. A gang of nomadic hill bandits would not attack a Russian Zim and a truck large enough to carry a company of soldiers unless they had a very strong motive. Men accustomed to fighting on horseback would realize they could not accurately fire rifles at a gallop. The bandits were only interested in keeping them pinned down long enough to move in for the kill.

Manning switched his FAL to full-auto and opened fire. A three-round burst struck a bandit in the chest. A pyramid-shaped wound appeared, and the impact knocked the man out of the saddle. The Canadian marksman quickly shifted his aim to another bandit and blasted the Mongol aggressor with a trio of 7.62 mm messengers. The third bandit hit the ground, blood spurting from his bullet-torn neck.

The bandits closed in fast. Soon they were within accurate pistol range. Major Alekseyev held his Makarov in both hands, aimed and fired. A bandit screamed when a 9 mm round punched through his breastbone, dropping his Tokarev and slipping from the saddle. His foot was trapped in a stirrup. The horse galloped past the Zim and the truck, dragging its wounded master across the merciless hard ground.

David McCarter and Rafael Encizo appeared from the rear of the truck. They hit the bandits from both sides of the vehicle. The Ingram M-10 and H&K MP-5 sprayed more than a dozen rounds. High-velocity 9 mm parabellums chopped into flesh. Four bandits convulsed on their mounts. An unfortunate horse raised its head at the wrong moment and took a bullet between the eyes. The beast died instantly and toppled to the ground, throwing off its startled rider. More bandits fell, their bodies ravaged by Phoenix Force fire.

Captain Tsedenbal used an open car door for cover as he fired his Stechin at the attackers. The Mongol had exhausted an entire twenty-round magazine and had yet to bring down a single opponent. Tsedenbal had never been in a firefight before, and he had never really expected to be in one. After all, Mongolia had not been involved in a conflict since the Communists had taken over in 1921. If the Chinese invaded, the Russians would assume most of the responsibility of driving them back. Mongolia's armed forces consisted of fewer than fifty thousand troops and airmen. The Mongolian air force had only fifty-three aircraft. The Soviets would not expect them to repel the Chinese, so the Mongols would simply let the Russians protect them.

Tsedenbal had never considered that a bunch of damn bandits might attack an official government car and a military truck. His hands shook as he fed a fresh magazine into the butt of the Stechin. This should not be happening, he thought sourly. Bandits were supposed to prey on peasants and farmers. That was part of the natural balance of the universe.

Then Tsedenbal's universe came to an abrupt end. A 7.62 mm round pierced the window of the car door and struck Tsedenbal in the forehead. The bullet split his skull, sliced through his brain and burst open the back of his head. The Mongol officer fell against the frame of the Zim and slumped lifeless to the ground.

Figures appeared behind the charging horsemen—more bandits on foot. The enemy was launching a combination cavalry and infantry attack, a battle plan that had not been used in major warfare since the American Civil War. However, the bandits used the tactic well. While the defenders were concentrating on the horsemen, the infantry caught the two KGB agents off guard. Phoenix Force, veterans of a thousand battlefields, had expected the enemy to have a backup team.

Katz saw a bandit yank at something in his fist. A hand grenade, the Israeli realized. As the bandit raised his arm to throw the grenade, Katz snap-aimed his SIG Sauer P-226 and squeezed off two shots. Both 9 mm rounds drilled into the bandit's rib cage, splintering bone and piercing a lung. The Mongol dropped the grenade and fell back, clutching his wounded side. Two bandits desperately dashed for the fallen grenade in an effort to pick it up and throw the explosive egg at the Phoenix Force group.

It was a bad outfield play. The bandits bumped into one another. Their hands awkwardly groped for the grenade. Fingers clawed dirt near the blaster. At last, one man closed a fist around the grenade—a split second before it exploded. The blast tore him apart, killed his partner and finished off the wounded bandit. Horses rose on their hind legs. The animals were accustomed to gunfire, but the explosion was more than they had been trained to ignore. Riders were thrown from their mounts. Animals and men bolted in panic, running in all directions.

Some ran straight for the Zim and ZIL-150 truck. Calvin James aimed his Colt Commander and fired two rounds into the nearest opponent. The force of the big 185-grain hollowpoint slugs lifted the guy off his feet and pitched him to the ground. Rafael Encizo nailed another bandit with a three-round burst from his H&K machine pistol. The Mongol twisted in a violent spin and fell on his face. Gary Manning fired his FAL and pumped three high-velocity hornets into the face of a third bandit. Most of the man's head vanished in a spray of blood, brains and skull fragments.

Two bandits simultaneously hurled grenades at the Zim. Katz bolted from the car and dived under the ZIL-150 for cover. Major Alekseyev followed his example. Boris Abakumov tried to do likewise, but the KGB agent was too slow. A sharp-eyed bandit gunman saw Abakumov run for the truck. The Mongol outlaw trained his Simonov carbine on the fleeing figure and shot Abakumov in the back. The KGB man cried out and fell near the rear of the Zim.

The grenades exploded. The blast blew the big Russian automobile apart. Gasoline ignited, and flames spewed across the cab of the ZIL-150. Burning metal debris crashed to earth. So did the charred and bloodied remains of Boris

Abakumov and Professor Sudoplatov. The chemist had never left the interior of the car.

Dzhambin grabbed a fire extinguisher from the front seat of the truck and sprayed foam on the flames that shrouded the cab. McCarter and John Trent covered the Mongol while he fought the fire. The British ace and the American ninja blasted three bandits before they could gun down Dzhambin. McCarter's M-10 cut two attackers across the torso with a long column of 9 mm rounds. Trent fired a single .45 slug from his Colt pistol. The big Remington semijacketed hollowpoint projectile smashed a bandit under the nose, shattering his upper jaw and driving bone splinters into the man's brain.

The bandits had already lost half their attack force. Some had exhausted their ammunition. Only three men remained on horseback. Some drew knives or pistols as the battle continued at close quarters. The odds were still in favor of the bandits. Eighteen strong, they outnumbered the defenders by more than two to one.

But Phoenix Force was used to taking on odds a lot worse than that. Katz remained under the truck as bandits swarmed around the vehicle. He aimed his SIG Sauer upward, between the legs of an attacker. The Israeli squeezed the trigger. A parabellum slug ripped through the bandit's testicles. The man shrieked in agony and collapsed to the ground, legs thrashing wildly as he clawed at his ruined manhood. Massive shock rendered the bandit unconscious.

Another bandit turned sharply when he heard the report of Katz's pistol. He saw his comrade fall, blood covering his crotch. But the man failed to see Katz until he stared down to find the muzzle of the Israeli's pistol pointed at him. Katz fired the P-226. A 9 mm slug caught the bandit under the jaw. The bullet punched through soft flesh, drilled into the roof of the man's mouth and burrowed into his brain.

Vikor Alekseyev slid from under the truck and fired his Makarov pistol upward at the closest bandit. The bullet hit the Mongol goon in the solar plexus and burned upward to burst the guy's heart. The bandit fell, and Alekseyev scrambled to stand as another bandit lunged with a knife aimed at the Russian's throat.

The KGB officer weaved from the path of the blade. His left hand seized the bandit's wrist above the knife as his right shoved the Makarov into the Mongol's stomach. He squeezed the trigger. The report of the pistol was muffled by the bandit's body. The bullet punched through the bandit as if he was a cardboard dummy. The shock made muscles freeze. The bandit simply stood rigid, unable to struggle or even cry out.

Alekseyev thrust his arm and slammed the butt of the Makarov into the bandit's face. The blow knocked the Mongol to the ground where he passed out and began to bleed to death. Alekseyev turned to see the barrel of a To-karev rifle aimed at his face. A bandit on horseback pointed the weapon at the Russian and smiled as he prepared to pull the trigger.

The bandit's head suddenly snapped to the side. His ear touched his shoulder, but he did not feel the contact. A parabellum round had split his right temple and had blasted the left side of his skull into a gory debris of bone and brain matter. His corpse fell from the saddle. The Tokarev went off when impact with the ground shoved the trigger into the dead man's finger. The bullet shrieked into the sky.

David McCarter had exhausted the thirty-two-round magazine of his Ingram machine pistol. There had been no time to reload, so the British warrior had quickly drawn his Browning Hi-Power from shoulder leather. He had seen that the bandit was about to waste Alekseyev. McCarter had aimed and fired, relying on years of combat training and experience. The pistol champion had placed the bullet right on target and had watched the outlaw fall.

"I just saved a bloody KGB agent's life," McCarter muttered. "This mission is really absurd."

Another bandit on horseback galloped around the nose of the ZIL-150. He rode past Dzhambin and failed to notice the Mongol soldier until Dzhambin attacked. The driver had finished putting out the flames on the hood of the truck. He lashed out with the closest available weapon, swinging the fire extinguisher and hitting the bandit under the ribs.

The blow knocked the outlaw from the back of his mount. The bandit crashed to earth, his breath driven from his lungs. He tried to raise his Simonov carbine, but Dzhambin's boot stamped the bandit's weapon and pinned it to the ground. The Mongol outlaw stared up to see Dzhambin raise the fire extinguisher overhead. The soldier brought it down hard, smashing the bandit's face. The man's skull cracked, and blood and brains leaked from the back of his head.

John Trent had moved toward the flames and smoke of the wreckage that had formerly been the Zim automobile. He crouched among the burning chunks of metal and upholstery while the bandits charged forward. The ninja allowed them to pass him, then rose from his camouflage to attack from behind.

Trent stuck his .45 pistol into his belt and grabbed the hilt of his *ninja-do* with both hands. He crept behind two bandits and struck with the deadly blade. A diagonal sword stroke split the nape of a bandit's neck and severed his spinal cord. The man was dead before he hit the ground. The second bandit turned and saw Trent lunge forward. The tip of the *ninja-do* plunged into the outlaw's throat. Seven inches of sharp steel punched through the man's windpipe, popped apart vertebrae and pierced the back of his neck.

Another bandit saw Trent and swung an old Model 1933 Tokarev pistol at the ninja. Trent immediately released his sword with its blade still firmly lodged in the throat of the man he had just eliminated. The ninja followed a basic principle of martial arts: the fastest way to move one's body from an attack is simply to collapse on the ground.

The ninja dropped a half second before the bandit's Tokarev barked. Two 7.62 mm messengers whistled above Trent's prone body as the ninja drew his Colt and returned fire. Trent pumped two big .45 slugs into the upper torso of his would-be assassin. The bandit staggered, fell to one knee and then tumbled onto his back—dead.

Rafael Encizo fired the last rounds from his H&K machine pistol into the chest of a Mongol gunman armed with an AK-47. The bandit fell back and knocked a Tokarev rifle from the hands of one of his comrades. The bandit snarled something in Mongolian and pulled an old Nagant revolver from his belt. A weapon designed in 1895—although used by the Russian military as late as 1945—the Nagant was as big as a British Webley, although it fired a diminutive 7.62 mm cartridge and featured a unique seven-round cylinder.

Encizo recognized but did not waste time thinking about his opponent's weapon. All that concerned him was the fact that the Mongol hoodlum was trying to kill him. The Cuban warrior charged forward and chopped the barrel of his empty MP-5 across the gunman's wrist. The Nagant fell from numb fingers. Encizo quickly rammed the muzzle into the bandit's solar plexus. The guy doubled up as the Phoenix pro pulled a Cold Steel Tanto from a belt sheath.

The Cuban slashed out with the big knife. The thick, ultrasharp blade of the Tanto sliced open the side of the bandit's neck, severing the carotid artery and the jugular. Blood gushed from the terrible wound as the Mongol outlaw crumbled to the ground. No sooner had the man hit the ground than another bandit attacked Encizo, wielding a fighting dagger with a nine-inch blade.

The Phoenix fighter met his opponent's charge, the steel Tanto dancing in the light of the flames that had licked the wreckage of the Zim. The Mongol knife artist realized Encizo was no stranger to knife fighting. The Cuban held his blade low in an underhand grip with the cutting edge aimed at the bandit. The Mongol's left hand streaked out as if to grab for Encizo's wrist. The Cuban slashed, but the bandit withdrew his hand and lashed out with his dagger.

Encizo raised the empty MP-5 in his left hand. The steel frame blocked the bandit's knife thrust. Encizo's right arm whipped forward, and the edge of his Tanto sliced the nerve center at his opponent's armpit. The Mongol screamed and dropped his dagger, blood oozing under his arm. Encizo executed a backhand sweep, slashing the knife across the wounded man's throat. Crimson spilled onto the bandit's shirt front as he stumbled backward. The Mongol pawed at his slit throat. His eyes rolled upward, and he sank to the ground as if suddenly bored with life and willing to accept death—not that he had a choice.

Gary Manning fired a three-round burst from his FAL rifle and drilled the trio of 7.62 mm slugs into the face of an attacker. Bullets burst the guy's eyeballs in their sockets and burned through his brain before finding the back of his skull.

A large shape loomed up in the Canadian's peripheral vision. Manning turned sharply to face the last bandit on horseback. The Mongol outlaw lashed out with a Simonov carbine. He had used all his ammo and was holding the weapon by the barrel, using it as a club. The wooden stock missed Manning's head, but it connected with the FAL and knocked the rifle from the Phoenix pro's grasp.

Manning leaped forward and seized the Mongol before his opponent could swing the empty carbine again. The Canadian grabbed the bandit's shirt front and hauled him out of the saddle as the horse bolted out from under him. Manning jammed a hand into the startled man's crotch and lifted him overhead like a weight lifter performing a military press.

Another bandit saw this as an ideal opportunity to rush forward and plunge a knife between the Canadian's ribs. He charged toward Manning, but the Phoenix strongman hurled the first bandit at the knife man. Mongol outlaw crashed into Mongol outlaw and both men hit the ground, dazed. Manning did not give them a chance to recover. He rushed forward and stomped on the neck of one bandit, crunching vertebrae under his boot heel. The other outlaw gazed up to see Manning's fist rocket into his face. The punch broke his nose and knocked him out cold.

Calvin James pumped two .45 caliber slugs into the belly and chest of a gun-wielding bandit. The guy went down, and James saw the slide to his Colt had locked back to reveal the empty breech. He reached for a fresh magazine and pressed the release catch to dump the spent mag from the butt of his Commander.

Suddenly a bandit attacked, swinging an empty Tokarev rifle like an axe. James sidestepped the attack and hooked a tae kwon do kick at his opponent's gut. The bandit doubled up with a groan, and the stock of the Tokarev struck the ground hard. James chopped the butt of his Colt into the man's kidney. The bandit howled in pain but suddenly whirled and lashed out with the rifle.

The wood stock struck James's forearm. The blow stunned the ulna nerve, and James's fist opened, the Commander falling from his hand. The Mongol outlaw raised his Tokarev and swung a kick at the black man's groin. James shifted a leg to protect himself, and the bandit's boot hit thigh muscle, but the outlaw slashed the Tokarev at the Phoenix fighter's face.

James ducked under the butt stroke and rammed a fist into his opponent's solar plexus. He hooked a heel-of-the-palm blow at the man's forearm to keep the bandit off-balance as he shuffled to the outlaw's side. James drove a knee at the guy's abdomen, and the Mongol doubled up once more. The black man chopped the side of his hand across the nape of his opponent's neck. The bandit fell on his face. James kicked him behind the ear to make sure the guy would not get up for a while.

The last bandit tried to bury a knife in Dzhambin's right kidney. The Mongol soldier turned as the blade flashed. Sharp steel cut Dzhambin along the rib cage. He cried out in pain and pumped an elbow into the face of his attacker. The bandit staggered from the blow, blood trickling from a nostril. He prepared to lunge with the knife, but David McCarter shot him between the eyes with his Browning Hi-Power.

"Well, pil-grim," McCarter remarked like John Wayne, as he blew smoke from the muzzle of his pistol, "I reckon that wraps it up."

"Hardly," Yakov Katzenelenbogen replied. "This is just the beginning. This attack wasn't happenstance. Somebody sent those bandits to kill us."

"And you still believe this TRIO organization is responsible?" Alekseyev asked. The Russian fumbled in his pocket for his cigarettes.

"More than ever," the Israeli confirmed. "Whoever sent the bandits must have been watching us at the installation. They must have had an idea who we were and decided they had to get rid of us fast."

"How could they know who you are behind those damn masks?" the Russian demanded as he lit a cigarette.

"TRIO probably has a general description of us," Katz answered. "Just as your people in the KGB have. TRIO is worried, although they might have less reason to be than they realize.''

''Dzhambin isn't hurt badly,'' Calvin James, the unit medic announced. ''Knife just grazed him. Still, I think somebody else should drive the truck. Our Mongol friend did pretty well in a firefight. So did you, Major.''

''We're sorry about Abakumov and Professor Sudoplatov,'' Manning told the KGB officer. ''Nobody knew anything like this would happen.''

''I was responsible for them,'' Alekseyev said grimly. ''I should have arranged better security.''

''It wasn't your fault, Major,'' Katz assured him. ''You have no reason to feel guilty. However, we must concentrate on the mission now, so that their deaths were not in vain.''

''You are right. Let's get out of here,'' Alekseyev replied.

8

Colonel Vasily Pushkin grimly listened to Major Alekseyev's report. The KGB director of special operations in the Mongolian People's Republic was not pleased with the story, nor was he happy about the masked stranger Alekseyev had brought into his office at the Soviet embassy in Ulan Bator. The man called himself Gray and was supposed to be some sort of superspy or ultimate warrior working for the Americans.

"If I didn't have orders directly from the Kremlin that I am to cooperate with you people," Pushkin declared, glaring at the two men who sat facing his desk, "I would have you arrested. That includes you, Comrade Alekseyev."

"Don't even think of it, Colonel," Katzenelenbogen warned.

"You dare threaten me?" Pushkin demanded. "Might I remind you that this embassy is the property of the Union of Soviet Socialist Republics?"

"If you try to arrest us," Katz said mildly, "this embassy will be a pile of smoking rubble. But let's not be unpleasant, Colonel. There's been enough unpleasantness already."

"A KGB agent and a noted Soviet scientist have been killed," Pushkin declared, "and an officer of the Mongolian People's Army. I'm going to have to do a lot of explaining to the Khural as well as to Moscow. That means I want some answers from you men that make more sense than what I've heard so far.''

"We can only tell you what happened," Alekseyev stated.

"And the only explanation you have is that an alleged Oriental crime syndicate is responsible," the KGB colonel scoffed. "Something called TRIO? At least, that's what this American coward who hides behind a mask claims."

"I'm wearing this mask because we're enemies, Colonel," Katz replied. "My group and I have fought the KGB on several occasions. Your organization has been involved in some of the most fiendish and corrupt conspiracies we've ever encountered, including a KGB operation in Greece that concerned a CBW weapon called the Proteus Enzyme. I don't believe the KGB or the Soviet government have changed very much. After all, your people were producing the VL-800 formula here in Mongolia."

"Then why are you helping us if we're enemies?" Pushkin asked suspiciously. "If indeed you really *are* helping us."

"We have our reasons, and if you don't know about them, that's because the Kremlin doesn't feel you have a need to know," Katz told him. "For now we'd better concentrate on how we're going to deal with TRIO."

"You should be able to tell us how to do that, Gray," Pushkin sneered. "Obviously you know all about this crime syndicate."

"Actually," Katz began, "we know very little about TRIO. Apparently it was formed some time in the late seventies. About the same time MERGE was created."

"MERGE?" Pushkin frowned.

"MERGE is another international crime network," Katz explained. "Factions of the Mafia joined forces with the Colombian syndicate that deals largely with cocaine, the Corsican syndicate, which is active in Western Europe and deals in heroin, and the so-called Mexican Mafia, which is active in Mexico and parts of the southwestern United States.''

"And you've encountered MERGE in your adventures?''

"Once or twice,'' Katz confirmed. "TRIO is similar to MERGE, although it is comprised of Asian criminals, who are well organized and very professional.''

"Don't you know where their headquarters is located?''

"No idea,'' Katz admitted. "We suspect they might have floating headquarters. The leaders probably travel from one country to another. They might supervise a major operation and stay in the area long enough to get the mission off the ground, but they seem to hand the duties of leadership to subchiefs and move on to a new locale. They certainly wouldn't keep a major headquarters here in Mongolia. Far too risky.''

"Criminals don't operate in a Communist country because our system gives people equality and order,'' Pushkin said smuggly.

"Your system is a police state,'' Katz replied. "The KGB is the largest intelligence organization in the world. The Soviet GRU is the second largest. Together the USSR intel outfits have close to two million personnel.''

"That is because we have enemies in the West who threaten our country,'' Pushkin declared.

"Then why is only one-tenth of the KGB and GRU used in foreign service?'' Katz inquired. "The vast majority of your operations are conducted within the Soviet Union. The Kremlin has its spies concentrating on the Soviet people, eighty-five percent of whom are not members of the Communist Party and have no say about how the USSR operates. The Kremlin is terrified of its subjects because, if Moscow falls, it will be the Soviet people who pull it down. Of course, they can't revolt against communism unless they can organize and they can't do that because the KGB, the

GRU and millions of paid informers are constantly spying on them.''

"Lies and propaganda," Pushkin said, his eyes narrowed with anger. "The Soviet Union offers greater freedom than the imperialist government of the United States—"

"The Soviet Union is a one-party government," the Phoenix Force commander stated. "Only members of the Communist Party have any say about the government. In the United States there are two major political parties, but one doesn't have to be a Democrat or a Republican to vote. There are also several smaller political parties—the Libertarians, the U.S. Labor Party, even the American Communist Party. A man named Gus Hall ran for President of the United States on the Communist party ticket. He even campaigned on television. If that doesn't offer freedom of choice, what does? In America a person can buy copies of *Das Kapital* or *The Communist Manifesto* in bookstores or read these works by Karl Marx in a public library. In the Soviet Union, books and literature are censored. Citizens in your country can't read copies of the U.S. Constitution or the Declaration of Independence."

"Subversive material," Pushkin remarked. He squirmed uncomfortably in his chair.

"Leaders of the SDS and the Black Panthers wrote articles that endorsed the overthrow of the U.S. government," Katz said with a shrug. "But even these books were printed and sold to the public. Perhaps because the majority of Americans would never support such politics. Americans can see both sides of any issue or political system, if they care enough to look. That isn't a system that runs on fear and ignorance. The Soviet government terrorizes its people with the secret police and threats of Siberian labor camps and government asylums for dissidents. The Communists refuse to allow the public to read material that criticizes their system or offers alternative forms of government. What freedom can you claim for the Soviet Union, Colonel Pushkin?"

"Gentlemen," Major Alekseyev said quickly. "Let's not argue about these political matters. We should concentrate on the VL-800 formula and whether or not this TRIO organization stole it."

"I'm convinced TRIO is responsible," Katz declared. "If the KGB wants to pursue the idea that the Chinese stole the formula, you're welcome to do so. But my team is going after TRIO. We'll let you know how our mission turns out—"

"Wait a moment," Pushkin insisted. "I didn't say we wouldn't pursue the possibility that TRIO is responsible. Now, why would these Asian hoodlums want the formula?"

"Blackmail, murder, to sell to other countries," Katz said with a shrug. "Any number of ways they can make a profit with it. TRIO is clever and well organized with branches all over the world. They'll find a market for the formula. Although, I must admit, I'm surprised they did something this rash. Ripping off a Soviet installation in a Communist country is very risky. Perhaps they just assumed the USSR didn't know about them and would be busy blaming the Americans or the Chinese."

"But you don't believe the formula is still here in Mongolia because this is a 'terrible police state' associated with the 'evil empire' of the Soviet Union?" Pushkin sneered.

"At last we can agree on something," Katz replied with a smile. "The fact is, a crime syndicate would have difficulty functioning in a country with so many strict government controls. Criminal organizations couldn't operate in Nazi Germany, largely because the Nazis were ultimate criminals working for the state. It has been said that the

Mafia planned to assassinate Mussolini because they couldn't conduct business in a Fascist country—''

"You're comparing communism to those damn dictatorships?" The KGB colonel was furious.

"I don't want to argue with you," the Israeli sighed. "But you must admit that government controls under communism are as extreme as they were under Hitler or Mussolini. The last public execution in the Soviet Union, sometime in the 1960's, involved a man who worked the black market. International crime networks would obviously avoid the Soviet Union and her satellite nations."

"They'd feel more at home in the United States," Pushkin commented, "where anyone can get a gun."

"The wrong people can always get weapons," Katz said with a shrug.

"This argument about our two countries isn't solving the problem," Alekseyev declared. "We need to find the VL-800 formula. If TRIO has it, we need to find them."

"They wouldn't stay in Mongolia," Katz declared. "And the USSR would be even worse for their needs. Same would be true about Communist China. That means they'd head for the coast . . . either the Sea of Japan or the Yellow Sea."

"And where would they go from there?" Pushkin inquired.

"Your people believed the Red Chinese were responsible," Katz mused. "So your investigation concentrated along the border. Did anyone consider the possibility they may have fled to North Korea instead?"

"We did," Pushkin confirmed. "One theory was that the thieves might be CIA or Japanese Kempai agents. In which case we thought the bastards would probably head east toward Japan or south to American installations in South Korea."

Katz rose from his chair and approached a map of the world that hung on a wall. The Israeli gazed at eastern Asia.

He noticed several red pins stuck in the map along the coast of the Sea of Japan. Many more were lined up along the border by mainland China. Only a few marked the coast of North Korea by the Yellow Sea.

"Is this a chart of KGB personnel emplacements set up to prevent the thieves from escaping?" Katz asked.

"Da," Pushkin confirmed. "I put the pins in the map this morning because I thought you people might want to examine it. Needless to say, I don't make a habit of keeping a wall chart of KGB activities. Frankly, I don't care to give you any more details unless I receive authorization from Moscow."

"The Sea of Japan is covered pretty well," the Phoenix Force commander remarked, "but the Yellow Sea isn't. Most of the personnel seem to be concentrated along the border at South and North Korea. The coast along Korea is wide open."

"Hardly," the KGB colonel insisted. "There were hundreds of Soviet and Korean operatives stationed there."

"But it's still the weak point in the net," Katz stated. "Check the dates on the time these blockades and observation posts were set up. If the stations at the Yellow Sea were among the latter posts and if they weren't reinforced, it suggests a good possibility that it's the route that the thieves used. Naturally we'll check with Kempai and the CIA to see if any likely ships reached Japan or South Korea."

"How could they tell if the ship was carrying TRIO gangsters with our VL-800 formula?" Pushkin inquired.

"The samurai short sword suggests yakuza are among the TRIO thieves," the Israeli explained. "That means they're Japanese and probably have identification. If they arrived in Japan or Korea, they'd certainly be questioned about the fact their vessel came from the direction of Mongolia and the Soviet Union. There's bound to be a record of that."

"But you don't think they went to Japan or Korea?" Alekseyev asked. "You suspect they headed down the Yellow Sea? Correct?"

"Suspicions aren't good enough," Katz replied. "What we need are facts. But since the weakness is at the Yellow Sea, it suggests the enemy headed south. Possibly to Korea, but I suspect TRIO would want to get as far away from Mongolia and the Soviet Union as possible. Maybe they'd head for Taiwan or Hong Kong."

"You think they could get that far?" Pushkin frowned. "Why not head for the Philippines?"

"Why look for trouble?" Katz smiled. "Look, if they could reach the South China Sea, there are virtually thousands of harbors they could choose from—Taipei, Sinchu, Hong Kong, about a hundred islands."

"We might never find them," Alekseyev said grimly.

"Not if we don't start looking for them," Katz replied.

9

Wang Tse-tu sat on his throne and gazed at the column of smoke that rose from the cobra-shaped incense burner. The obese Chinese seemed to be consulting the smoke as if expecting to find the answer to some grievous problem drifting in the fragrant mist. He shook his head slowly. Wang Tse-tu knew well how to deal with obstacles in business, but the problem that troubled him now was with the organization.

Wang Tse-tu did not look like a typical organization man. He wore a green *mang p'ao* dragon robe with a long purple jacket and an ornate court collar trimmed with gold. A Mandarin cap with a peacock feather tassel was perched on his round head, and a *pu fang* coat of arms hung from a gold chain around his neck. The amulet bore the symbol of TRIO, a three-headed black serpent.

However, Wang Tse-tu was the *ling shyou* of the Black Serpent Tong, the Chinese section of TRIO. He was one of the most powerful and feared men in Asia. The tong leader had inherited his position after the death of his father. For thirty-three years Wang Tse-tu had ruled one of the largest and most successful criminal societies in the Orient with branches extending to the United States and Western Europe. When the Black Serpent Tong joined forces with the Snake Clan and the New Horde, Wang Tse-tu became even more powerful.

Wang Tse-tu had learned that the key to holding power is not to grab for too much too soon. He feared that Tosha Khan had violated that rule and had jeopardized all of TRIO in the process.

"The Vacpalenee Lagkech 800 formula is probably the most valuable commodity that has ever fallen into our possession," Tosha Khan declared. "The potential for profit is limitless. Yet you seem displeased, my brothers."

Tosha Khan was not as surprised at the response as he pretended. The leader of the New Horde had not expected the others to be pleased when they learned what he had done. However, the Mongol crime czar did not care what they thought. He had seized the opportunity fate had offered. Success belonged to the bold, and the timid were only fit to follow their leaders.

Tosha Khan was a bold man, a general commanding troops in the field. He wore the uniform of a Mongol conqueror. A metal breastplate covered his thick chest. Bracelets of chain mail were bound to his wrists, and he wore a brass helmet with hornlike decorations at the crown. The blood of greatness ran through his veins. He was descended from the great Genghis Khan. The others would do well to remember that, he thought.

Shimo Goro had never been impressed with Tosha Khan's stories of his esteemed ancestry. Tosha Khan had no proof that he came from a line of bastard offspring of Genghis Khan. However, Shimo Goro was indeed descended of an honorable and noble family.

The proof leaned at the armrest of Shimo's throne. It was a thirteenth-century *katana*, a samurai long sword. The weapon had been crafted by the great swordmaker Hashigo Naifu. Shimo Karada, a great samurai warrior, had wielded the sword on the battlefield. Karada had become a *ronin* or mercenary samurai, and later a yakuza. A thief with honor.

The leader of the Snake Clan wore a less elaborate costume than his companions. Shimo was dressed in a black kimono with matching *hakama* culottes and a gold obi sash bound around his waist. The Japanese *obyan* considered the ritual of wearing traditional costumes absurd, but he understood the benefits. Ritual costume evoked reverence, and the showmanship and symbolism impressed the many followers of TRIO.

"You should have consulted us before taking action, Tosha Khan," Wang Tse-tu declared. The three master criminals of the greatest Asian syndicate in the world conversed in English. It was a concession of equality, a neutral language. They did not know one another's native tongues.

"Time was important," the Mongol declared. "I had to order my men to act immediately or it would have been too late to seize the formula from the Russians."

"*Your* men?" Shimo Goro replied, raising his bushy black eyebrows. "Need I remind you that you ordered several of my yakuza and some of Wang Tse-tu's tong to participate in the raid on the installation? A number of them were killed in the process."

"But the formula arrived safely here in Hong Kong." Tosha Khan smiled. "I've had chemists working on it. They analyzed the VL-800 formula, and they assure me that producing it in volume will not present any problem."

"That's wonderful," Shimo sneered. "We don't need a damned biochemical weapon to begin with, but you expect us to be delighted that you plan to make more of it. For what purpose, Tosha Khan? We are businessmen, involved in a profitable international market of goods and services. We do not need killer viruses or invisible nerve gas."

"I thought you understood, Mr. Shimo," Tosha began. "The VL-800 formula causes victims to die from pneumonia. They lose all natural immunities and simply get sick and die. It is a perfect means for eliminating enemies without creating suspicion.''

"Eliminating individuals is simply a necessary part of our profession,'' Wang Tse-tu announced, raising an index finger with a fingernail nearly as long as the digit itself. ''It has to be done occasionally, but we hardly need a biochemical weapon capable of wiping out an entire city.''

"Or a country,'' Shimo added. ''Is that what you had in mind, Tosha Khan? Do you plan to unleash this VL-800 on anyone in particular?''

"Don't be coy,'' the Mongol said. ''Please, speak your mind, Mr. Shimo.''

"Tosha Khan,'' Wang Tse-tu began wearily. ''We are well aware of the fact you despise the Soviet Union. You resent the control the Russians have in Mongolia. I'm certain if Mr. Shimo or I had been born in your country, we would feel the same way toward the Russians.''

"I have not suggested using the formula in the Soviet Union,'' Tosha Khan insisted.

"But you didn't mind stealing it from the Soviets,'' Shimo declared. ''Do you think the Kremlin is going to simply shrug and say 'How terrible. We've been robbed. Perhaps we should report the theft to Interpol'? You of all people should know how the Soviets will react. The KGB is probably hunting us at this very moment.''

"The KGB doesn't know anything about us,'' Tosha Khan told him. ''They think the Communist Chinese stole the formula. By the time they realize their mistake, it will be too late.''

"You are certainly underestimating the KGB, Tosha Khan,'' Shimo stated. ''The Soviet intelligence service is probably the largest and most ruthless clandestine organization in the world. We are not espionage agents, and you are getting us involved in an area outside our expertise. That is very dangerous, Tosha Khan.''

"Don't worry about the KGB," Tosha Khan insisted. "The New Horde has operated in Mongolia and Eastern Europe for twenty years, and the Russian spies haven't done anything about us yet."

"You never stole a Soviet secret weapon before," Shimo replied. "I say the best thing we can do is get rid of the VL-800 formula. Burn it with thermite and destroy it."

"That would be throwing away a fortune," Tosha Khan declared. "We can sell the formula to foreign governments. Or sell it to political revolutionaries and terrorists. We can even sell it back to the Russians."

"Absolutely not," Shimo told him.

"Mr. Wang," Tosha said, turning to the Chinese master criminal. "It appears we need a deciding vote. Do you side with Mr. Shimo or with me?"

"I don't agree with either of you entirely," Wang replied. "Tosha Khan, you were wrong to begin this business without discussing the matter with us. You may have jeopardized our entire organization. The risk is not justified by the potential for profit. However, I do not agree with Mr. Shimo either. To destroy valuable merchandise would be foolish. As you said, Mr. Shimo, some of our people have already died getting this formula. It would seem a futile effort if we did not make use of the VL-800 formula."

"That's going to cost us more lives," Shimo said grimly.

"This business includes an element of risk," Wang stated. "We've all been doing this long enough to know that. Now, we'll have to decide how to best use the formula to make the largest possible profit with the least amount of risk."

"Thank you, Mr. Wang," Tosha said with a nod.

"Very well," Shimo sighed. "But I want to state officially that I am opposed to biochemical weapons. I also wish to exercise my right to refuse to recruit more of my yakuza for a mission that I regard as less than stable."

"Will you be sending your men back as well?" Wang asked.

"The yakuza already committed to this operation will stay," Shimo replied. "I have given my word that they would be stationed in the Hong Kong area, and here they shall stay. However, I will not bring reinforcements from Japan. If the mission goes badly, that is karma."

"I can agree to those terms," Tosha Khan stated.

"Very well," Wang nodded. "Now let's decide how to handle this matter and who we'll put in charge of the mission."

"I already have my choice," Tosha Khan said proudly. "My son Temujin has arrived from Mongolia. He speaks Cantonese and Mandarin fluently. I have trained him since childhood. He is an excellent commander and a fine warrior."

"I'm sure he is," Wang Tse-tu assured Tosha Khan. Actually the Chinese tong leader doubted that Temujin was as impressive as his father claimed. Wang Tse-tu had four sons of his own, and while he regarded them all as perfect examples of manhood, he realized that a father's opinion of his own son was biased.

"Temujin brought some interesting news from Mongolia," Tosha Khan began. "The Russians have been investigating the site of the installation where the VL-800 was being produced. Six strange men accompanied the Russians. Temujin does not believe they were Soviets, because they wore masks. He said their general physical description fits that of the mysterious five-man team that destroyed our operation in the Philippines last year."

"How long have you known about this?" Shimo demanded. His hand reached for the hilt of the *katana* by his chair.

"Temujin told me about this personally only two hours ago," Tosha Khan explained. He had not wished to tell the others because he knew they would be disturbed by the news, yet he knew they would find out about it sooner or later. It was better they heard it from him now than discovered he had remained silent about the matter.''

"There may be no connection," Wang Tse-tu stated. He noticed Shimo was prepared to draw his sword. TRIO infighting could rapidly lead to their downfall. "Temujin said there were six men. Not five."

"There were six in San Francisco," Shimo reminded the Chinese. "But what information we've been able to acquire suggests the same group was involved in both incidents. The two greatest defeats TRIO has suffered were at the hands of those bastards. Now, Tosha Khan wants us to go ahead with this germ-warfare scheme, although he knows our worst enemies have joined forces with the KGB to try to track us down."

"Please allow me to finish," Tosha Khan said mildly. "My son realized these men might present a serious threat to our operation. So he contacted a gang of bandits who occasionally work under contract for the New Horde, although they know no details about the organization. The bandits ambushed the six masked men and their Russian friends while they were crossing a section of the Gobi Desert. There is no cover in the Gobi, and the bandits numbered more than thirty men. I'm certain our enemies no longer present a problem."

"Does Temujin know for certain that these bandits destroyed the enemy?" Wang Tse-tu inquired.

"He had to leave immediately," the Mongol answered, "in order to reach Hong Kong in time to take command of this operation. But there is no doubt the ambush was successful—"

"In other words," Shimo snapped, "the answer is no. The six professional killers might still be alive. Perhaps the KGB did not know about TRIO, but those six American butchers know about us. If they are working with the KGB, we may be facing the worst threat to our organization since the encounter with the Triad when we first created TRIO."

"Mr. Shimo," Wang Tse-tu began. "If you will recall, we managed to avoid bloodshed with the Triad. We came to an understanding with them. An agreement was made, and TRIO and the Triad have not had any confrontations since."

"This is not the sort of situation we can negotiate our way through," the yakuza boss insisted.

"No," Wang Tse-tu agreed. "But the same principle of keeping a cool head and dealing with the situation in a rational manner does apply. We do not know that these are the same men. We do not know that they survived the bandit ambush. We do not know that they are going to be any more successful at locating our base of operations than the KGB has been. It is logical to prepare for trouble, but it is destructive to worry too quickly about matters that might not exist."

"But it is far more dangerous to ignore a threat to our organization," Shimo insisted.

"Gentlemen," Tosha Khan announced. "I suggest we set up observation posts at airports and large airstrips to see if these six mystery men arrive in Hong Kong. If they do, we'll simply eliminate them."

"And draw more attention to TRIO operations," Shimo complained. "Killing them in Hong Kong will draw the attention of the authorities. It is more apt to compound our problems than to solve them."

"We must leave Hong Kong within two hours," Wang Tse-tu reminded the others. "Let's spend that time determining exactly what plan of action best suits this situation."

10

The Soviet TU-144 airliner arrived at the international aiport in Kowloon. Commercial aircraft from the Soviet Union were rarely seen in Hong Kong . . . and were not very welcome. Naturally Phoenix Force and the KGB had contacted the authorities in advance. A reception committee was waiting for the Aeroflot plane when it arrived a few minutes before noon, Hong Kong time.

Phoenix Force was still accompanied by John Trent and Major Alekseyev. Captain Yuri Zhdanov and Lieutenant Vladimir Savchenko were also assigned to the group. Since the two KGB officers had been working on the VL-800 investigation in Mongolia already, Colonel Pushkin had decided to send them to replace the slain Boris Abakumov and Professor Sudplatov. Zhdanov was less than happy about the assignment, but Savchenko seemed quite pleased to have an opportunity to visit Hong Kong.

The members of the reception committee were not very glad to see Phoenix Force and their Soviet companions. Hong Kong was a center of capitalism in the Far East, although it was positioned literally along the coast of mainland China. Although technically a British dependency, Hong Kong had a thriving economy that dealt in trade and commerce with the Western democracies and had recently established good relations with Communist China.

Naturally the Hong Kong authorities were not thrilled at the arrival of KGB agents in Kowloon. The Russians were supposed to be there for a mission that concerned the safety of the entire world. If the Soviets had not been accompanied by an elite team of professionals—although no one seemed certain what they were supposed to be professionals at—that had been given top-level clearance directly by the President of the United States, the Hong Kong officials would never have given the KGB permission to land in Kowloon.

"My name is Colonel Charles Hunntington-Smythe," a husky middle-aged man with a handlebar mustache announced as he coldly greeted the arrivals. "Hong Kong Security Intelligence Service."

Hunntington-Smythe's accent revealed a Cambridge education, although the Briton had been born and raised in Hong Kong. He was strongly dedicated to his homeland, and he took his job very seriously. Greeting KGB agents turned his stomach. He did not care much for a team of hotshot Yanks muscling into his jurisdiction either.

"This is Kauo Yvet-sang." Hunntington-Smythe indicated a wiry Asian dressed in a white linen suit and narrow houndstooth necktie. "He's my aide. A very good man."

"A pleasure to meet you," Major Alekseyev declared as he offered his hand to the SIS officer.

Hunntington-Smythe ignored it. "And this is Gerald Crane," he continued. "American CIA."

Crane nodded at the group. He was a tall blonde with broad shoulders and a V-shaped torso. He wore an expensive pastel jacket, a T-shirt and sunglasses. The guy looked like he was understudying Don Johnson of *Miami Vice*.

"Hey, Colonel," Crane began. "If we're gonna talk about the Company, let's do it someplace that isn't out in the open."

"What are you worried about, Crane?" Hunntington-Smythe asked dryly. "The KGB is right in front of us. If they can know who we are and what we do, who cares if the general population overhears anything?''

"We care," Katzenelenbogen told him. "Now let's get to a secure area."

The group moved from the runway and entered the airport. The building was crowded with Asians, Europeans, Arabs and Americans. Tourists and businessmen, military personnel and airline pilots mingled with the crowds. The airport was slightly busier than most, but Phoenix Force did not feel the enormous presence of Hong Kong's massive population until they reached the street.

Hundreds of people walked the streets. Hong Kong's 403 square miles was populated by more than five million people. After the miles of emptiness of Mongolia, the crowded streets of Kowloon were claustrophobic.

Hunntington-Smythe led the group to a tour bus parked at the curb. Phoenix Force, Trent and the three KGB officers had carried their gear off the plane; they had not had to clear customs. They loaded their bags into the bus and seated themselves. A Chinese driver with large buckteeth smiled and nodded at his passengers. He started the engine and pulled into the driveway. Within minutes they were creeping through a traffic jam that moved only slightly faster than a glacier.

"Well, isn't this a cozy bunch?" Crane began, fishing a pack of cigarettes from his jacket pocket. "CIA, SIS, KGB and whatever the hell you guys belong to. What are you? Some special branch of the National Security Agency? Didn't think those boys liked to get their hands dirty."

"We're just a bunch of dudes who hang around together and play cowboys and Indians with real guns," Calvin James said with a shrug. "We don't make a lot of money, but we sure have a lot of fun."

"Uh-huh," the CIA case officer grunted.

"I'd like to hear some explanations," Hunntington-Smythe declared. "So far, all I know is that the SIS has been ordered to cooperate with you chaps in every way possible. That is, with you fellows working for Washington. There's a limited amount of information I intend to share with the KGB. Frankly, I don't understand why you're working with the Soviets or what this mission is about."

"Something about a dangerous substance smuggled into Hong Kong. Correct?" Kauo Yvet-sang inquired. The SIS colonel's aide sounded as British as Hunntington-Smythe.

"That's a long story," Major Alekseyev said with a sigh.

"We've got time before we reach Victoria," Hunntington-Smythe replied. He turned to face Phoenix Force. "And I want to hear it from *you*. I have a problem trusting Soviet agents."

"The story started last month," Yakov Katzenelenbogen began, taking a pack of Camels from his pocket. "At a remote Soviet installation in Mongolia."

Katz had donned a different prosthesis device. This one had three hooks at the end of the "arm." The hooks functioned as fingers and could perform many of the tasks flesh-and-blood hands accomplish. Katz used the hooks to pull a cigarette from the Camel pack and raised it to his lips as he took his lighter from another pocket.

Phoenix Force had made another change when they had arrived in Hong Kong. Reluctantly the team had decided to remove the clear plastic masks they had worn since the mission had begun. They did not like showing their faces to the Russians, well aware that the KGB agents would memorize every detail of their features. However, circumstances made the masks too great a liability in Hong Kong.

Katz told Hunntington-Smythe and the others about the VL-800 formula and sketched in some general information about what had happened in Mongolia. He also explained how they had determined that TRIO had brought the deadly CBW chemicals to Hong Kong.

"Approximately twelve hours after the installation was attacked," Katz continued, "a ship sailed into the Yellow Sea. It had all the necessary papers and government permission to transport beef and wool from Mongolia to North Korea. It moved right along the edge of Korean waters, then it apparently vanished. The Koreans were told that it had been ordered back to the Soviet Union due to some administrative problem. Since the shipment of Mongolian goods was scheduled, and the skipper had made deliveries in the past, no one was terribly suspicious at first."

"However, the ship never returned to port," Alekseyev stated.

"Is that right, Mr. Gray?" Hunntington-Smythe inquired.

"It was abandoned," Katz answered. "The ship drifted to the coast of the People's Republic of China. Naturally the Chinese wanted more details about the vessel before they reported the incident to the Mongolians and the Soviets. They apparently took the ship apart looking for evidence of explosives, drugs, whatever. However, all they found was beef, wool and a bunch of empty cabins."

"What happened to the crew?" Crane asked. "And the VL-800?"

"We're fairly certain the crew boarded a South Korean fishing vessel that was in the area at the time," Katz explained. "The fishermen had been warned that they were getting too close to the Communists' zone, but they didn't seem concerned. Of course, the Soviets didn't suspect that the crew from the Mongol ship had gotten on board a Korean vessel. We wouldn't have known about it either if we hadn't compared information logged by the Communist North Koreans and the pro-West South Koreans. We might never have found out if CIA, NSA, KGB and Korean intelligence forces on both sides hadn't contributed data.''

"Then this same ship sailed to Hong Kong?" Hunntington-Smythe frowned.

"To Taiwan," Katz answered. "But it claimed to be a Japanese fishing vessel that had gone off course. It stopped in Changhua Harbor to repair its engine and get diesel fuel. The crew did all the work, and the Taiwanese confirmed that the members of the crew were Japanese...or at least the men they met were Japanese. However, it was noted that, while the ship was supposedly called the *Mishima* and flew a Japanese flag, the legend at the rear of the vessel was written in Korean.''

"The *Ch'orok Pit Mogyoil*," Lieutenant Savchenko stated. "The Korean fishing vessel that we believe picked up the crew from the Mongol ship."

"And the stolen VL-800," Alekseyev added.

"The *Mishima* left Taiwan and headed southwest," Katz concluded. "That means they were headed for China, Vietnam, Kampuchea or Hong Kong. Only one place would make any sense for TRIO to use as a base of operations."

"So we should check for the *Mishima*?" Crane asked. "You know, hundreds of ships come into the seaports here every day. That job is gonna be a mother. Still, with the help of a computer we should be able to find out where the *Mishima* finally docked.''

"Don't count on it being the *Mishima* any longer," Manning warned. "TRIO probably changed the name again. Since they have Chinese members as well as Japanese and Mongolians, they might claim the ship is Taiwanese.''

"And knowing TRIO," David McCarter added, "the ship was probably scheduled to make a delivery or pickup. Don't count on them making any mistakes. That's not TRIO's style."

"My God," Hunntington-Smythe rasped. "This is like looking for a needle in a haystack. And a needle disguised as a piece of straw at that!"

"It isn't as hopeless as it seems," Encizo assured him. "After all, we've managed to track them here."

"You make it sound as if Hong Kong was some little hick town back in the States, José," Crane commented. "We've got more than five million regular citizens here, and that ain't including all the businessmen, bankers, and tourists who are here for a visit."

"Won't be easy," James said with a shrug. "But it won't be impossible either. New York City and Los Angeles have larger populations than all of Hong Kong put together, but you can still find dudes who try to hide there. It's all a matter of lookin' in the right places."

"New York or Los Angeles or Mexico City might have larger populations than Hong Kong," Hunntington-Smythe remarked, "but we've got the greatest density of population in the world."

He pointed at the rows of office buildings, skyscrapers and apartment houses that crammed the skyline. "If we were to drive in that direction about half a mile from here," the SIS colonel began, "we would arrive at the Mong Kok district. The population distribution is unbelievable—more than 650,000 people per square mile. People live on rooftops. It's said that 104 people were living in a single room when we had the housing crisis back in 1959. Don't think it's going to be easy finding individuals here."

"Gee whiz," James said with an exaggerated pout. "I guess we'll just have to give up and go home, huh? If you'd been listening, Colonel, you might have noticed I said it won't be easy, man."

"Excuse me," John Trent began. "I admit that I'm not as experienced in these matters as the rest of you gentlemen, but wouldn't it be logical to search for TRIO in much the same manner as one would search for any other sort of criminal?''

"So you suggest we contact the police?'' Crane snorted. "Not such a great idea, fella. Our security will go right in the toilet if we do that.''

"I suggest quite the opposite,'' Trent said, smiling. "I think we should contact some criminals. The competition always knows its rivals better than anyone else.''

"You think we could ask one of the Triad to help us?'' Hunntington-Smythe scoffed. "We're not talking about General Motors and Ford. These are criminal syndicates, my friend.''

"But they regard themselves as businessmen,'' Trent insisted. "Gentlemen's agreements are made. This is my territory. That belongs to you. Don't cross me and I won't cross you. The Chinese tong learned a long time ago that it was advantageous to divide the power rather than fight over it. It's good business to avoid bloodshed even if it means the competition gets some business you might have had otherwise. Still, they're the competition. If they have problems, it doesn't bother you. Especially if their actions might hurt your own business. And you don't mind helping others who might cause more problems for the competition.''

"Is this a theory, or do you know this shit works?'' Crane asked sourly as he ground his cigarette under a shoe.

"It can work,'' Trent said with a nod.

He did not tell them that his Uncle Inoshiro, who had trained him to be a ninja, was currently living in San Francisco. Inoshiro was a subchief for a yakuza clan. Most of their activities were perfectly legal, but others were not. Inoshiro dealt in minor-league black market, bootleg videotapes and other petty but profitable crime. Trent had never gotten involved with yakuza operations, but he understood them very well. The yakuza and the tong had an understanding in San Francisco. Trent was unfamiliar with Hong

Kong, but he knew that people were much the same any-where in the world.

"I think I know a chap who might be able to help us," McCarter announced cheerfully. "That is, if he's still alive."

"Oh, God," Manning groaned. "Not another one of your friends in low places. I swear, you know the weirdest people in the strangest places..."

"But they usually turn out to be pretty reliable," McCarter said, grinning. "Don't they? Eccentric perhaps, but dependable."

"He has a point," Encizo commented.

"Yeah," Manning muttered, "at the top of his head."

"When do we meet this friend of yours?" Hunntington-Smythe inquired. He was surprised to discover McCarter was British. He wondered how many of the others were nationalities other than American. There might be hope for these bloody hotshots after all.

"You don't," McCarter replied. "My friend wouldn't care to have SIS or CIA or any other sort of copper poking into his business. He trusts me...at least he used to, but if I show up with all you blokes, he'll run like a fox with the hounds on his arse."

"You ought to take at least one man, just in case," Katz told him.

"I speak Chinese," Lieutenant Savchenko announced eagerly. "I might be quite an asset."

"No offense, mate," the Briton said. "But if I have to have just one fellow for backup, I'd prefer somebody I've worked with before."

"And somebody who isn't KGB?" Savchenko asked dryly.

"That, too," McCarter admitted. "I don't remember what the hell your cover name is..."

The Briton was looking at Trent.

"I think I'm supposed to be Collins," the American ninja replied with a shrug. "I'm the lucky choice to get to meet your friend?"

"You wouldn't feel that way if you'd ever met any of his friends before," Manning commented.

"What about you guys?" Trent asked.

"Who said we're his friends?" Manning answered.

"Yeah, man," James added with a grin. "We got our reputations to think of."

McCarter gave them instructions to do something of an obscene nature. Hunntington-Smythe rolled his eyes toward heaven. Any hope he had for this group seemed to be evaporating rapidly.

11

David McCarter had been in Hong Kong before, when he was with the Special Air Service. A gang of terrorists had been raising hell in Victoria and Kowloon. Every time the police had gotten near the radicals, cops had been killed, and the terrorists had gained new members from the street gangs of bullyboys who regarded crime as a way of life and murder as an act of courage.

Hong Kong is a British colony. The governor is appointed by Great Britain, but Hong Kong generally governs itself, with a forty-eight member legislative council, a sixteen-member executive council and a supreme court. However, it had been the governor who had requested assistance from Britain to deal with the rising wave of terrorism.

The SAS was instructed to handle the task as quietly and covertly as possible. They had spent more than a year in Hong Kong hunting down terrorists. More often than not, the SAS had had to kill the bastards; survivors had been turned over to the authorities. The street gangs had seen that their super heroes were not so special after all. They had been disappointed and disillusioned, but most of them had continued their life of crime, simply transferring their hero worship to other hoodlums and sadists.

As far as the SAS had been concerned, the mission had gone quite well. It had taken a bit longer than they had first expected, but the results had been effective and not a single SAS trooper had been killed. Of course, the assignment had been very hush-hush. Only a handful of people had ever known about it, and that was exactly how the United Kingdom and Hong Kong had wanted it.

Hong Kong had not changed much since then. It had had a thriving economy when McCarter had been stationed there, and as far as he could tell, the only difference was an increase in the number of businesses and banking interests. There were more buildings, huge modern structures of concrete and steel. The most valuable real estate in the world was found in Hong Kong. A one-room apartment often rented for two thousand dollars a month. A small office building was worth millions.

"Hard to believe this island was just a haven for smugglers, pirates and opium merchants a hundred and forty-five years ago," McCarter remarked as he and Trent sat in the back seat of a taxi that worked its way through heavy traffic in the capital city of Victoria, a city that was usually referred to simply as Hong Kong.

"The world has changed everywhere," Trent replied. "Although this is incredible. Yet I wonder what effect this hectic pace and crushing population has on the people."

"The citizens of Hong Kong seem to take it in stride," the Briton stated. "Of course, they've evolved into sort of social hybrids. Britain acquired this property in 1898. Signed a lease with China for ninety-nine years. We've had ninety years to corrupt these folks with our Anglo-European concepts. The people of Hong Kong don't really consider themselves to be either Asians or Europeans. They tend to think they've got the best of both worlds."

"A lot of people in Japan think the same way," Trent remarked. He noticed a ricksha being pulled by a man dressed in a traditional coolie outfit, complete with a conical hat of woven rice reeds. Behind the ricksha was a Rolls-Royce.

"In Hong Kong they have an expression," McCarter mused. "They say the East lives in the past, the West lives in the future, but Hong Kong lives for the present. Maybe that atittude helps them cope with the stress and uncertainty.''

''Maybe we should adopt that notion,'' Trent commented. He glanced out the window, searching for a street sign. The taut canopy of a merchant who sold fish and squid blocked the American ninja's view. ''Are you sure this friend of yours will still be at this address?''

''If he isn't, we'll just kick over a few rocks until we find him,'' McCarter said with a shrug.

Although Trent had failed to find a street sign, the cab-driver had no difficulty locating the address. He steered the taxi into a narrow alley. Several trash cans were lined up by the door of a small restaurant. Some children rummaged through the garbage. They watched the two strangers emerge from the cab. McCarter paid the driver.

''Hau bu hau!'' the children cried, holding their hands out in hopes the tourists would toss them some coins.

''Hey, mister,'' one kid yelled in English. ''You want meet girl? Take you see private show. Nice girl there.''

''No, thanks,'' McCarter said gruffly. He dipped a hand into his jacket pocket. ''Just get out of here and go hang around somebody else.''

The Briton held out a fistful of coins and dropped a few into the greedy hands of each child. Their faces beamed, but they noticed the harshness in McCarter's expression.

''That's all you get,'' he added. ''Don't come back for seconds. Now get out.''

''Dzou-chyu!'' Trent added sharply. *''Dung bu dung?''*

''Hau,'' the kids assured him.

They bolted from the alley. McCarter walked to a metal door in a brick wall. The Briton hammered his fist on the door and then stepped clear of it. Trent followed his example. The Briton carried his briefcase with the M-10 Ingram machine pistol inside. He also had his Browning Hi-Power in the Bianchi shoulder holster under his left arm. Trent was armed with his Colt Commander, *manrikigusari* fighting chain, some *shaken* throwing stars and a few other ninjutsu devices.

"*Shum-mau-ren?*" a voice demanded from the opposite side of the door.

"Mao's ghost," McCarter growled. "It's a dirty old Brit, you bloody bugger."

"McCarter?" the voice inquired.

"Of course I am," the Briton replied. "But don't take my word for it. Check through a peephole or a window."

"Not necessary," the voice chuckled. "I'd recognize that whiny lemon-sucking voice anywhere."

The door opened. A small, portly Chinese smiled up at them. He held a Sterling machine pistol canted against his shoulder. Pudgy fingers waved the pair into the room. The interior startled Trent. He had expected to enter a boiler room or the back room of a tavern. However, the room was adorned with silk-screen prints, jade carvings and delicate crystal figurines.

"This is Hsin Li," McCarter said, introducing the Chinese to Trent. "He's an old friend and informer. A wise man who keeps a hand on the pulse of Hong Kong and knows all the dirty business that others believe are secrets."

"I'm not just an informer anymore, McCarter," Hsin Li declared as he gestured at the fine furniture, expensive stereo-television unit with videotape recorder and assorted works of art. "Can't you see that I've gone up in the world?"

"So you have," the Briton said, nodding. "What sort of work are you into these days? Gunrunning?"

"You mean this?" Hsin Li patted his Sterling subgun. "This is just for home security."

"Very nice," McCarter said. "So what are you doing?"

"I'm sort of an unofficial social director for visiting dignitaries," Hsin Li explained. "I make certain VIP tourists and certain locals enjoy themselves while they're in our fine capital city of Victoria."

"Does that mean you're a pimp, drug pusher or both?" McCarter asked dryly.

"David," Hsin Li frowned. "You know me better than that. I'm not a brute who would peddle women like cattle, and I abhor drugs—"

"But you know people who don't mind doing that sort of thing," McCarter said. "Is that right?"

"Well, yes," Hsin Li admitted. "After all, that's free enterprise. Supply and demand. My customers have expensive tastes in entertainment. I simply arrange for them to meet with individuals who can fill their . . . needs. If I didn't do this, someone else would. Someone with fewer principles who wouldn't care what sort of ladies the visitors met or the quality of the substances they used."

"You're obviously a man of great principles," Trent said dryly.

"I'm glad you appreciate that," Hsin Li said, smiling. "I like your friend, David. Why don't we all have some French brandy before we discuss whatever business brings you here?"

"Because we don't have very much time, Hsin Li," McCarter replied. "We need information. Just like the good old days."

"Will I get paid?" the Chinese inquired, sinking into a large leather armchair. "After all, my services always have a price."

"I remember," McCarter assured him. "Just don't get too greedy. You'll take what we pay you, and don't try to blackmail me, Hsin Li."

"Would I do such a thing to an old and dear friend?" the Chinese hustler asked in an injured voice.

"I know you would," McCarter told him. "But don't try it with us, Hsin Li. That could be hazardous to your health, mate."

"Then I'll have to get a decent payment from the beginning," Hsin Li said, smiling. "But I'm certain you'll pay me a fair price for my valuable knowledge."

"What can you tell us about an organization called TRIO?" the Briton inquired.

"Excuse me?" Hsin Li stared at McCarter and raised his eyebrows. "Did you ask me a question? Does that mean I'm working for you? Then I must insist on a one-hundred-dollar office fee...."

"Hong Kong dollars or American currency?" McCarter asked.

"American dollars," Hsin Li answered. "Or fifty British pounds, if you prefer."

McCarter tossed two fifty-dollar bills into the hustler's lap. "Tell me about TRIO."

"I've heard of it," Hsin Li replied, folding the money and sticking it in his pocket. "Heard it's supposed to be some sort of international crime syndicate that combines some tong societies with Japanese yakuza members. Probably a myth."

"That's hardly giving us our money's worth," Trent commented. "You're telling us less than we already know."

"I can only give you information about what I know," Hsin Li said with a shrug.

"You don't want to earn any more money?" McCarter sighed. "You've certainly changed, Hsin Li."

"Ask me for details about something else," Hsin Li urged. "Uh...I'd rather not discuss anything connected with the Triad. Now that can certainly be hazardous to one's health."

"What about the Black Serpent Tong?" Trent inquired.

"That's almost as bad," Hsin Li replied.

"A thousand dollars interest you?" McCarter asked.

"Won't even pay for my funeral," Hsin Li replied.

"Are you really that worried?" McCarter asked.

"Make it two thousand," Hsin Li said with a shrug.

"Let's hear what you can tell us about the Black Serpent Tong first," the Briton insisted.

"All right," Hsin Li began. "Hong Kong waterfront. You'll find Lung Harbor there. It's a Black Serpent Tong front. They're running a smuggling operation. Drugs, guns, stolen merchandise, I'm not sure what all they're involved with. Those storage houses could hold anything."

"Storage houses?" Trent asked. His pulse quickened. "There are storage houses at the harbor?"

"Of course," Hsin Li confirmed. "Are you two looking for something special?"

"The less you know," McCarter replied, "the better off you'll be. What else can you tell us?"

"Just that the Black Serpent Tong is one of the largest and best-organized tongs in Asia," Hsin Li warned. "Their operations are not limited to Hong Kong. The Black Serpents have branches in Thailand, Taiwan, possibly even inside the People's Republic of China."

"They're bigger than that," McCarter said with a nod. "I think you ought to know that the Black Serpent Tong is just part of a larger organization."

"You mean TRIO is for real?" Hsin Li glared at him.

"That's right," the Briton confirmed. "If you decide to find out more about the Black Serpent Tong, you'd better know what you'll be poking your nose into."

"Thanks for telling me," Hsin Li said glumly. "Don't expect any more information from me."

"Then," McCarter said as he counted two thousand dollars and handed it to Hsin Li, "don't expect any more money either."

"Fair's fair," Hsin Li said with a nod.

"Well, thanks for the information," McCarter said. "Take care of yourself and maybe I'll see you again before we leave Hong Kong."

"No offense, David," the hustler replied, "but I'd rather you didn't."

"I guess I can live with that." The Briton turned to Trent. "Let's go. I'm sure Hsin Li would like to be alone with his money."

Hsin Li unbolted the door and opened it. McCarter and Trent stepped across the threshold into the alley. Both men stiffened. They sensed something was wrong immediately, even before they noticed the driver was no longer seated behind the wheel of his taxi. The alley was too quiet. Too still.

The alley seemed deserted. Even the cab appeared to be empty. McCarter and Trent glanced about, first left, then right. Then they looked up. Two men were positioned on the roof directly overhead. Both aimed pistols at the Phoenix pro and his ninja companion.

McCarter and Trent dived to the pavement. The Briton leaped to the right while Trent jumped to the left and rolled toward the cover of the taxi. They had separated so as not to present a single easy target. The gunmen on the roof tried to track their quarry through their gun sights. They squeezed triggers. The pistols hissed loudly, but neither McCarter nor Trent were struck.

The Briton held his briefcase in one fist and drew his Browning Hi-Power with the other hand. He extended his arm and pointed the Browning at the figures on the roof. The blade of the front sight lined up with a gunman's head. McCarter snapped off the safety and fired his pistol. The Browning roared, and the gunman's skull popped open.

A 115-grain parabellum slug punched through the gunman's head. Brains and blood splashed the face of his companion. He dropped his pistol and hastily wiped the gory debris from his face. McCarter fired another 9 mm round at the remaining gunman as Trent unsheathed his Commander and fired a .45 missile at the same target.

McCarter's bullet struck the lip of the roof and ricocheted off stone to strike the gunman in the side of the face. The round had little energy left when it slashed the assailant's right cheek, barely breaking the skin. The man cried out, more from alarm than pain. He weaved away from the edge of the roof, but did not move fast enough. Trent's .45 slug hit him in the center of the chest. The big 185-grain projectile crushed his sternum and pulverized his heart. The man sprawled across the rooftop and gasped a final desperate breath before he died.

The two gunmen were only part of a hit team. The rest of the assault group swiftly attacked. Two Chinese assailants rose from behind the trash cans. One aimed a bulky pistol at McCarter while the other jumped into the open and charged, wielding a club in his fist. Another club-swinging opponent lunged at Trent from the rear of the taxi. Two more Chinese charged through the mouth of the alley, each man armed with a fighting staff roughly five feet long.

McCarter raised his briefcase to shield himself from the club-wielding attacker and aimed his Browning at the pistolman stationed by the trash cans. He realized he was too late. The gunman's pistol hissed. A projectile struck McCarter's briefcase as he fired his Browning.

The British ace was astonished when his case did not burst apart from the enemy's bullet. He looked down and recognized the reason instantly. The gunman had not fired a bullet at McCarter; it was a tranquilizer dart.

However, McCarter had fired a high-velocity semijacketed hollowpoint slug at the ambusher. The bullet hit the Chinese triggerman at the bridge of the nose and knifed through his skull. The man collapsed behind the trash cans. An ugly stain of crimson-and-gray brain matter marked the wall above the garbage containers.

The man with the club kept coming. He swung his weapon at the Phoenix warrior. McCarter awkwardly blocked the attack with his case. The cudgel struck hard. McCarter felt the briefcase jerk from the blow. The handle snapped, and the briefcase hurtled to the end of the alley.

McCarter reacted swiftly, reflexes preempting thought. He wanted to take at least one attacker prisoner for questioning. Although he could have easily shot the club-wielding opponent, McCarter held his fire and slashed the barrel across the assailant's wrist. The club fell from the man's grasp, but his other hand quickly grabbed McCarter's wrist above the Browning.

The Chinese hit man shoved McCarter's pistol toward the ground and whipped the Briton's face with the back of his fist. McCarter's head bounced from the blow, and he tasted blood. The assailant twisted McCarter's wrist and forced his fist to open. The Browning fell at their feet.

McCarter swung a left hook at the side of his opponent's jaw. He followed with a knee to the man's abdomen. The Chinese groaned, but held on to McCarter's arm. He suddenly stepped to the right, twisted his upper body and hauled McCarter over his hip. The Briton's back hit the pavement hard. The Chinese bent a knee and jammed it into McCarter's stomach with all his weight behind it.

The Briton gasped as the wind was driven from his lungs. His opponent raised a fist and swung it like a hammer at McCarter's face. A hard forearm block met the man's wrist and stopped the fist before it found its target. McCarter's other arm streaked forward and drove a *ming chuan* "ram's head" punch to the point of his opponent's chin.

The blow toppled the Chinese from McCarter's prone body. The Asian hit the pavement, but quickly started to rise. McCarter braced himself with the palms of his hands and pivoted on the small of his back. The Chinese was in a crouched position, about to straighten his legs and back, when McCarter lashed out with his boot. The kick slammed into the hit man's face. The Chinese fell, moaned softly and passed out.

John Trent had been just as busy as McCarter. A Chinese lashed a cudgel across the American ninja's forearm. The blow jarred the ulna nerve, and Trent's Colt Commander fell from numb fingers. The assailant's left hand slashed a *shuto* chop at Trent's neck. The ninja raised a shoulder to block the hand stroke, but his opponent thrust the end of the club into the American's midsection.

Trent groaned and started to double up from the blow. He quickly swung a roundhouse stroke to his opponent's head. The heel of his palm hit the guy between the right ear and temple. The blow stunned the Chinese aggressor. Trent snap-kicked the man in the lower abdomen and quickly grabbed the attacker's arm to prevent him from swinging the club.

The ninja pushed the guy's arm down with his left hand while his right launched a punch under the Asian's chin. Trent's half-closed fist struck hard. The fingers were bent at the second row of knuckles. The panther punch hit the man in the throat. A knuckle crushed the thyroid cartilage. The Chinese dropped his club and staggered backward, both hands reaching for his throat. Trent turned sharply and slammed a powerful side kick at the injured man's chest. The blow propelled his opponent into another assailant. Both men fell to the ground.

The Chinese who had received the panther punch to the throat could no longer offer any threat to Trent or anyone else. His windpipe had collapsed, and he was rapidly dying. However, two opponents remained, and each wielded a five-foot fighting staff made of rock maple.

A wooden shaft slashed at Trent's skull. He ducked beneath the whirling staff and reached into his jacket. The Chinese stickfighter lunged, stabbing the end of his staff at

Trent's solar plexus. The ninja dodged the stroke and pulled his *manrikigusari* from his belt. The hit man raised the staff and swung it toward Trent's face. The American ninja pulled the chain taut, and steel links blocked the fighting stick.

Trent hooked a kick at his opponent's side, the toe of his shoe striking the Chinese under the ribs. The man gasped and fell against the frame of the taxi, but his partner came to the man's assistance. The second stickman swung his staff in a roundhouse stroke aimed at Trent's head. The ninja took the blow on his left shoulder. The impact knocked him onto the hood of the car.

A staff slashed at him. Trent rolled from its path, and the hardwood shaft struck the frame of the cab near the windshield. Trent tried to roll to the opposite side of the automobile to put the vehicle between himself and his opponents. However, the other stickfighter had dashed to the front of the cab and thrust his weapon at the ninja's groin.

Trent wiggled away, and the butt of the fighting staff struck the windshield hard enough to smash a deep crack in the thick glass. In a kung fu or ninja movie, the hero would escape by executing a fancy backflip. But such acrobatics were more impressive than practical, and they were almost impossible without trampolines and mats. Trent simply scrambled onto the roof of the car. It did not look very impressive, but the tactic got him out of the way of another staff stroke that smashed a foot-long section of the windshield.

A staff whipped Trent across the left thigh muscle. He clenched his teeth, hissed from the pain and lashed out with his *manrikigusari*. A weighted end of the chain struck the stickman in the face. The man staggered backward, one hand reaching for his bruised and bloodied cheek.

The other Chinese attacker thrust his staff like a lance, trying to stab Trent in the throat with the hard blunt end. The ninja's *manrikigusari* swung again. The chain wrapped around the wooden shaft. Trent caught the weighted ends and pulled to trap the staff with the steel links. His opponent tried to yank the stick free, but Trent held the staff captive and lashed a foot at the Asian's face.

The heel of his shoe crashed into the jaw, breaking the hinge at the left side of the mandible. The Chinese released his staff and stumbled backward. He flapped his arms weakly like a wounded bird. The man uttered a moan and fell unconscious.

The other stickman snarled with rage as he swung his weapon in a sweeping move at the roof of the taxi. Trent jumped down from the car to avoid the attack and landed on the other side of the vehicle, away from his enraged opponent. The Chinese suddenly tossed his staff aside and stooped to pick up something from the pavement. He smiled as he held the Colt Commander that Trent had dropped during the battle.

"Wang-pu-tan!" the Chinese growled as he circled around the taxi in a wide arc, keeping well out of the range of his opponent's weighted chain.

Trent had already guessed what the Chinese had found and scrambled to the rear of the cab. The Asian hastily fired the big pistol. A .45 slug shattered glass from a back door window. The Chinese had not had much experience with firearms, and the hefty recoil of the .45 caliber pistol startled him. His arm rose with the kick. He awkwardly grabbed the weapon with both hands, hoping to get a better, steadier grip.

Trent kept his head down as he removed a *metsubushi* from his jacket pocket. A ninja "sight remover," the *metsubushi* was simply a hollowed-out egg filled with flash powder and black pepper. He held the egg in his left hand and opened a leather pouch on his belt with his right, drawing two *shaken* throwing stars from the sheath.

The Chinese moved toward the rear of the taxi. Trent hurled the *metsubushi* at his opponent's position. The Asian fired the Commander at the blurred shape of Trent's arm, but the ninja had hastily ducked behind the frame of the automobile. A bullet shattered glass from another rear window of the taxi. Shards fell near Trent's position.

The *metsubushi* exploded on impact. A brilliant flash of white light and a small cloud of stinging black pepper rose into the face of the startled Chinese. He uttered a sound that resembled a half-choked scream. Trent immediately rose and hurled a *shaken* at his opponent.

Sharp steel points struck the Chinese in the side of the skull near his left eye. A metal tip pierced the sphenoid bone. Trent threw the other steel star. The *shaken* struck the guy in the neck and punctured the carotid artery. The Chinese hit man was dead before he hit the pavement.

Silence followed. McCarter and Trent glanced about, searching for more opponents, but they had finished off the last of the hit team. Dozens of voices chattered beyond the alley. Spectators had wisely stayed clear of the battlefield, and no one wanted to get closer in case the fighting was not finished. Sirens wailed as police cars headed for the site.

Hsin Li had pulled his door shut and had probably barricaded it. The hustler had no intentions of sticking his neck out for anyone. McCarter imagined that Hsin Li was probably crouched behind a sofa with his Sterling subgun in his fists, trembling in terror. *I hope the authorities question him* the Briton thought sourly.

"You all right, mate?" McCarter asked Trent as he returned his Browning to shoulder leather.

"A few bruises, but nothing broken," the ninja replied, retrieving his Colt Commander from the lifeless hand of a dead Chinese. "I'd say we certainly got a reaction from someone."

"Yeah," the Briton agreed. "Bloody well like to know why."

12

'You can't be shooting down people in broad daylight in Hong Kong!" Colonel Hunntington-Smythe declared. 'This isn't Dodge City, for Christ's sake!"

"My men acted in self-defense," Yakov Katzenelenbogen replied, seated across from Hunntington-Smythe in the man's office at the headquarters of the Security Intelligence Services. "What did you expect them to do?"

"Hell," Hunntington-Smythe sighed. "I don't know. The chief of police was on the phone. He's very upset about what happened. Five men were killed, Mr. Gray. The police want answers. They don't care much for us keeping secrets from them."

"Maybe we can share some information with them," Katz suggested. "We could use some help from the police when we check out Lung Harbor."

"Are you sure the Englishman's contact is telling the truth about the place being a Black Serpent Tong operation?" Crane, the CIA agent, asked as he slumped into a chair. He had removed his jacket to reveal a shoulder holster rig with an S&W .357 Magnum revolver sheathed under his left arm. "Could be he set up your boys for the hit men."

"That wouldn't make much sense," Katz answered. "The fellow is a criminal, or at least he has connections with criminals who wouldn't want to deal with him if they knew the police might be nosing about where he lives. Hsin Li wouldn't have arranged the hit to happen right outside his own door.''

"But how did TRIO find out about us?" Major Alekseyev wondered as he poured himself a cup of tea. "Their intelligence must be far better than we realized."

"Or we've got a security leak big enough to sail a battleship through," Crane suggested, lighting a cigarette.

"I wouldn't be surprised if we have a security leak," Captain Zhdanov commented. "KGB, CIA, SIS and whoever Gray and his people are. It would be remarkable if we didn't have security leaks. We're enemies and we're openly sharing information that should be top secret. I still don't understand this."

"Any time you want to return to Mother Russia, pal," Crane remarked. "Go ahead. I don't like fuckin' around with you commies anyway."

"I don't care for working with you people either," Zhdanov said crossly. "Why is the CIA even involved in this business? It started as a KGB operation—"

"Yeah," Crane growled. "Because you guys were turning out biochemical weapons that got out of hand. What the hell are you doing here? Haven't you Russkies caused enough trouble already?"

"The KGB has been cooperative with us," Katz stated. "And they alerted us to the VL-800 threat in the beginning. We've been trying to work together on this mission. After all, if TRIO wins, we all lose."

Kauo Yvet-sang entered the office. Colonel Hunntington-Smythe's aide placed a folder on his commander's desk. "The results of the analysis of the drugs used in the hypo darts the ambushers fired at our friends," he announced.

"I don't have time to read this," Hunntington-Smythe complained. "Was it tranquilizers or poison? Did they intend to capture those two or kill them?"

"Tranquilizer," Kauo Yvet-sang answered. "Phenobarbital mixed with some other chemicals and water."

"So the tong intended to kidnap them," Alekseyev mused.

"Except they weren't tong," Rafael Encizo announced as he appeared in the doorway. "I just came from the SIS computer identification and information section. Three of the dead men have been positively identified as members of SAD—the Social Affairs Department."

"That's Chinese intelligence," Hunntington-Smythe said in a stunned voice. "*Communist* Chinese intelligence!"

"That's right," Encizo said with a nod. "And two of the assailants have been identified as members of the diplomatic corps of the People's Republic of China. They were attached to the Chinese embassy right here in Victoria."

"Oh, no," the SIS colonel groaned. "There's going to be an international stink."

"Were the diplomats among the dead or the living?" Kauo Yvet-sang inquired.

"One's dead and the other is having his jaw wired together so we can interrogate him," Encizo answered as he moved to the teapot. "Don't you have any coffee?"

"This is terrible," Hunntington-Smythe muttered.

"It's not that bad," the Cuban assured him. "I'll drink tea if I have to."

"Damn it," the SIS officer snapped. "Hong Kong has established vital relations with the People's Republic. Do you realize how important it is that we keep a good rapport with mainland China? They're going to own Hong Kong in eleven years!"

"Own it?" Zhdanov raised his eyebrows.

"A slight exaggeration," Hunntington-Smythe admitted, "but *only* slight. The British signed a lease with the Chinese Imperial government for Hong Kong back in 1898.

The lease is up in 1997, and Hong Kong will revert to Chinese sovereignty.''

"We'll have to get used to being the Hong Kong Special Administrative Region of China," Kauo Yvet-sang added. "That will be our new title when the change occurs."

"That doesn't mean Hong Kong will become a Communist puppet," Crane explained. "That is, if the Red Chinese keep their word according to the agreement between England and China."

"What agreement is that?" Zhdanov inquired.

"In 1984," Hunntington-Smythe began, "China and Great Britain agreed to terms for Hong Kong's future. The Chinese will assume responsibilities for defense and foreign affairs, but Hong Kong is supposed to retain its own economic, social and legal systems."

"For at least fifty years," Kauo Yvet-sang added, "according to the agreement."

"We Russians had some agreements with the Chinese, too," Alekseyev commented. "Don't count on them keeping their word."

"The ChiComs have improved a lot since Mao died," Crane remarked as he ground out his cigarette in a glass ashtray. "We're hoping they'll adopt more capitalistic traits until communism becomes as dead as the Ming Dynasty."

"China is still a long way from that," Katz stated. "Peking still enforces government control of just about everything. Then again, so do a number of non-Communist governments. We must discover how the Chinese intelligence organization is involved and why it tried to kidnap Nelson and Collins," Katz stated, thinking of McCarter and Trent's close call.

"Do you think we can get the Chinese prisoners to answer those questions?" Alekseyev asked.

PULL THE PIN ON ADVENTURE.

... get 4 explosive novels plus a digital watch

FREE

Free digital watch—on time and on target

Rugged digital calendar watch displays exact
time, date and running seconds with flawless
quartz precision. Water-resistant, too. Comes
complete with long-life battery and one-year
warranty (excluding battery). Best of all, it's
yours FREE!

Peel off grenade from
front cover and slam it
down here

PULL THE PIN ON ADVENTURE

Rush my 4 free books and my free watch.

Then send me 6 brand-new Gold Eagle novels (2 *Mack Bolans* and one each of
Able Team, Phoenix Force, Vietnam: Ground Zero and *SOBs*) every second
month as they come off the presses. Bill me at the low price of $2.49 each
(a savings of 13% off the retail price). There are no shipping, handling or other
hidden costs. I can always return a shipment and cancel at any time.
Even if I never buy a book from Gold Eagle, the 4 free books and the watch
are mine to keep.

166 CIM PAJJ

Name _____ (PLEASE PRINT)

Address _____ Apt. No. _____

City _____ State/Prov. _____ Zip/Postal Code _____

This offer is limited to one order per household and not valid to
present subscribers. Price is subject to change.

PRINTED IN U.S.A

The most pulse-pounding, pressure-packed action reading ever published

Razor-edge storytelling. Page-crackling tension. On-target firepower. Hard-punching excitement. Gold Eagle books slam home raw action the way you like it—hard, fast and real!

"This isn't the Soviet Union," Hunntington-Smythe said sharply. "You Russians aren't going to use any crude torture tactics here."

"I didn't suggest that," the KGB major replied. "But we might use scopolamine or some other truth serum."

"Won't do any good," Calvin James announced as he entered the room. "I came from the clinic. We finished wiring broken bones and stitchin' up cuts on those two dudes who survived their run-in with Nelson and Collins. Truth serum won't work on them."

"How can you be sure?" Zhdanov demanded. The KGB captain was a racist, and he put little stock in what the black man had to say.

"When the Chinese were sedated so we could operate," James began, "they started to yak away about their names and what they did for the government. One guy was still trying to talk with a busted jaw."

"Did you get the information?" Kauo Yvet-sang asked, confused about James's previous remark.

"Why bother?" the black commando said with a shrug. "It's all bullshit. Those dudes have obviously gone through special training under hypnosis that programs the subconscious to relay a cover story if they're subjected to any kind of sedative or truth serum."

"You're a hypnotist," Encizo said, recalling a previous mission when James had used this skill to get information from Iranian terrorists in Turkey. "Can you beat Peking's programming?"

"I don't know," James confessed. "It'd take at least a week to break down subconscious training. Maybe longer. Maybe not at all. Whoever worked on those guys did a good job."

"I'm not surprised," Katz commented. "The SAD is very efficient, perhaps the most underrated intelligence outfit in the world. The SAD is remarkably small, considering the huge population of mainland China, but they're very good at their job. The Chinese have always valued quality personnel more than quantity in intelligence.''

"The ChiComs who tried to grab your boys weren't so impressive," Crane remarked.

"Kidnapping people isn't a regular part of intelligence," Katz replied. "You know that as well as I do, Mr. Crane. Besides, they didn't realize they were trying to capture a pair of tigers. If they had, they would have armed all their people with Bio-Inoculator pistols. Even then they probably wouldn't have succeeded. The Social Affairs Department is good, but my people are better."

"I was in a firefight with Gray's team in Mongolia," Alekseyev remarked. "He's not bragging."

"Well, if you blokes are so damn great," Hunntington-Smythe said crossly, "perhaps you can tell us what the hell we should do next. Your bloody President seems to think you can all walk on water. He's managed to convince the governor of Hong Kong to put you in charge of this mission. So what shall we do? Do you need to go up to a mountain and talk to God first or do you already have the answer?"

"First we talk to the SAD and see what they have to say about this," Katz replied simply.

"That's great," Crane said, shaking his head. "How the hell do we do that, your holiness?"

"Contact the Chinese embassy," Encizo told him. "The fact that some of the men involved in the ambush were with the embassy proves the SAD has agents there. Besides, almost every major country has spies working out of embassies all over the world. Why should the Chinese be any different?"

"Yeah," James added, "and you guys seem to forget that none of us committed a crime. The SAD sent agents to try to kidnap two of our buddies who responded to a violent threat in self-defense. The goddamn SAD has some explaining to do, not the other way around. Quit acting like wimps. We've got a valid complaint and a right to get some answers.''

"What if they don't care to give us any?" Kauo Yvet-sang inquired.

"Then they'd better not fuck with us anymore or we'll send some more of their agents back to 'em in a box," James replied.

"You sure there isn't any coffee?" Encizo asked hopefully.

LO HUNG-CHIN AGREED to meet Katz, Colonel Hunntington-Smythe and Major Alekseyev in a public place in one hour. The security consultant for the Chinese embassy suggested the Lan Kao restaurant a few blocks from the embassy. The others agreed.

The Phoenix Force commander, the SIS officer and the KGB agent rode to the meeting in a government limousine driven by Kauo Yvet-sang. The big car crept through the busy marketplace. Rickshas and bicycles comprised most of the traffic. Crowds filled the streets. Beggars and street merchants avoided the government vehicle. Some of the older Asians bowed their heads solemnly. Despite one hundred and fifty years of British influence, Hong Kong is still part of the Orient, and her people are largely Asian. English is the official language of Hong Kong, but Chinese is the tongue most of the citizens speak.

Chinese culture is still the foundation of Hong Kong's people. Centuries of history, art and literature and the traditions of one of the oldest civilizations of the world still influence Hong Kong. Just as the people of mainland China regarded Mao Tse-tung as a sort of twentieth century version of an emperor, so the people of Hong Kong regarded government officials with a special brand of reverence.

Some bow with respect; others bow because it is simply what one does in the presence of rulers. In ancient China, the lower classes were forbidden by law to raise their heads and look directly at anyone associated with the Royal House.

The crowds were smaller as the limo approached Embassy Row. The columns of majestic embassy buildings surrounded by ornate fences and gates somehow suited a city called Victoria. The quiet, neat and orderly section of diplomacy was a stark contrast to the marketplace. Some referred to it as "terribly British." Most people who said this had spent little time in England and none at all in East London or Piccadilly Circus or Soho.

The traffic was scarce, but the vehicles were worth noticing. Bentleys, Rolls-Royces, other limos, were the creatures of the road at Embassy Row. As the limo rolled past the Embassy of the People's Republic of China, a large black sedan emerged from a driveway and followed them. Katz grabbed a briefcase that contained an Uzi submachine gun with a folding stock. Alekseyev reached into his jacket, fingers touching the butt of his Makarov pistol.

"Do you think this is trouble?" Colonel Hunntington-Smythe asked tensely.

"Let's find out," Katz declared. "Pull over to the curb and stop."

The SIS officer told Kauo Yvet-sang to follow the Israeli's instructions. He reluctantly obeyed. The colonel's aide reached under his seat and opened a compartment that contained a Sterling subgun...just in case. The sedan came to a halt behind them, and two Asians, dressed in suits, with sunglasses and straw hats emerged from the vehicle.

"I am Lo Hung-chin," the elder of the pair announced. "I believe you gentlemen wish to speak with me."

Hunntington-Smythe opened a door and slid out. "I thought we were supposed to meet at the restaurant, Mr. Lo."

"This is more desirable," the SAD case officer stated, gesturing toward the sedan. "Shall we talk in my vehicle?"

"That's hardly neutral ground," Katz stated, climbing from the limo.

"There is a special radio transmitter in my car," Lo Hung-chin explained. "It produces a wavelength that scrambles other radio frequencies. Thus neither your people nor mine nor anyone else can listen to our conversation by electrical eavesdropping devices. The doors and frame are reinforced steel, making it most difficult for one to listen in with a . . . rifle microphone, I believe you call it."

"And the windows are tinted glass to prevent anyone from looking in," Katz noticed.

"To guard against lipreading by unfriendly agents of foreign governments," the Chinese said, smiling. "They are all around us, you know."

"Nice private place for a murder, too," Alekseyev remarked.

"Don't be absurd," Lo Hung-chin replied. "We would not kill anyone here. If we wanted you dead, we could have done it at the marketplace. Yes?"

"Let's talk," Katz announced.

Katz, Hunntington-Smythe and Alekseyev followed Lo Hung-chin to the sedan. The SAD agent's companion stood by the limo, watching Kauo Yvet-sang while the others climbed inside Lo's vehicle.

"Straight to the point," Katz declared. "A team of SAD agents attacked two of my people. Why?"

"They meant to capture your men," Lo Hung-chin replied, "not kill them. We wanted information. We wanted to learn more details about the VL-800 formula that was supposedly stolen last month."

"How did you—" Alekseyev began. He stopped himself before he could complete the sentence.

"The Soviets set up an installation in Mongolia near the Chinese border," Lo said with a shrug. "Does it surprise you that we took an interest in this and learned as many details as possible?"

"You said the SAD was good, Gray," Alekseyev muttered.

"Oh?" Lo Hung-chin turned to Katz. "How nice of you."

"You Chinese have been involved in espionage longer than anyone else," Katz replied. "Sun Tzu wrote the first textbook on the subject back in . . . 500 B.C., I believe?"

"Closer to 510," the Chinese said, nodding. "You refer to the *Ping Fa*, the *Principles of War*. An excellent book. Have you read it?"

"Indeed," Katz assured him.

"It is good to speak with an educated man," Lo declared.

"We're trying to find the people who stole the formula," Katz said. "Do you know who they are?"

"If we knew that, we would not have attempted to kidnap your friends," Lo answered. "That turned out to be a very bad choice of action. Your people must be very well trained, Mr. Gray."

"The best," Katz confirmed. "What's your interest in this matter, Mr. Lo?"

"Our interest is simple self-preservation," the SAD man replied. "The Soviets may not be our enemies, but they are certainly not our friends. Thus we are concerned when they produce new biochemical weapons close to our borders, weapons that might be used against us in the future. Even an accident could be lethal to millions of Chinese. Something like the Union Carbide chemical leak in India in 1984. If the wind blew the VL-800 across our border, who knows what destruction would occur."

"So you stole it?" Alekseyev inquired.

"Certainly not," Lo replied. "Although we considered that choice of action. Perhaps we would have done it if someone else had not done so first."

"What does the SAD plan to do here in Hong Kong?" Colonel Hunntington-Smythe asked.

"Apparently the formula is here," Lo answered. "That means it is still a great threat to my nation. This island is located by our coast, Colonel. It is very dangerous for you and for us."

"Are you familiar with an organization known as TRIO?" Katz asked.

"TRIO?" the Chinese said, frowning. "It is a criminal syndicate. Very large and well organized. They operate here in Hong Kong, Taiwan, Thailand, even within mainland China."

"What can you tell us about their activities in Hong Kong?" Katz inquired hopefully.

"Unfortunately we don't even have details about what they are doing in mainland China," Lo admitted. "Are you saying that TRIO stole the formula?"

"A strong suspicion, Mr. Lo," the Israeli replied.

"Let us make an agreement, gentlemen," the Chinese suggested. "If you will release our two agents who are currently your prisoners, the SAD will attempt to learn more about TRIO, and we shall share this information with you."

"Sounds all right," Hunntington-Smythe said with a nod. He did not bother to tell the Chinese that the SIS did not want to hold the SAD agents anyway. "You've got a deal."

"And," Lo continued, "we also want the formula to make the VL-800 for our own CBW arsenal."

"I'm afraid we can't agree to that," Alekseyev declared.

"I suggest you get authorization," Lo stated. "Mainland China is interested only in a balance of power. The Soviet Union has the VL-800 formula. I assume the United States must have it or they wouldn't be cooperating with the

KGB. Most probably England now has it or the governor of Hong Kong would not sanction your activities here. To maintain the balance of power for the safety of the entire world, the People's Republic should have the formula as well."

"Help us with the mission and you'll get it," Katz declared.

"You can authorize this?" the Chinese asked with surprise.

"You have my word," the Israeli confirmed.

"Well, I think we have a deal, gentlemen," Lo smiled.

"But I have a condition for sharing the formula with the People's Republic," Katz added. "Your government will have to agree to participate in an international research committee to find an antidote for the VL-800 formula. I suggest this committee consist of scientists from the Soviet Union, the United States and other countries including your own. Find an antidote, share it with everybody else and render the VL-800 harmless as a CBW weapon for anyone to use against another nation."

"What an extraordinary notion," the Chinese said with amazement. "Will all the governments of the other nations involved agree to this?"

"If they don't," Katz answered, "I suggest we go public. You fellows might not be able to do that, but I can. Threaten to reveal the details about a deadly CBW device created by the Soviets and shared with the Americans, the British and the Chinese. The superpowers can either cooperate to find an antidote or they can all have world opinion turned against them."

"Your own people might kill you if you do this," Alekseyev warned.

"They might try," Katz said with a shrug. "But I doubt it. I think we can make this work. What do you think, Mr. Lo?"

"I'll speak with my superiors," the Chinese replied. "Well, this has certainly been an interesting conversation. I wonder how it will all turn out?"

"We'll let you know," Katz told him, opening the car door.

"Oh, Mr. Gray," Lo added, "the SAD won't forget that two of your friends killed five of our people. For now, we'll let it go as an unfortunate misunderstanding. However, if we ever have reason to cross swords with your group again . . . well, we won't be so gentle."

"Thanks for the warning," Katz replied as he slid from the car. "Just remember, my people are used to playing rough."

13

By eight o'clock that evening, the Hong Kong police had blocked off most of Lung Harbor. The cops had been told only that an international smuggling ring was operating there. Colonel Hunntington-Smythe told the chief of police in Victoria to let SIS and agents of "Interpol" handle the close work. The police would maintain a security ring around the harbor to capture any hoodlums who might attempt to escape.

"Bear in mind that these men are highly dangerous and probably well armed," the SIS officer warned. "Make certain your men have firearms and that they're ready to use them."

Phoenix Force, John Trent and the three KGB agents prepared for the raid. They donned black camouflage uniforms. Katz armed himself with his Uzi, SIG Sauer P-226 pistol and a .380 Beretta for backup. McCarter stuck with his favorite weapons—an M-10 Ingram and Browning Hi-Power. Manning carried his FAL assault rifle and an Eagle .357 Magnum autoloader. James selected an M-16 assault rifle with an M-203 grenade launcher attached to the underside of the barrel, in addition to his .45 caliber Colt pistol. Encizo carried his Heckler and Koch MP-5 machine pistol, a Walther PPK in shoulder leather and a 9 mm S&W pistol on his hip.

Besides their firearms, Phoenix Force also carried both fragmentation grenades and SAS-style flash-bang concussion blasters. Manning hauled additional explosives in his backpack, with pencil detonators in his pockets. Encizo carried his big Cold Steel Tanto on his belt and a smaller Gerber Mark II fighting dagger in an ankle sheath. Calvin James had his pet blade, a Jet Aer G-96 combat dagger, in a sheath under his right arm, clipped to his Jackass Leather shoulder holster rig.

John Trent wore the traditional black costume of a ninja, with a cloth mask and hood that concealed his head and face except for a narrow gap for his eyes. His split-toed *tabi* boots were designed for climbing, and his *gi* jacket had concealed pockets that contained *shaken* throwing stars, *metsubushi* sight removers, and two spare magazines for his Colt Commander. He carried the pistol in shoulder leather under his left arm. The *ninja-do* sword was thrust in a black obi sash around his waist, and his *manrikigusari* was tucked in the sash at the small of his back.

Major Alekseyev, Captain Zhdanov and Lieutenant Savchenko carried their Makarov 9 mm pistols and Sterling submachine guns supplied by the Hong Kong SIS. Kauo Yvet-sang and Gerald Crane were also armed with Sterlings.

The assault force congregated by the police barricade. Colonel Hunntington-Smythe raised a pair of Bushnell binoculars and peered down at Lung Harbor at a small ship docked there. Track lights mounted on the storage houses illuminated the pier. Crates were stacked along the harbor, and husky stevedores hauled burdens to the gangplank of the vessel.

"I count nine...no, ten men," the SIS officer announced. "Make that eleven. Probably more on the ship and in the buildings."

"We'll find out," Katz replied. "Does Kauo Yvet-sang have our warrant?"

"I'll give it to him," Hunntington-Smythe stated. "The search warrant is made out for the SIS, with Interpol attached, to search for alleged contraband, including drugs, illegal firearms and other dangerous substances. That means a senior SIS officer should deliver the warrant to Po Chiangping."

"There could be violence," the Israeli warned. "Are you sure you're up to it?"

"I don't think I'm much older than you, Mr. Gray," the SIS colonel said defensively. "I'm fifty-two years old."

"Actually," Katz replied with a shrug, "you're a few years younger than I am. That isn't the point. You've been deskbound for a long time. When was the last time you were in the field or even at a firing range?"

"I can take care of myself," Hunntington-Smythe declared, taking a snub-nosed .32 caliber revolver from a holster on his belt.

"Can't you do better than that thing?" Manning remarked. "It's not a combat weapon. The caliber is too small for stopping power, the barrel is too short for accuracy and it only holds six rounds. You won't be able to reload it as quickly as an autoloader."

"But revolvers don't jam," Hunntington-Smythe said as he opened the cylinder and checked his revolver.

"Any weapon can jam," the Canadian told him. "You want to carry that peashooter for backup, that's up to you. But, you'd better take along something with some decent stopping power and a range greater than six feet."

"This will do," the SIS colonel said with annoyance, clearly offended by the younger man's advice.

"Give me the warrant," Katz ordered.

"You're not SIS," Hunntington-Smythe complained.

"You're not ready to go into combat," the Israeli insisted. "Now give me the warrant. I'm not going to have you jeopardize this operation out of personal vanity."

"Here," the SIS officer hissed through clenched teeth as he thrust the search warrant into Katz's hand. "You'd better not make any mistakes, Gray."

"He doesn't make many," Rafael Encizo commented. "I think we're ready to roll. Everybody has been briefed."

"Let's do it," Katz said with a nod, and Phoenix Force and its allies moved into position.

Katz, McCarter and Kauo Yvet-sang went forward. They headed straight for the center of the harbor. Encizo, Alekseyev and Lieutenant Savchenko formed a line of defense behind them. James commanded another backup team with Gerald Crane and Captain Zhdanov. Gary Manning, the rifle expert, remained at the rear. Trent would do what a ninja does best. He would penetrate the enemy position in his own fashion.

Several stevedores saw three heavily armed figures approach the harbor. Two of them started to dash to a storage house, but Kauo Yvet-sang shouted a warning in Chinese. The stevedores stopped abruptly and raised their hands over their heads.

"We're with the Security Intelligence Service and Interpol, Special International Enforcement Division!" Katz announced in a loud voice. "We have a search warrant—"

"I am Po Chiang-ping," a tall, pole-thin Asian declared in crisp English as he stomped from a small shacklike building across from the storage houses. "I am the company manager of this harbor after 6:00 p.m. What do you want?"

"We've been informed of illegal activities that are specified in the warrant, Mr. Po," Katz replied. "Please do not resist. We have the harbor surrounded."

"No one intends to resist," Po said with disgust as he jammed his hands into his pants pockets. "Let me see that warrant."

"Of course," Katz said, using the tri-hook of his prosthesis to pull the document from his shirt pocket.

Po reached for it with one hand, but suddenly drew a small .25 automatic from his pocket. He tried to grab Katz's prosthetic arm, planning to pull the Israeli off-balance to jam the .25 against his head and threaten to kill Katz if the others did not drop their weapons.

It was a clumsy tactic that did not have a chance of success against Yakov Katzenelenbogen. The Israeli was faster than Po. The steel hooks of his prosthesis snared Po's wrist before he could grab the Israeli. Katz chopped the stubby barrel of his Uzi against the fist holding the diminutive .25 caliber handgun. The little pistol fell to the boardwalk.

Katz applied pressure with the hooks and twisted forcibly. Bone crunched, and Po screamed as his wrist was pulverized in the viselike metal grip. Katz slammed the frame of his Uzi against the side of the Asian's skull and knocked him out cold. Po Chiang-ping fell senseless at Katz's feet.

This was a signal for all hell to break loose.

Four stevedores near the trio launched a desperate attack. Armed with knives and grappling hooks, they charged Katz, McCarter and Kauo Yvet-sang. The tactic was virtually suicide. David McCarter immediately hosed the attackers with a long spray of 9 mm rounds from his Ingram M-10. Parabellums chopped into the chests of two opponents, kicking their bodies into backward arcs ending in death.

Kauo Yvet-sang hesitated as the other two leaped toward him. He raised his Sterling in time to block a grappling hook, but the force of his opponent's charge toppled the SIS lieutenant. Both men fell to the boardwalk, the stevedore on top of Kauo Yvet-sang.

The muscular stevedore placed a hand on Kauo's Sterling and shoved it against the SIS man's chest to pin him as the hook rose. The hood planned to bury the sharp tip in

Kauo's face. The SIS agent suddenly bent a knee and pumped it into his foe's kidney. The stevedore fell forward, and his hook was thrown off target. Kauo Yvet-sang heard metal bite into wood less than an inch from his head.

Kauo's hands streaked out to slap his palms into the stevedore's ears. The man cried out in pain from a ruptured eardrum. Kauo swiftly slashed the side of his hand across his opponent's windpipe. As the stevedore tumbled off Kauo Yvet-sang, his hands clutching his throat, the fourth attacker prepared to plunge the seven-inch blade of his knife into the SIS agent's heart.

McCarter's Ingram fired a three-round burst. The impact hurled the knife artist away from the fallen Kauo. The stevedore fell, and Kauo Yvet-sang rose to one knee in time to train his Sterling subgun on a group of gun-toting figures who suddenly emerged from a storage house. The SIS man triggered his weapon, and tong enforcers screamed as bullets tore their bodies to bits.

Kauo did not take out the group alone. Rafael Encizo and the two KGB agents under his command supplied additional firepower. Encizo nailed two opponents with a volley of H&K projectiles while Major Alekseyev and Lieutenant Savchenko burned two more with Sterling slugs. The tong soldiers melted to the planks, their flesh ravaged by more than thirty 9 mm rounds.

A figure armed with an old British-made Sten Mark I submachine gun emerged from the tiny office building. He aimed his weapon at Katz and McCarter, and suddenly his forehead exploded with a splitting headache. The 7.62 mm missile tunneled through his brain and killed him before he could hear the report of Gary Manning's FAL rifle. The Canadian marksman swiftly swung the muzzle of his weapon toward movement at the window of a warehouse. A figure used the barrel of a rifle to shatter glass and prepared to aim at the Phoenix pair on the dock.

"Not today," Manning rasped as he squeezed the trigger of his FAL twice.

Two rounds struck the would-be assassin in the center of the chest. The figure dropped from view.

"Not ever," Manning added. Switching the selector switch to full-auto, the Canadian commando jogged closer to the battle.

Calvin James realized Captain Zhdanov and Gerald Crane had little, if any, combat experience. That was why they had stayed to the rear. The KGB captain and the CIA agent who secretly wanted to be the star of *Miami Vice* could get themselves killed if they wanted, James thought, but Phoenix Force did not intend to let the pair interfere with the mission.

The only problem, as James saw it, was what the hell to do with the green troopers. The solution was supplied when enemy gunmen started to smash windows to aim their weapons at the raiders. James ordered Zhdanov and Crane to open fire at the building. Sterling full-auto slugs chewed at the walls and windowsills. A couple rounds even struck one of the gunmen. All James wanted his men to do for the moment was pin down the enemy.

The black badass pointed his M-16 at a different target. Several figures were darting about on the ship docked at Lung Harbor. Several shapes carried firearms, and two were busy setting up a Type 67 light machine gun on the deck. The Type 67 was manufactured in the People's Republic of China. Obviously TRIO had gun-smuggling connections with the mainland.

James aimed his assault rifle carefully, the butt braced at his hip and the barrel canted up. He triggered the M-203 attached to the rifle. A 40 mm explosive shell was hurled from the grenade launcher. It sailed into the ship and blasted the deck spart, the explosion crushing the Type 67 chattergun and ripping its team limb from limb. Two opponents were pitched over the handrail by the force of the blast. They splashed into the water and floated lifeless on the surface.

Katz, McCarter and Kauo dashed for cover. They ran toward the stacks of crates, but that sanctuary was already occupied. Two enemy gunmen opened fire at the trio. Kauo threw himself to the boardwalk and fumbled with his weapon. Katz landed on his belly and braced his Uzi across the forearm of his prosthesis. The Israeli returned fire with deadly accuracy. One gunman tossed his Type 56 assault rifle in the air. He lowered his outspread fingers toward his bullet-shattered face, but he died before they reached it.

McCarter yanked the pin from an SAS concussion grenade and hurled it at the crates while Katz covered him, letting loose a barrage of Uzi slugs. The flash-bang blaster exploded. Three crates tumbled from the stack. A tong buttonman stumbled from cover and collapsed, blood pouring from his nostrils and ears.

Kauo bolted for the crates. He suddenly spun about, dropped his Sterling subgun and sat down hard. The SIS man clasped his left hand to the fountain of blood that bubbled from his bullet-punctured right bicep. A gunman on the roof of a storage house had seen Kauo go down and aimed his Sten Mark I at the SIS agent, determined to finish the job.

Yakov Katzenelenbogen and David McCarter raised their weapons and opened fire. Twin streams of 9 mm rounds slashed the gunman. His bullet-riddled body slid down the roof and tumbled from the eaves to the ground. McCarter dashed to Kauo, grabbed the back of the guy's collar and dragged him to the cover of the crates. Katz supplied cover fire with his Uzi as he followed.

"Think we should let them know they're all under arrest?" the Briton commented as he removed a spent magazine from his Ingram machine pistol and reached for a fresh clip.

"Maybe later," Katz replied. "I don't think they feel like listening right now."

TWO BLACK SERPENT TONG ENFORCERS opened the rear door to a storage house and crept outside. The pair hoped to either ambush the assault force from a new direction or, better yet, to reach one of the small boats tied under the pier to escape the carnage. Instead, they found themselves face-to-face with a startling vision—a figure dressed in black, complete with a ninja mask and hood.

John Trent swung his *ninja-do*. The sword deflected the barrel of the closest man's M-3 greasegun. Trent turned his wrists and slashed the edge of the long blade across the hoodlum's throat.

Blood spurted from the lethal wound as the first opponent fell. His comrade tried to aim a Type 51 pistol at Trent as the ninja raised his sword again. The blade descended before the tong goon could squeeze the trigger. Sharp steel split open the gunman's face from the crown of his head to the bridge of his nose. He died on his feet. Trent yanked the sword from his opponent's skull and allowed the corpse to fall.

Trent crept to the door and cautiously peered into the storage house. The place was filled with columns of crates and stacks of large bags marked in Chinese and English as containing rice. There were several corpses sprawled on the floor, but three hoodlums were alive and well and busy trying to pry the lids from two crates. One man was using an iron crowbar while the other two clawed at a wooden box with stevedore hooks.

"Just couldn't wait till Christmas, huh?" Trent remarked as he stepped toward the trio.

Alarmed by the mysterious figure who had seemed to materialize from nowhere, the stevedores attacked with the tools in their hands. As one man raised his crowbar, Trent stepped forward and punched the tip of his *ninja-do* into the hollow of his opponent's throat. The crowbar fell, and the man dropped to his knees, hands clutching his streaming throat.

Another stevedore swung his hook. Trent's blade blocked the attack. The hood pulled, trying to snare the sword and yank it from Trent's grasp. The ninja suddenly stepped back and yanked his sword downward. The razor edge sliced fingers fisted around the handle of the stevedore hook. The tong flunky shrieked as the hook, and three of his fingers, hit the floor.

Trent thrust his fists forward and slammed the butt of his sword under the man's jaw. The tong goon's teeth clashed together, and he fell unconscious. The third stevedore attacked with a steel hook in each fist. Trent made a backhand sword sweep at the man to force him to jump back. The ninja needed the room to wield his sword.

The ninja raised the blade overhead as his opponent assumed a bow-and-arrow kung fu stance, stevedore hooks poised like two great talons. Trent guessed that his opponent was waiting for him to attack. When he delivered the sword stroke, the tong goon would try to trap the blade with the two hooks. Of course, it was a guess, but an informed one. If he was wrong, he'd have to live with it—he hoped.

Trent executed a quick chopping motion with the sword. The stevedore raised the hooks and crossed the steel talons to block the attack before he realized it was a feint. Trent suddenly stepped to the right and slashed the sword across the tong's wrists. The hooks fell to the floor with fists still clenched to the handles. Blood jetted from the stumps at the ends of the stevedore's wrists. He howled in agony until Trent whipped the back of his fist at the tong's face. A big knuckle hit the guy between the eyes, and he fell senseless at the ninja's feet.

CALVIN JAMES FIRED another M-203 grenade at the ship. The explosion shattered thermite across the fly bridge and deck, the burning fluid covering the vessel. The tactic was ruthless but necessary. If the VL-800 formula was aboard the ship, it might already be leaking. James could not take that risk, so he opted to burn the ship and everything it carried.

Unfortunately this included any crew members who failed to escape the merciless thermite. Several men dived overboard. Others scrambled down the gangplank to the pier. A couple were trapped on the ship. They shrieked but their suffering was brief. Gary Manning shot one man with a trio of FAL rounds through the head. James picked off the other guy with a three-round burst of 5.56 mm slugs from his M-16 rifle.

Major Alekseyev and Lieutenant Savchenko fired at the gunmen stationed at the windows of the only storage house that still contained battling tong followers. While the KGB agents kept the enemy busy, Rafael Encizo ran to the cover of a forklift, crouching behind it. The Cuban pulled the pin from a concussion grenade and hurled it into a window. He ducked low and covered his head.

The grenade exploded. Glass burst from the windows, the door popped open and two tong enforcers tumbled across the threshold. Encizo and Savchenko headed for the building. Major Alekseyev covered them, watching for lurking adversaries. A tong gunman, not noticing the KGB case officer, pointed a Type 68 rifle at Encizo and Savchenko. Alekseyev saw the barrel of the gunman's weapon appear at the corner of the storage house. The Russian raised his Sterling subgun and waited for the killer to show his face. When the tong hitter's head poked behind the rifle, Alekseyev opened fire. The man's face vanished beneath a veil of blood, and tumbled to the ground.

The two dazed goons who had been thrown from the building started to rise. Both were unsteady on their feet and clearly disoriented. Blood trickled from their nostrils. One man placed a hand to his head, trying to muffle the pain of a shattered eardrum.

"Stay down," Encizo instructed as he slammed a fist to the jaw of the nearest man.

The guy obeyed. He hit the ground and passed out. The other tong enforcer reached for a Chinese Tokarev pistol in his belt. Lieutenant Savchenko grabbed the man before he could draw the weapon. The big Russian wrapped a brawny arm around the hood's throat and drove a heel-of-the-palm stroke behind an ear. The tong's head jerked violently from the blow. Vertebrae cracked when his neck broke. Savchenko released his opponent, and the man's limp body wilted to the boardwalk.

Encizo dashed to the door. He carefully peered inside and, seeing several unconscious and dazed Chinese sprawled on the floor, gestured for Savchenko and Alekseyev to come forward. The Russians advanced, and Encizo removed some unbreakable plastic riot cuffs from his belt. Alekseyev held his Sterling submachine gun ready while Savchenko and the Cuban warrior bound the wrists and ankles of the stunned tong members.

Only a handful of Asian goons who had bolted from the ship to the boardwalk remained. Without cover, they were caught in the open with only two options—surrender or die fighting. They chose the latter.

The tong members opened fire. Gary Manning and Calvin James answered it with their assault rifles switched to full-auto. Bullets slashed the hoodlums. Bodies fell, but the tong gunmen continued to fire at the raiders. Captain Zhdanov boldly rose and placed the stock of his Sterling submachine gun to his shoulder.

Eight bullets slammed in his chest. The Russian officer was propelled six feet by the impact and fell lifeless to the boardwalk. Manning and James continued to hose the enemy with high-velocity slugs. Katz and McCarter contributed to the firepower, creating a deadly crossfire. Within seconds the last of the tong flunkies lay dead on the blood-spattered pier.

"All right!" Katz shouted to his team. "That's it! Round up the prisoners and let's see what we've got!"

14

"Congratulations, Gray," Colonel Hunntington-Smythe said dryly. "You and your team killed a great many people for nothing."

The SIS officer tossed a clipboard on his desk and rose from his swivel chair. He glared at Yakov Katzenelenbogen and Major Vikor Alekseyev who sat across from Hunntington-Smythe. The SIS officer jammed a finger at the sheet clipped to the board.

"This is a list of what was recovered from Lung Harbor," Hunntington-Smythe announced. "Opium, firearms manufactured in Taiwan and mainland China, merchandise, which is probably stolen...but no VL-800 formula."

"That still isn't 'nothing,'" Alekseyev commented. "It proves the tip about the Black Serpent Tong was accurate. It was a criminal operation, just as we thought it was—"

"But not the *right* one," Hunntington-Smythe complained. "The enemy has been warned. They'll be twice as difficult to find now. You've really botched this mission, Gray. I intend to make a complete report about this fiasco to the governor. You might be an influential character with whatever outfit you work for, but your career is finished as of now!"

"Slight exaggeration, Colonel," Katz said. "The mission isn't over yet."

"What do you suggest we do now?" Hunntington-Smythe demanded. "Your only lead went sour, Gray. You know that as well as I do. Time for you and your friends to go home. And same goes for you and your KGB friends, Major.''

"Friend," Alekseyev corrected. "Captain Zhdanov was killed. The lieutenant and I aren't leaving until this mystery is solved, Colonel.''

"I can have you deported," Hunntington-Smythe warned.

"Not right away, you can't," Alekseyev insisted. "Until the governor agrees to throw us out of Hong Kong and sends us back to the Soviet Union, Savchenko and I will continue our mission. The honor of my country is at stake, Colonel. I don't intend to back off simply because you're ready to quit.''

"Honor of your country?" the SIS officer scoffed. "You Russians don't know what the word 'honor' means—''

"Let's stop name-calling, Colonel," Katz said sharply. "Major Alekseyev deserves better than that. I don't like communism—especially the Soviet brand of Communism—any better than you do, but the major is not responsible for the policies of the Kremlin and he didn't have anything to do with the VL-800 formula. Major Alekseyev and his men have risked their lives trying to help us locate it. They deserve respect as men of courage, regardless of their politics.''

"We've all been prepared to risk our lives for this mission," Hunntington-Smythe snapped. "I would have actively participated in the raid on Lung Harbor, but you refused to allow me to do so.''

"And I told you why," Katz said without apology. "I didn't wish to insult you, Colonel, but I couldn't let you participate. You're not a field commander. Not anymore, at least. But you don't have to be. Your experience and expertise as a shaker and a mover with the brass here in Hong Kong makes you far more valuable to us here, behind that desk, than you would have been at the pier. The connections you have with the government and the police have been a great help to us. We still need that help, Colonel."

"I see," Hunntington-Smythe sighed. He realized Katz was trying to salve his wounded ego, yet much of what the Israeli said was true. The SIS officer was not too stubborn to appreciate Katz's wisdom. "What do we do now?"

"Interrogate prisoners and hope we get something valuable from them," Katz replied. "Personally, I'm exhausted. Would it be possible for us to set up some cots or sleeping bags here?"

"Of course," the SIS colonel answered. "I suppose we could all do with a few hours' sleep. My poor wife probably doesn't remember what I look like by now. Think I'll go home to her before she decides to get a replacement. We'll tackle this mess anew in the morning."

"Interrogations had better start tonight," Alekseyev suggested. "The tong members we captured should not be allowed to rest or communicate with each other."

"We'll sleep in intervals," Katz agreed. "That way we can get some rest without allowing the prisoners to sleep. I'll also talk to Mr. Johnson about the possibility of using scopolamine on the prisoners."

"Johnson is the black man, right?" Hunntington-Smythe said, frowning. "Are you certain he knows what he's doing with that stuff? Scopolamine is a very powerful truth serum. It can kill a man if the dosage is too strong."

"Mr. Johnson has used scopolamine on captives in several previous missions," Katz stated. "He's never lost a patient."

"I won't argue," the SIS man replied wearily.

"Speaking of patients," Alekseyev began. "Any word from the clinic about the condition of Kauo Yvet-sang?"

"Yes," Hunntington-Smythe confirmed. "His bicep muscle was damaged, but no serious internal bleeding or broken bone. He ought to be all right."

"Glad to hear it," the Russian said, rising from his chair. "Well, I'm going to talk to Savchenko and tell him how things are going."

"I have to talk to my people, too," Katz added. He and Alekseyev moved to the door. "See you in the morning, Colonel."

"Of course," Hunntington-Smythe replied. "Oh, Major? Thanks for asking about Kauo."

"You're welcome," Alekseyev said with a nod. After he and Katz left the office, the Russian whispered. "Why did he thank me for asking about his aide?"

"I think he wanted to let you know he thinks you might be human after all," Katz said, smiling. "Of course, he doesn't know you as well as we do."

"Thanks a lot," the KGB man muttered, but he realized Katz was joking. For some reason, this pleased him.

Rafael Encizo and Calvin James met the Phoenix Force unit commander and the KGB officer in the corridor. They asked "Mr. Gray" to speak with them privately. Alekseyev left the three Phoenix fighters and continued to search for Savchenko.

"What is it?" Katz asked, taking a pack of Camels from his pocket.

"Calvin and I want to know something," Encizo answered. "And we want a straight answer. Okay?"

"You need to ask?" the Israeli inquired, firing a cigarette.

"Back at the harbor," James began. "You put me in charge of Zhdanov and Crane. Neither one of them is an experienced field agent. Well, the Russian got killed—"

"Nobody's blaming you for that, Cal," Katz assured him.

"That isn't what's bothering me," James insisted. "You forced me to stay at the rear instead of getting into the middle of the battle. I couldn't just leave those two to fend for themselves. You gave me the milk run, Yakov."

"Yeah," Encizo stated. "Me, too. You put me with Alekseyev and Savchenko."

"They're experienced agents," Katz reminded him.

"And they could cover for me," Encizo declared. "Clever move, Yakov. You gave us the safest jobs during the raid without being obvious about it."

"Nobody had a milk run during the raid," Katz assured him.

"You and McCarter took the greatest risk," James said. "Gary stayed at the rear because he's a skilled sniper. But you wanted us in the background because you figured we might freeze. Right?"

"Neither of you has ever frozen in combat," the Israeli replied. "I put you in charge of other, less-experienced men for the raid and you think I'm giving you an easy job? What do you regard as difficult, my friends? Wrestling polar bears while blindfolded?"

"Come on, Yakov," Encizo began, pulling a glove from his right hand. He held the palm open to display the puffy circular scar in the center of his palm. "This has you worried. Doesn't it?"

"Seems to be healing nicely," Katz commented.

"Look, man," James said. "Rafael and I were tortured by those assholes at the Vatican. After something like that happens, a dude is usually washed-up for work in the field."

"Not necessarily," Katz replied. "But I'll level with you. I would have preferred to give you men time to rest and recover from the experience before going into the field again. It would have been better if we could have done some training exercises before this mission, but there just wasn't time. For that matter, Trent should have had more time to recover from being shot by friendly fire during the Vatican affair. That was a nasty experience, too, but not as bad as being tortured.''

"But you still claim we didn't get a milk run during the raid on the harbor?" Encizo inquired.

"That's right," Katz insisted. "You two held up fine during the firefight in the Gobi with those bandits. You worked as smooth as silk during the raid. I'm not worried about how you'll cope with pressure in the field. You've already proven you can handle it.''

"I have to admit," Encizo began. "I was really rattled when we landed in Moscow. The idea of being captured and worked over by the KGB had me sweating bullets.''

"Good Lord," Katz said, laughing. "We *all* felt that way. Don't worry if you're human. Our line of work requires a special sort of man with special abilities, but we're still just flesh and blood with all the emotional and psychological baggage that goes with being human. Thank God we've got it. Otherwise, we'd probably be like some of the scum we come up against. Spiritually dead. Unable to feel compassion or care if what we're doing is right or wrong.''

"So we were worried about nothing, huh?" James asked hopefully.

"We all have to be a bit concerned about what stress and battlefield fatigue do to us," Katz answered. "I've seen men who became so paranoid and overconditioned they couldn't safely walk the streets of a city. If a fellow reached in a jacket for a wallet or cigarettes, the overwrought warrior thinks the stranger is reaching for a gun and immediately attacks. If someone bumps into him in a crowd, the poor devil whirls to confront his 'opponent' and goes for the throat.''

"Sort of like attack dogs that get to a level where nobody can safely handle them," James remarked. "Eventually their owners have to have them destroyed.''

"The same thing can happen with people," Katz confirmed. "But none of us is in any danger of that just yet."

"Have you talked to McCarter lately?" Encizo commented.

"David handles the balance as well as any of us," the Israeli assured them. "Don't forget, he has a live-in girl friend back in London. None of the rest of us have managed to sustain a relationship with a female since we joined Phoenix Force. Don't worry about McCarter. He's got his head together, even if it doesn't seem so most of the time."

"I hope so," James said, grinning. "What's our next move?"

"We'll take turns getting some sleep," Katz replied. "We've got some prisoners to interrogate, but I think it's unlikely any of them know a damn thing about the VL-800 formula. They were involved in a Black Serpent Tong smuggling operation. No reason for them to know about anything else the tong is up to. They probably don't even know about TRIO."

"Doesn't look very good right now," Encizo sighed.

"It could sure look a lot better," Katz was forced to agree.

15

Temujin paced the tile floor of Chou Minchuan's office, muttering in his native tongue. Chou Minchuan did not understand Mongolian, but he guessed Temujin was growling about the mission.

Chou Minchuan was a subleader of the Black Serpent Tong. He was forty years old, a bit paunchy at the waist and prematurely gray. Temujin did not worry Chou Minchuan. The Chinese regarded himself as a businessman. The tong supplied people with items that they could not get through legal channels. Like any other business, the tong relied on customers' interest in order to exist. He saw nothing particularly evil about the tong. It was simply a business with profits and losses, sales and agreements, developing new markets and the necessary termination of customer services, even though this occasionally meant terminating the customer.

The Chinese gangster did not like Temujin. He regarded Mongols as barbarians, as uncouth louts who did not understand the principles of good business and profit investments. Traditional animosities notwithstanding, Chou Minchuan got along fine with the yakuza members of TRIO. The Japanese understood business. They had embraced the twentieth century and were rapidly moving into the twenty-first. The Mongols, in Chou Minchuan's opinion, were still backward savages who believed only in brute force as a method of conquest.

Temujin was a typical example of this, the Chinese thought. The young Mongol was dressed in baggy fatigue uniform trousers and shirt. He wore a sheepskin vest and boots made of goat hide. Temujin carried a pistol and fighting dagger on his belt, as if he expected to plunge into battle right there in Chou Minchuan's office. Absurd, the tong subchief thought sourly.

Of course, Temujin was young. Too young to be commanding other men. He was the son of that lunatic Tosha Khan, who dreamed of reviving the Mongol Empire. Did that fool really believe the Chinese and Japanese members of TRIO would ever allow him to do that? Even if it was possible, the tong and yakuza elements would prevent the Mongols of the New Horde from carrying out such a scheme. Self-preservation was a very powerful instinct.

"They're here," Temujin said sharply, addressing Chou Minchuan and Akira Osato in thickly accented Mandarin Chinese. "The raid on Lung Harbor was carried out by the same men who were at the installation site in Mongolia, the same men who have been a thorn in the side of TRIO for more than a year."

"You may be right," Akira Osato began. The Japanese spoke softly, his voice calm. Osato was a man of great discipline. He had trained his voice and facial muscles to conceal his emotions. Chou Minchuan admired his skill. "But this only proves the enemy has no idea where we have the VL-800 formula. It is safe, Temujin-san. There is no need to fear."

"I fear no man!" Temujin said angrily.

"Fear was a poor choice of word," Akira Osato said. "Rather, there is no need for concern that the enemy will discover the formula before it is too late."

"You aren't thinking of destroying it?" the Mongol demanded. "I know Shimo was opposed to this operation, but my father and Wang Tse-tu voted in favor of it. Shimo fi-

nally saw the value of the formula and agreed to participate.''

"Reluctantly agreed," Osato said softly. "Shimo-sama
only agreed because it is essential that all members of TRIO
work together. Mongol, Chinese and Japanese must cooperate. Otherwise we shall all perish together.''

"You do not approve of the plan to use the formula to
bring our enemies to their knees?'' Temujin asked.

"Whether we approve or not has nothing to do with
this,'' Chou stated. "We have been ordered to protect the
formula and arrange for its covert sale to foreign governments. However, your father stole the VL-800 from the
Russians without consulting the other leaders of TRIO.
That was inconsiderate.''

"How dare you criticize Tosha Khan!'' the Mongol
snapped, his hand reaching for the gun on his hip.

"Brother Chou merely states that your father has put us
in an awkward position,'' Osato remarked. "He suddenly
acquired a commodity that we had no market for. His original idea was to use the formula to blackmail the Soviet
government or even to use it aggressively against the Soviet
people. This would clearly be too dangerous to attempt.
Selling the formula to other governments is the best way to
make a profit, but even that involves more risk than our
usual operations.''

"The potential for profit is great,'' Chou said, trying to
calm the angry young Mongol. "Providing, of course, we
can make the sales successfully. Selling to governments,
especially those of Third World countries, is always a risky
business. Politicians are cheats and liars by nature. Many of
them might contact Moscow before agreeing to the sale.
This causes many hazards that should be obvious, Temujin.''

"But you still have to obey orders," the Mongol sneered. "And I say we should also kill the team of butchers from America."

"You tried that in Mongolia," Osato commented. "It did not work very well then."

"I left the task to bandits," Temujin replied. "This time we shall use our own people and do the job correctly."

"If these men are the same individuals who destroyed our operations in San Francisco and the Philippines," Chou mused, "then our own people have tried to kill them in the past."

"So, you're afraid?" Temujin said with contempt.

"There is no point in killing them," Osato answered. "Our contact within the SIS has already informed us that the commandos—or whatever they call themselves—have no idea where to find the formula. They do not present a problem to us at this time."

"The fact they are still alive is a problem," the Mongol insisted. "One does not deal with enemies by ignoring them. You find out who they are, where they are, and crush them."

"No action will be taken against them unless they seem to be close to learning details about us," Chou insisted. "The subject is closed, Temujin. Our main concern at the present is to secure foreign markets for the VL-800 and arrange the sales."

"Then I'll leave you gentlemen to your computers and telephones," Temujin muttered as he stomped from the office.

"Mongols," Chou hissed with disgust. "They would turn back the clock to the twelfth century."

"And they have no patience," Osato added. "No spiritual discipline."

Chou smiled and nodded. He was glad to be working with someone with whom he had so much in common.

TEMUJIN MET with Yumjaagiyin and Khorloin, two of his most trusted lieutenants, Mongols who had belonged to the New Horde since Tosha Khan had first established the organization. Their loyalty was clearly to the Horde and its founder, not to TRIO. They were honored to serve Temujin, the son of the great Khan, and they obeyed him without question.

Yumjaagiyin and Khorloin followed Temujin outside the main house. Tosha Khan's son did not trust the Chinese and Japanese who outnumbered his small Mongol group. He did not feel comfortable discussing private matters with his men within the walls of Chou Minchuan's house. The three Mongols moved across the parade field. The shadows of night seemed to envelop them with a cloak of security.

"You know that our enemies have followed us here from Mongolia," Temujin told his men. "They are in Hong Kong, hunting us at this moment. I spoke with Chou and Osato. They choose to ignore this threat. They are like the ostrich. Those fools would bury their heads in the sand while their enemies closed in with guns and nets."

"The Chinese have always been weaklings and the Japanese have always been corrupt," Khorloin hissed, proving that prejudice was a universal form of stupidity.

"They're afraid to take direct action," Temujin continued. "If my father was here, he would have their heads cut off. Unfortunately, I cannot punish them... yet. Later, I shall ask permission to personally execute those cowards."

"Is there nothing we can do about the commando team that threatens to destroy us, Temujin?" Yumjaagiyin inquired.

"Not if we listen to Chou and Osato," the Mongol subchief answered. "But I have no intention of allowing their cowardice to rob my father and my people of this great victory. That is why I have brought you here to speak in confidence. I have a mission for you."

"Tell us what we must do," Khorloin replied, ready to obey before he heard the task.

"There is a petty hoodlum in Hong Kong," Temujin began. "I have his name and address. The man is an informer who has already been contacted by the enemy. It is believed he gave them the information about the Lung Harbor episode being a tong operation. I want you to go to this man and force him to help us lay a trap for these Westerners who dare stalk us like animals. I will also tell you how to locate some tong enforcers to assist you. Do not tell the Chinese I sent you. Tell them the orders come from Chou Minchuan. By the time they find out otherwise, the trap will already have sprung shut on our enemies. They shall be dead, and Chou will be busy trying to take credit for the success of my plan."

"It shall be done, Temujin," Khorloin assured him.

"Of that I have no doubt," the Mongol subchief said with a smile.

16

The sun rose and splashed the skies above Hong Kong with gold and pink. A halo of light glowed around white cloud formations. The pale blue firmament flowed overhead like a message of hope and a promise of salvation.

Yet the light of dawn brought no illumination for the problems that confronted Phoenix Force. They had questioned prisoners, poured over SIS and police reports concerning tong activities and checked the records of Black Serpent enforcers both living and dead. Nothing seemed to offer even a slight clue as to the location of the VL-800 formula.

At the insistence of Manning, Encizo and James, a large coffee urn had been set up in Colonel Hunntington-Smythe's office. The Canadian sat at a table, wearily leafing through lists of merchandise delivered at Lung Harbor over the last three weeks. Lieutenant Savchenko stirred a glass of hot tea. Like most Russians, he thought tea tasted better in a glass than a cup. The KGB officer was searching through the criminal records of some of the men who had been killed during the raid. He sipped his tea and sighed.

"I wonder if any of this is getting us to any place," he remarked.

"To any place?" Gary Manning looked up from his papers. "You mean 'is getting us anywhere'?"

"That is what I said, is it not?" Savchenko replied. "It is an odd expression. You Americans have many strange expressions. Where are you from in the United States? New York? California? Washington, D.C.?''

"I've been to a few places from time to time," Manning replied. "I'm not really sure where home is these days."

"I have always wanted to go to the United States," the Russian said, smiling. "Is it true they have television networks that the state does not own?"

"Yeah," the Canadian replied. "In fact, the TV news media tends to criticize the government and the President. Regardless of who happens to be in office or what the government policies happen to be, some members of the media will condemn and others will praise whatever's going on. Not always a fair balance of the two, but I'd say the criticisms are usually more plentiful than the praise."

"They really do that in the United States?" Savchenko raised his eyebrows. "And in England and Canada as well?"

"In Canada?" Manning said, smiling. "Yeah, of course. And in England, Australia, a few other places. In America they have the FCC—Federal Communications Commission—that sets standards for profanity, nudity and anything that isn't considered proper for network broadcasts. Even then, some cable channels show programs that include so-called adult material. But they don't ban anything for political reasons."

"Anything?" Savchenko asked, his eyes open wide.

"Well, nothing I know about anyway," Manning said with a shrug. "Of course, freedom of speech and freedom of the press are part of the First Amendment of the U.S. Constitution."

The telephone on Hunntington-Smythe's desk rang. Manning answered it. "Colonel's not here right now," he announced. "He'll probably be back in a couple of hours."

"I have to talk to David McCarter," a voice declared from the earpiece. "I understood I could find him at this number."

"Jesus," the Canadian rasped. "Hold on. I'll get him."

"Is something wrong?" Savchenko asked, noticing the angry expression on the Canadian's face.

"One of my partners is an idiot," Manning muttered. "Would you mind finding Mr. Nelson and asking him to get his ass in here? He's got a telephone call."

"Nelson is the Briton, yes?" Savchenko inquired.

"The guy with the British accent and the lobotomy scar," Manning replied.

The Russian was confused by the remark, but he left the office and successfully located "Mr. Nelson." McCarter entered with a bottle of Coca-Cola in his hand. The Briton was puzzled by the expression on Manning's face as the Canadian shoved the telephone receiver at him.

"Way to go, jackass," Manning growled. "Remind me to talk to you about maintaining our security."

"What?" McCarter began, but decided to worry about Manning later. He took the phone and spoke into the mouthpiece. "This is Nelson."

"Who?" a vaguely familiar voice replied. "McCarter? This is Hsin Li—"

"Bloody hell," McCarter groaned. "How the hell did you get this phone number? For that matter, how did you know I'd be here?"

"My connections," Hsin Li's voice replied. "Isn't that where you usually do business when you're in Hong Kong?"

"Where I—" the Briton began. "What's going on, Hsin Li?" the Briton questioned, showing his impatience by the tone of his voice.

"I have some information for you," the Chinese declared. "Not the sort of thing I want to talk about over the phone. Meet me at the Green Dragon Restaurant in the Shiang District at six o'clock tonight. I'll explain everything then."

"The Green Dragon Restaurant?" McCarter frowned.

"They serve excellent sweet-and-sour pork," Hsin Li stated. "I order it every time I eat there. Recommend it. May as well have a good meal while we discuss my fee."

"All right," McCarter agreed. "I'll be there."

Hsin Li hung up.

"Something is very wrong here," the Briton commented as he placed the receiver in the phone cradle.

"You can say that again," Manning growled. "What's the matter with you? Giving somebody the phone number to this office—"

"I didn't give him the bloody phone number," McCarter snapped. "If you had been listening, you might have heard me ask where the hell he got it."

"Yeah," Manning was forced to admit. "You did. Who was on the phone anyway. The informer guy? Li?"

"Hsin Li," the British ace confirmed. "He wants to meet me at a restaurant tonight. Told me how he always orders the sweet-and-sour pork when he's there."

"So?" the Canadian said with a shrug.

"Hsin Li is a member of a Buddhist sect that doesn't believe in eating meat," McCarter explained. "That rascal would lie, cheat, steal and sell his grandmother to a brothel if he could get enough money for her, but Hsin Li has always been a strict vegetarian."

"You think he's trying to warn you something's wrong," Manning asked.

"That's what I figure," McCarter answered with a nod. "Hsin Li was pretty rattled when we had our first conversation. He was reluctant to tell me about the Black Serpent Tong, and he nearly had a heart attack when I told him TRIO wasn't just a bullshit story. He told me not to expect to hear from him again. Then John and I had that donnybrook with the SAD. That would have convinced Hsin Li *never* to talk to me again."

"But he just contacted you," Manning commented. "And *somebody* gave him the phone number."

"Probably the same people who forced him to make the call," the Briton mused. "Bet you ten quid there was a gun pointed at his head when he phoned."

"So TRIO knows we're working with the SIS," Manning said with a frown. "How the hell did they find out? Did they figure it out from last night's raid or what?"

"I don't know," McCarter replied. "If so, somebody must have seen Hunntington-Smythe at the police blockade and guessed he was connected with us."

"And they just happened to know the phone number?" Manning shook his head. "Well, I suppose they could have found out somehow."

"A lot of coincidences," McCarter said. "Personally, I don't believe much in coincidence. On top of everything else, how did TRIO know about Hsin Li in the first place?"

"Maybe they've been watching us since we arrived in Hong Kong," Manning suggested.

"I doubt it," McCarter replied. "If they had, TRIO would have shut down the operations at Lung Harbor before we hit them. They lost a fortune in opium and other contraband. There's only one explanation that fills in all the holes, mate."

"Yeah," Manning agreed. "Somebody we've been working with is a mole for TRIO. There's a goddamn informer in our group."

"An informer?" Savchenko asked with surprise. The Russian had just entered the office in time to hear the tail end of the conversation. "Are you sure of this?"

"We're sure," McCarter sighed. "And we don't want to broadcast it."

"Are you certain you haven't broadcast this already?" Savchenko inquired. "There could be hidden microphones in this office."

"Not now," Manning announced as he took a small metal disc from his pocket. "I dusted for bugs earlier. Found this under the colonel's desk. It's a miniature transmitter, powered by a quartz battery that I've already removed."

"Why didn't you tell me about that before?" the Russian said, frowning.

"Because you're KGB, Vladimir," Manning replied. "I figured you planted it."

"Actually..." Savchenko looked down at the floor. "I did. Nothing personal. It is part of my job...not a part that I like, I assure you."

"That's all right," McCarter said with a sigh of relief. "I was afraid the informer had done it. That would have meant our suspects would include everybody in the bloody building...up to and including the cleaning lady."

"Who do you think the informer is?" Savchenko inquired.

"What matters right now is who it *isn't*," Manning stated. "The only people we can be sure we can trust are the members of our original team. Anybody who has been in Hong Kong longer than we have could be working for TRIO."

"So what do we do?" the Russian asked helplessly.

"We start planning how to outfox some foxes," McCarter replied with a grin.

17

The Green Dragon Restaurant was located near the bay. Customers enjoyed the view of Chinese junks sailing gracefully past the wide picture windows of the restaurant—the Green Dragon had little else to boast of. The Shiang District was a tough area.

Shabby buildings, most likely brothels, opium dens and private gambling joints where bets were placed on life-and-death struggles between animals, men and occasionally women, lined the streets.

Life was cheap in the Shiang District. Women who cheated their pimps were left in alleys with their throats cut. Gamblers who welched on bets were found in the bay, floating facedown. Desperate drug addicts, vicious thieves and other criminals prowled the streets.

David McCarter and John Trent entered the Green Dragon at precisely 6:00 p.m. Both men wore dark jackets and pants and black knit caps. McCarter wore paratrooper boots, but Trent wore black sneakers. An observant spectator could see the bulges of pistols carried in shoulder leather beneath their jackets. They wanted onlookers to know they were armed. The enemy would already assume this, so concealing the weapons would not give McCarter and Trent the element of surprise with any TRIO gunsel. However, the numerous street hoodlums avoided confronting the pair because they noticed both men were packing.

The decor of the Green Dragon Restaurant was impressive only to someone with an unusual affection for papier-mâché. A long snakelike dragon stretched across the wall behind a plywood bar. Crudely made dragon heads hung on the walls above most of the tables. The papier-mâché reptiles had been painted dark green, but dots and streaks of white peeked through the faded colors.

There were roughly thirty people in the dining room and bar. The majority of them clustered around the bar, perched on stools as they downed cheap whiskey and puffed putrid cigarettes. Some undernourished hookers tried to lure some patrons from the bar, but none of the males seemed very interested. The women were not discouraged. They knew if they waited long enough some of the men would change their minds as alcohol blurred their vision and impaired their judgment.

"Hey, honey-boy," a feral-looking harlot called to McCarter. "You got ten American dollar? Wanna fuck? Ten dollar."

"No, thanks," the Briton replied. "Left my penicillin supply at the hotel."

The customers at the bar looked like members of a convention of cutthroats. Two wicked-looking characters had entered the restaurant a half hour before McCarter and Trent. They sat at the bar, barely speaking to one another and totally ignoring the other patrons. The pair stood out among the crowd because they were Caucasians. One man was built like a lumberjack and carried a knapsack tucked under his arm. The other was middle-aged, but tough. His right arm rested on the counter—a big steel hook gleamed from the end of his sleeve.

Manning and Katz barely glanced at McCarter and Trent. The Briton and the American ninja did not acknowledge their partners as they moved to the dining room. Major Alekseyev and Lieutenant Savchenko sat at a table. They paid little attention to their meals as they conversed in whispers, glancing about as if concerned someone might eavesdrop. The Russians glared suspiciously at McCarter and Trent as the pair passed their table.

"There's Hsin Li," McCarter rasped when he spotted the hustler. "Looks like he's got company."

"He doesn't seem too happy about it," Trent added.

Hsin Li was seated at a table in a corner. Two young Asians with granite faces and black steel eyes, sat with the hustler. A dark bruise marred Hsin Li's right cheek, and a brown stain of dried blood ran from his nose to his upper lip. McCarter and Trent approached the table.

"Come across a couple of old school chums?" the Briton inquired.

"They were in the neighborhood," Hsin Li replied in a hoarse voice. "They're very eager to meet you."

"At least you are punctual," Khorloin remarked as he stared up at McCarter. The Mongol's eyes were narrowed into mere slits. A drooping mustache accented the frown etched into his features. "Sit down."

"Shouldn't we exchange introductions first?" McCarter inquired.

"Sit," Khorloin repeated. He moved a hand from beneath the table to display a .380 Astra Constable in his fist. "If I have to say it again, I'll put a bullet through your guts. Nobody here would care if I killed you, Englishman."

"I think you're wrong about that," McCarter replied. "I also think you'd rather talk to me than shoot me. Dead men can't tell you a hell of a lot."

"What will we have to say to each other?"

"You tell me," McCarter invited. "Might help if I know what you want. Might as well talk to me, because you aren't going to use that thing."

"Why not?" Khorloin smiled. "If I shoot you, nobody here will tell the police anything. No one will see anything.

That's the way things are here. Everybody has their own individual reason not to cooperate with the police. Most of them are involved in activities they don't want the authorities to know about.''

Two men dressed in white uniforms entered the restaurant. The tall black man and his Hispanic companion headed straight for the bar. The two ''sailors'' carried laundry bags slung over their shoulders. Calvin James and Rafael Encizo both ordered beer.

"U.S. Navy to the rescue," McCarter mused. "Things could get a bit sticky for all of us."

"Blood is sticky," the Mongol warned.

"Yours or mine?" the Briton asked as he shoved his hands into his coat pockets. "Or everybody's?"

"Yours for certain," Khorloin answered. "And keep your hands in plain view."

John Trent suddenly headed to a door on the opposite side of the room. Khorloin demanded he return to the table.

"I need to use the bathroom," Trent replied. "I'll be back."

"Get back here, you half-breed bastard!" the Mongol snapped, aiming his pistol at the ninja.

"Calm down," McCarter warned. He held his left fist in front of his face so Khorloin and the other TRIO goon could see the hand grenade he had taken from his pocket.

"What do you think you're doing?" the Mongol asked. His voice was still harsh, but he lowered his pistol.

"I think I'll probably blow us all to hell if I let go of this grenade," McCarter said with a smile. "Take a good look, mate. The pin is out. If I let go of the spoon, this sucker will explode in six seconds. Figure you can reach safety by then?"

"You don't think I'd sacrifice my own life for our cause?" Khorloin asked, his body trembling with rage.

"I think you'd rather stay alive," McCarter replied. The Briton seemed calm, but he did not like the way Khorloin was shaking. The bastard might pull the trigger without meaning to.

"Khorloin syan-shing," the Chinese thug at the table began. *"Ching, syau-syinn!"*

"Bau shwo!" Khorloin snapped. He noticed Trent had entered the rest room. Two Asians immediately followed the American. Khorloin smiled thinly. "Put the pin back in the grenade, Englishman. Let's talk."

The Mongol lowered his pistol and slipped it under the table. McCarter still held the grenade in his fist. He made no attempt to return the pin to the charging handle.

"I'll just hold it for a while," the Briton explained.

"McCarter, are you insane?" Hsin Li rasped. "I mean, even crazier than I always knew you were?"

"Now how would I know how crazy you think I am?" McCarter replied with a shrug. "Let's let Hsin Li leave. He isn't really involved in any of this, you know."

"He is now," Khorloin stated. "There are no innocent bystanders. Only people who are too stupid to realize what side they're on. Maybe I'll let you live if you tell me where to find the rest of your people, McCarter."

Calvin James staggered through the dining room and headed toward the rest room, muttering something in a slurred voice. The TRIO enforcers who had followed Trent opened the door and prepared to enter. James tried to move faster and still maintain his drunken sailor act.

Suddenly Yumjaagiyin stepped in his path. The stout Mongol held up his hands to warn James not to come any closer. Patrons decided to leave before violence erupted. The hookers, particularly sensitive to danger, were the first out the front door.

"Time to leave," the bartender told Katz and Manning. He was bigger and more muscular than most Chinese. A jagged scar marked his bald bullet-shaped head. Other scars on his knuckles suggested he had dealt out more punishment than he had received.

"Haven't finished my beer," Manning replied, raising the mug to his lips.

Katz glanced about, making a quick survey of the people who remained in the restaurant. Besides the men of Phoenix Force, Trent and the two KGB officers, Katz counted sixteen. They were all Asian males between the ages of twenty-three and thirty-six. The hardness in their eyes and their menacing attitude revealed that all sixteen were likely members of TRIO. Except poor, terrified, Hsin Li, who looked like he might welcome a massive coronary.

The bartender swung a paddle-sized hand and knocked the beer mug from Gary Manning's grasp. Glass exploded when the mug crashed into a wall. The bar man glared at Manning.

"I tell you get out!" he snapped. "You and your cripple friend. That goes for you too, sailor."

"Wh…what you be…bein' so shitty…uh…for?" Encizo asked, stumbling over his words as he weaved from his barstool in a drunken manner.

"You get that black monkey boy and leave," the bartender told Encizo. "You sailors shouldn't be in a place like this anyway. There's a whorehouse across the street. Go there."

"I've had enough of you," Manning announced, drawing his .357 Magnum autoloader from his jacket.

The bartender's mouth fell open in astonishment. He started to raise his hands in surrender. Manning slammed the barrel of his Eagle pistol across the guy's face. The blow knocked the bartender to his knees.

"My turn," Encizo muttered as he vaulted over the bar.

The Cuban landed, feet first, between the shoulder blades of the dazed bartender. The brutal stomp drove the man to the floor. His jaw smashed into wood, and his nose was crushed into a crimson smear. The bartender moaned softly and passed out.

Two Chinese goons at the bar jumped off their stools and lunged toward Manning. Knives flashed in their fists as they attacked the Canadian. Neither man paid much attention to Yakov Katzenelenbogen, whom they regarded as an "old cripple." An instant later, they knew they were very wrong.

Katz swung his right arm and smashed the hard steel curve of the hook across the closest opponent's jaw. The Chinese crud's head spun from the blow. Three teeth spewed from his mouth as he slumped unconscious.

The Second TRIO assailant lunged at Katz, knife aimed at the Israeli's belly. Katz sidestepped the knife thrust and slashed the side of his left hand across the tong hood's wrist. The knife fell from the goon's fingers. The Phoenix Force commander's right arm streaked out, and the hook snared the thug's neck. Katz slammed the heel of his left palm under the guy's jaw. The impact drove the hood's head and neck back into the hook. Sharp steel pierced flesh and muscle to splinter vertebrae and sever the spinal cord.

Another TRIO creep pulled a 9 mm Browning from his belt. Gary Manning promptly shot him. A 158-grain flat-nosed slug smashed through the man's chest and splattered his heart. The force of the magnum punch hurled the hoodlum's body into a wall. His corpse slid to the floor.

Since TRIO had expected to close the trap on only one or two opponents, a few of the goons involved had not bothered to carry weapons. A Chinese thug who had left his firearms at home attacked Manning with the only weapon he had—his body. The man was a kung fu expert. He charged toward Manning while the Canadian was busy blowing away the gunslinging hoodlum. The Phoenix fighter turned his Eagle .357 toward the blurred shape of the next opponent, but he was a split second too late.

The martial artist thrust a kick to Manning's hands, and the pistol sailed from the Canadian's fingers. With a war shout, the Chinese hood hit Manning with a roundhouse *ming-chuan* punch to the head, followed by a straight punch to the chin. Manning fell against the bar, his head throbbing from the blows. Kung fu and karate punches were delivered with the two big knuckles of the middle and index finger. It was a popular misconception that every punch or kick by a martial artist shattered bone as if it was glass. In a "breaking demonstration" the artist took time to concentrate on a single target, building up breath control and focusing all his energies on the object. A living opponent was a moving target—there was no time for concentration with a target that could hit back.

However, the kung fu artist hit very hard and very fast. He snapped a kick to Manning's midsection. The Canadian doubled up under the force of the blow. The Chinese goon slashed the side of his hand at Manning's neck. A brawny forearm broke the stroke.

Manning rammed his fist into the Asian's solar plexus. The kung fu man gasped for breath. The Canadian slammed a left hook at his opponent's face. The kung fu artist stumbled backward from the blow, but quickly lashed out a kick. Manning slapped a palm at the man's shin to block the attack.

The Chinese thug slashed a sideways hand chop at the Canadian's face. Manning ducked under the attacking limb and thrust another punch at his opponent's solar plexus. The kung fu fighter doubled up, rasping desperately as the breath was driven from his lungs. Manning rammed a fist into the man's kidney and quickly smashed the side of his hand at the base of the Chinese hood's skull. The Asian hurtled forward and crashed headfirst into the bar. Cheap plywood burst, and the man's head and shoulders vanished through the gap. The tong enforcer groaned and slumped into unconsciousness.

WHEN THE FIGHTING ERUPTED at the bar, David McCarter and Calvin James also burst into action. McCarter and Khorloin were faced with an apparent standoff, the Briton holding a grenade in his fist and the Mongol armed with a pistol. McCarter abruptly ended the stalemate. He tossed the grenade onto the table in front of Khorloin.

The Mongol stared at the grenade, startled that the Briton had apparently decided to kill himself along with the TRIO members. The Chinese enforcer with Khorloin desperately grabbed for the M-26 fragger. Hsin Li closed his eyes and clenched his teeth, bracing himself for the terrible explosion.

McCarter had thrown himself to the floor the instant he had dropped the grenade, his right hand drawing the Browning Hi-Power from shoulder leather. Khorloin reacted to the blur of movement and fired his pistol, but McCarter had already dropped from the path of the .380 slug, which sliced across the room.

The Briton held his Browning in a two-handed Weaver grip. Khorloin swung his Astra autoloader at McCarter. The Mongol's finger tightened on the trigger. A sizzling 9 mm projectile smashed through the center of Khorloin's forehead. The Mongol fell across the table, his Astra still clenched in his lifeless fist.

The Chinese seated beside Khorloin was confused and horrified. He had tried to grab the grenade, but hesitated when McCarter shot his Mongol companion. The Asian thrust a hand inside his coat to draw a weapon. It was the last mistake he ever made. McCarter shot him twice through the heart. The Chinese gunman tumbled from his chair and fell to the floor, his life spilling out from his punctured heart.

Hsin Li flinched from the sound of gunshots. He nearly fainted with relief when he realized he had not been shot. The hustler opened his eyes to behold Khorloin's corpse draped over the table, next to the unexploded grenade.

"Is this thing going to go off?" he asked in a trembling voice.

"Of course not," McCarter replied as he rose from the floor. "It's just a dud. No explosives. Not even a fuse."

"Oh..." Hsin Li replied. "Good."

YUMJAAGIYIN THOUGHT Calvin James was just a drunken sailor. He did not see James as a threat when he blocked the black man's path to the rest room. When the battle began, Yumjaagiyin discovered his mistake.

James's left fist shot out to jab Yumjaagiyin on the point of the chin. The Mongol's head bounced from the punch. James hit Yumjaagiyin with a hard right cross, opened his hand and swiftly slashed a karate chop under his opponent's sternum. The stunned Mongol groaned and raised his hands to fight back.

The black warrior clubbed his forearms into Yumjaagiyin's wrists to block the Mongol's attack. James smashed his fist in the guy's mouth. Yumjaagiyin staggered, his knees buckling as his body swayed unsteadily. James's left hand seized the Mongol by the forelock and pulled him down. The Phoenix fighter's right fist slammed a powerful uppercut at the Mongol's face. Yumjaagiyin's body sagged.

James shoved the unconscious Mongol aside and reached under his shirt for the Colt Commander tucked in the waistband of his trousers. Suddenly a Chinese goon dashed from a table and leaped toward James. The Asian swung a foot at James's head. The black commando dodged the kick and drew his pistol. The tong thug swatted a palm against the Colt to force the pistol toward the floor. His other hand thrust two fingers aimed at James's eyes.

The Chicago-bred badass bobbed his head forward to avoid being hit in the eye. The Asian's fingers poked James's forehead. The Phoenix fighter countered with a left hook at his opponent's face. The punch staggered the Asian. James pivoted on his left foot and launched a powerful side kick at his opponent's abdomen. The Asian folded from the kick. James slugged the barrel of his Colt across the tong goon's skull, and the Chinese hoodlum fell senseless at James's feet.

Two TRIO hoodlums drew pistols. Another pair turned over a table and ducked behind the wide wooden top for cover. Calvin James dropped to one knee and fired at the two enemy gunmen. The black fighting machine fired two rounds into the chest of the closest opponent. The impact of two .45 slugs smashed the hoodlum into a wall. His body slumped to the floor as another gunman aimed his weapon at James.

Lieutenant Vladimir Savchenko triggered his Makarov pistol, blasting a 9 mm bullet into the side of the Asian gunsel's head. The guy's skull burst, and brains spat from an exit wound the size of a quarter. The TRIO thug fell dead, but his two comrades behind the table had drawn weapons and prepared to open fire.

Major Vikor Alekseyev suddenly hit them with three 9 mm rounds, triggering his Makarov as fast as possible. The high-velocity projectiles punched through the flimsy wood tabletop. Two bullets drilled into the abdomen of an enemy triggerman. The Asian hood fell forward, tipping over the table.

The remaining hoodlum found himself without cover. He dropped to a prone position and pointed his pistol at the two Soviet agents. Rafael Encizo had stationed himself behind the bar and removed his H&K machine pistol from the laundry bag. He blasted the TRIO hit man with a volley of 9 mm slugs. Three parabellums ripped into the hood's back between the shoulder blades. Bullets punctured heart and lungs and severed his spinal cord. The guy was dead before he could blink.

THE TWO TRIO HOODS who followed John Trent into the rest room got a big surprise. The American ninja was waiting for them with his *manrikigusari* in his fists. The first man through the door received a hammerlike blow to the left temple. Trent had hit him with a weighted end of the chain in his fist.

The second thug lunged at Trent with a five-inch dagger in his fist. Trent lashed the *manrikigusari* across the guy's wrist. Steel links wrapped around the target, and a weighted end stung the man's nerve center at the base of a thumb knuckle. The knife fell from his grasp. Trent quickly rammed a knee into his opponent's groin and jammed an elbow stroke under the man's jaw. The TRIO goon's eyes rolled up in his head, and he slid senseless to the floor.

Trent heard the shooting outside the rest room. He put away the fighting chain and drew his Colt Commander. The American ninja emerged from the rest room with his pistol held ready, but the battle was virtually finished. The fighting had been fast and furious. Dead and unconscious TRIO members littered the restaurant floor.

"We have any prisoners?" Katz called out.

"Two or three," James replied as he knelt by the unconscious Yumjaagiyin and began binding his wrists with plastic riot cuffs.

"I've got one here, too," the Phoenix Force commander announced. "Let's round them up and get out of here."

18

"Where the hell have you guys been?" Gerald Crane demanded when Yakov Katzenelenbogen, Major Alekseyev and Gary Manning entered Colonel Hunntington-Smythe's office a few minutes after midnight.

"Oh, I suspect I know where they've been," the SIS colonel remarked sourly. Hunntington-Smythe sat behind his desk, stuffing tobacco into the bowl of a brier pipe. "I heard a news report on the radio about a big gun battle in the Shiang District. They found about a dozen bodies at some restaurant. Sounds like your people were busy this evening."

"As a matter of fact," Katz said with a smile, "you're right."

"Well, whoop-dee-do," Crane snorted. The CIA agent lit a cigarette and forced smoke out of his nostrils. "You hotshots just took off without tellin' any of us where you were going. We've been looking for you all day. Then I get a phone call, and I'm told to meet you jokers here. What's your big news? You've been killin' people at some fuckin' restaurant in the Hong Kong slum district."

"Mr. Crane was surprised when he got here," Hunntington-Smythe added. "He thought I knew what was going on, but I had been called at my home and told to return to my office. You said you had some important information for us, Gray."

"I do," Katz confirmed as he drew his SIG Sauer auto-loader from shoulder leather. The Israeli stepped forward and placed the pistol on Hunntington-Smythe's desk. "And I'll explain everything when everybody arrives."

"What's that for?" the colonel demanded, pointing the stem of his pipe at the SIG Sauer.

"The gun is on your desk, not in my hand," Katz replied mildly. "No reason to be alarmed by that. Just relax. We'll explain everything. . . ."

The door opened. David McCarter and John Trent escorted Kauo Yvet-sang into the office. The Chinese SIS agent's right arm was cradled in a sling. He appeared to be upset and confused by the situation.

"Kauo should be in the hospital," Hunntington-Smythe said angrily. "He was shot during the harbor raid, in case you forgot."

"He was going to be released from the hospital in the morning," McCarter replied. "We just brought him out a bit earlier."

"At gunpoint," Kauo spat. "And they refuse to tell me why."

"Don't feel paranoid," Crane remarked. "These guys aren't telling us anything either."

"We will now," Katz assured them.

"Getting a bit crowded in here," McCarter said. "We'll wait outside."

The Briton and Trent left the office. Kauo Yvet-sang took a seat, but Katz, Manning and Alekseyev remained on their feet. The Israeli lit a cigarette before he began the explanation.

"You're already aware that we were at the Green Dragon Restaurant this evening," the Israeli said. "The reason we were there is because a telephone call came through this office for Mr. Nelson. The call was from Hsin Li, Nelson's informer friend. He was the fellow who gave us the tip about the Black Serpent Tong operations at Lung Harbor. Remember?''

"I didn't recall his name," Hunntington-Smythe admitted, "but I know who you're talking about. What I'd like to know is why the hell Nelson gave the man the phone number to my office!"

"He didn't," Manning stated. "The men who forced him to make the call knew the number and they knew they could contact Nelson at this office. Fortunately Hsin Li managed to warn Nelson he was in trouble. The enemy wanted to lure Nelson into a trap, but we turned the tables on them."

"Why didn't you tell us about this?" Crane demanded.

"Because one of you three is an informer," Major Alekseyev announced. "You, Mr. Crane, or Colonel Hunntington-Smythe or Kauo Yvet-sang is a double agent working for TRIO."

"Double agent working for a bunch of hoods?" the CIA agent scoffed. "TRIO is a criminal syndicate, not a spy network. You KGB boys must get pretty paranoid, and I guess the same must be true about Gray and his pals. You find very many conspiracies during your missions?"

"A few," Katz replied with a shrug. "TRIO isn't a street gang, Crane. It's a powerful and sophisticated criminal organization that has adopted espionage tactics in order to successfully function in a covert manner. Not surprising they'd have informers within the police, law-enforcement organizations and the SIS."

"I'm not with the SIS," Crane said. "I'm CIA. You think TRIO could infiltrate the Company, for Christ's sake?"

"Why not?" Manning replied. "Everybody else has."

"You've been working with the SIS since we arrived," Katz told Crane. "That made you a suspect. The only other two who could be informers are you, Colonel. And you, Kauo Yvet-sang."

"This is outrageous!" Hunntington-Smythe declared. "That's the most insulting and offensive accusation I've ever heard!"

"Yeah," Crane added. "It's pretty goddamn sorry when you guys suspect us of being spies for TRIO, but you trust the goddamn KGB!"

"I assure you," Alekseyev chuckled. "Mr. Gray and his friends don't trust the KGB, but they knew we couldn't be informers. Whoever was working for TRIO must have been in Hong Kong before we arrived here."

"So we had to deal with the TRIO ambush scheme without telling you about it, gentlemen," Katz stated. "TRIO was at the restaurant in force. Of course, they didn't expect us to show up in a group. We caught them off guard. Had to kill most of them, but we managed to take five of them alive. You remember I told you Mr. Johnson is very skilled at using scopolamine? He's been busy with our prisoners. Luckily Lieutenant Savchenko and Mr. Collins speak Chinese fluently, so they've been able to interrogate the subjects under the influence of the truth serum."

"We got some valuable information," Alekseyev added. "One of the prisoners is a Mongol named Yumjaagiyin. He's a henchman for a man named Temujin, who is the son of a man who calls himself Tosha Khan. The khan is the leader of the New Horde, part of the three great criminal networks that comprise TRIO."

"You got this information from a Mongol criminal here in Hong Kong?" Hunntington-Smythe asked with amazement.

"Fortunately," Manning replied, "Lieutenant Savchenko speaks Mongolian. Yuma-what's his name . . ."

"Yumjaagiyin," Alekseyev supplied.

"Yeah, that guy," Manning said with a nod, "gave us the most important information of all. He told us where the VL-800 is located."

"And," Katz added, "he also gave us the name of the double agent...."

Kauo Yvet-sang suddenly bolted from his chair and grabbed for the SIG Sauer pistol on the colonel's desk. Crane jumped from his seat and seized Kauo's shirt from behind. The Chinese SIS agent bent his left elbow and pumped it back to strike Crane in the chest. The CIA operative fell to the floor as Kauo seized the pistol.

"It isn't loaded," Katz said with a sigh. "Did you really think it would be?"

"But this gun *is* loaded," Alekseyev declared, aiming his Makarov at Kauo. "And I'll use it if you give me half a reason."

Kauo Yvet-sang placed the SIG Sauer on the desk and raised his uninjured arm. Yakov stepped forward and retrieved his pistol. He held it in the left fist and pressed the magazine catch. An empty mag dropped from the well.

"Shit," Crane muttered as he picked himself up from the floor. The CIA agent rubbed his bruised chest and glared at Katz. "Why did you bait the fucker with the empty gun? If you already knew Kauo was the double agent—"

"Because we didn't know," Katz answered. He held the P-226 in the tri-hooks of his prosthesis as he shoved a magazine loaded with fifteen 9 mm parabellums into the butt of the pistol.

"Bau-shir!" Kauo Yvet-sang exclaimed. "But you said—"

"We lied about that," Manning told him. "None of the hoods we interrogated knew about the TRIO spy within the SIS. So we hoped you'd panic and expose yourself when we claimed one of them had told us who you were."

"My God," Hunnttington-Smythe said, shaking his head. "Why, Kauo? You've been my aide for two and a half years. Why did you agree to spy on us for TRIO?"

"The answer is simple," Crane growled. "M-O-N-E-Y. Right, Kauo? You little shit—"

"Money had nothing to do with it," Kauo said defensively. "I was born to a family that has belonged to the Black Serpent Tong for more than a century. My father was a member of the tong and his father before him. You do not understand the loyalty we have to our tong. To you, we are simply criminals."

"That definition seems good enough to me," Manning told him. "You can defend your actions—and the tong's—when you go to court."

"I'll never stand trial," Kauo replied. "I won't live that long."

"Maybe you will and maybe you won't," Crane commented. "I can think of worse things than you gettin' offed while you're in prison, asshole."

"What about the TRIO headquarters?" Hunntington-Smythe asked Katz. "Was that a lie, too?"

"No," the Phoenix Force commander replied. "The Mongol prisoner really did give us that information. We're planning to raid them just before dawn. Will you help us, Colonel?"

"A pleasure, Mr. Gray," the SIS officer assured him.

19

The British submarine *Manta* silently cruised twenty leagues beneath the surface of the South China Sea. It was headed for the small island of Chiwey-Wu. A strip of land roughly a mile in diameter, Chiwey-Wu was the property of a respected Hong Kong businessman and banker named Chou Minchuan. He employed a private security force of twenty-three guards, all licensed to carry automatic weapons.

Phoenix Force, Trent, their KGB allies and Colonel Hunntington-Smythe sat at the captain's table in the officers' mess. The cabin was as large as most living rooms, but Gary Manning was uncomfortable inside the submarine. The Canadian suffered from a mild case of claustrophobia. The sooner he got out of the underwater sardine can the better. Major Alekseyev and Lieutenant Savchenko were also uncomfortable inside a British military vessel, although the captain and crew were unaware that two of their passengers were Soviet agents.

"I must say," Captain Robert Bradsworth remarked as he sipped tea from a thick mug, "I've had some unusual assignments in my day, but this is one of the oddest and certainly the most sudden. Really no time to prepare at all, you know. Still, when the orders come directly from the Prime Minister, a chap doesn't question matters much."

"We're glad we could arrange this transportation," Yakov Katzenelenbogen remarked. "And we realize this is all very unorthodox, Captain."

"To say the least," Bradsworth agreed. "Most of the time, duty here is rather bland. Submarine patrols seem almost unnecessary since Mao died. The Chinese haven't been hostile toward Hong Kong and the Soviets haven't tried mucking about here much. Of course, the Americans have a fleet in Taiwan considerably larger than the naval forces Her Majesty has stationed here."

"Excuse me, Captain," Colonel Hunntington-Smythe said, glancing at his wristwatch. "But we should be pretty close to Chiwey-Wu by now. Perhaps we should get ready."

"The torpedo tubes are empty," Bradsworth stated. "There are six tubes. How many of you will be going ashore?"

"Eight," Hunntington-Smythe answered. "Everyone but me."

"All of you?" the captain glanced at Katz. A middle-aged man with a prosthesis had no business getting involved in an armed assault on some sort of enemy base, in Bradsworth's opinion.

"That's right," Rafael Encizo told the captain. "Six of us can leave simultaneously through the tubes. That'll leave just two men to follow."

"We'll let you out about three hundred meters from shore," Bradsworth declared. "The swim won't be too bad. After the first hundred meters, the water should be pretty shallow. Probably be able to wade the last hundred."

"What about our gear?" Alekseyev inquired. "We certainly can't carry it and swim that great a distance."

"We're putting everything on a scuba sled," Calvin James explained. "The gear will be sealed in waterproof bags and strapped to the sled. It has its own propellers, so it's easy to push through the water. One man can haul four hundred pounds of stuff on a scuba sled. Our stuff doesn't weigh nearly that much."

"I have some experienced frogmen among the crew," Bradsworth announced. "I'm certain I can get some volunteers to assist you—"

"Thanks, but I think we'd better use our own people," Katz answered. "Nothing against your men. Just for security. The fewer people who know any details, the better."

"Well, I don't know many details myself," the British officer said with a shrug. "Now, let me make certain I've got everything straight. We let you blokes out through the torpedo tubes and leave you to do whatever at the island?"

"Right," Manning confirmed. "Then come back in four hours. We'll fire a red flare to signal you to pick us up."

"If we don't see the flare, then I'm supposed to order my men to fire a missile loaded with incendiary explosives," Bradsworth said, frowning. "Enough to burn everything on the island into a cinder."

"Wait a minute, mate," David McCarter said sharply. "First you circle around the bloody island and look for either a flashlight signal in Morse code or two small campfires near the beach."

"Oh, yes," Bradsworth nodded. "And the Morse code message will be 'R.I.P.', I remember now."

"Don't bloody forget," McCarter warned. "I don't care for the idea of getting cremated because our damn flare gun didn't work and you didn't recall the alternative signals we'll use in an emergency."

"I won't forget," Bradsworth insisted.

"If he does, I'll remind him," Hunntington-Smythe assured the men of Phoenix Force.

"But if we don't send up any flares or use the other signal devices," Katz added. "Burn the island. That absolutely *has* to be done unless you see our signal."

"I understand," the captain nodded. "I don't understand why, but I understand the instructions."

"Good," Katz said. "Then let's get ready."

PHOENIX FORCE and its three allies were ejected from the torpedo tubes and swam to the shore of Chiwey-Wu. They waded to the beach, dragging the scuba sled with them. The beach was hardly a romantic spot for lovers. The sand was mostly mud, and slippery rocks extended along much of the coast. Had the waves been more powerful, the beach landing would have been hazardous.

The men removed their face masks and Emerson air tanks. McCarter unzipped the rubber "body bag" that contained smaller waterproof bags filled with their gear. The Briton eagerly found his and opened it. McCarter hated being unarmed under any circumstances, but to be unarmed at an enemy stronghold was especially upsetting.

"Damn," Katz rasped as he gazed up at the pale orb that poked above the horizon. Shimmering lights reflected on the water like diamonds on a velvet cloth. "Sun is rising."

"We're only ten minutes behind schedule," Encizo remarked, checking his wristwatch. "Maybe daybreak was earlier than we expected this morning."

"Well, we're here now, folks," Manning sighed. "Just have to do the best we can."

"Any major changes in the plan?" Alekseyev asked as he took his bag from the sled.

"Not really," Katz replied. "Except our chances of being seen by the enemy are greater than they were before. Do you know any ninja tactics of invisibility that might help us, Mr. Collins?"

"One way to be invisible is to blend with the shadows or with surroundings," John Trent replied. "Another is to be where your opponents aren't looking."

"Sounds nice," McCarter said. "But how is that going to apply to this situation?"

"How do I know?" Trent said with a shrug. "I haven't seen the enemy stronghold yet. I don't know which method will apply or how to best handle it."

"Yeah," James muttered as he pulled off his diving fins. "Give the dude a break, man."

All eight men wore black rubber diving suits. They exchanged flippers for combat boots from their gear bags. Trent donned his split-toe *tabi* footgear. They slid into shoulder holster rigs and shoved loaded pistols into leather. James and Manning assembled their assault rifles and screwed foot-long sound suppressors into the threaded muzzles of the weapons. Katz and McCarter also attached silencers to their Uzi and Ingram.

Trent wrapped his ninja hood and mask around his head. He donned his *gi* with the hidden pockets for weapons and spare magazines. The American ninja knotted the black obi sash around his waist and thrust the *ninja-do* sword into the cloth belt. He tucked the *manrikigusari* at the small of his back and attached a small black ditty bag to his right hip. Finally he removed a small black aluminum bow and a quiver containing six arrows.

The KGB armed themselves with Makarov pistols and Sterling submachine guns with ammo pouches containing spare magazines for their weapons. Savchenko had also added a bayonet to his weaponry. Encizo donned the same firearms and knives he had carried during the harbor raid. Manning slipped on his backpack of explosives.

McCarter had brought a Barnett Commando crossbow in addition to his Ingram and Browning. The Commando featured a skeletal steel stock and a cocking mechanism that allowed the bowstring to be pulled back and locked into place more rapidly and easier than that of a conventional crossbow. Phoenix Force and the two KGB agents also clipped grenades to their belts. Trent did not like explosives of any sort and carried only his *metsubushi* sight removers.

Calvin James, the unit medic, fastened a first-aid kit to his belt at the small of his back. Katz, Manning, Encizo and Alekseyev carried small one-shot flare guns and all eight men had GI issue "angle head" flashlights that they clipped onto belts or shoulder straps.

The team was ready for action. They filed out from behind the rocks and headed from the beach. The terrain was rugged. Chou Minchuan had probably purchased Chiwey-Wu cheap. It was a harsh chunk of rock, virtually worthless to anyone interested in tourism, crops or industry. However, the island was isolated and did not appear on most maps, thus it was ideal for TRIO's need for a secret base.

They soon found the estate. A stone wall surrounded the main house as well as two smaller buildings, which appeared to be a billeting hut and a warehouse. A Bell UD-1 helicopter stood on the parade field. Two guard towers were mounted on the walls. Sentries were posted in the towers. No doubt they were supplied with binoculars and two-way radios to communicate with their comrades inside the compound.

"Any brilliant ideas about how we're going to get close to that place without being spotted?" Alekseyev whispered to Katz as the strike force huddled behind a cluster of boulders a hundred yards from the compound.

There was no cover between the boulders and the wall of the stronghold. The Israeli turned to Trent.

"You said something about becoming invisible by not being where the enemy is looking," he reminded the ninja.

"Right," Trent said with a nod. "I'll make them look elsewhere. Somebody else will have to take them out, and *fast*."

Katz nodded. Trent crept along the length of the boulders, moving away from the others. McCarter placed a bolt in the groove of his crossbow. Manning switched the selector of his FAL rifle to semiautomatic. The Briton and the Canadian waited by the edge of the boulders.

Trent hurled a *metsubushi*. The eggshell burst on impact. Flash powder ignited, and a small cloud of black pepper rose from the earth. The TRIO sentries stared at the miniature explosion, wondering what the hell had caused it.

McCarter and Manning struck immediately. The Briton's Barnett sang a single shrill note as the bowstring snapped forward. Manning's FAL coughed harshly as a 7.62 mm slug hissed from the silencer-equipped barrel. The crossbow bolt struck a sentry in the chest. The steel tip pierced flesh, and the split fiberglass shaft splintered inside the guard. The bolt was loaded with two hundred cubic centimeters of cyanide, and the poison seeped into veins and arteries. The guard tried to yank the quarrel from his chest and opened his mouth to scream, but the powerful poison was already taking effect. He fell to the floor of the "crow's nest," twitched feebly and died.

His comrade was already dead. The Canadian marksman had hit his target in the bridge of the nose with a semijacketed soft lead slug with a mercury core. It exploded on impact. The top of the guard's skull vanished in a grotesque shower of assorted gore.

Phoenix Force and company dashed to the wall. The doors of the main gate were closed, probably bolted and possibly equipped with an alarm. Trent removed a pair of *shuko* from his ditty bag. He strapped the metal bands to his hands, curved thick blades jutting from the palms.

"Look for wires," Encizo told him. "Especially at the hinges. If you find any, cut 'em. That'll render most alarms useless. It might set the alarm off, depending on how it's wired, but we don't have time to be fancy. Just cut the wires and hope that does it. Okay?"

"I've got it," Trent assured him.

The ninja clawed the steel talons against stone. He dug his toes against the wall and pushed. He raised a *shuko*-clawed hand and hooked it on stone to pull himself higher and then used the other hand, continuing to pull with the talons and push with his toes until he climbed to the summit of the wall.

He dangled over the edge of the wall on the opposite side. The American ninja hung full length and dropped the remaining four feet to the ground. He moved to the gate. A thick steel bar was bolted across the doors. He searched for alarm wires, but found none. The ninja raised the bar and removed it from the doors, then pulled the gate open.

"Good work," Katz told Trent as he entered the compound.

"I try," the ninja replied, unbuckling the *shuko* from his hands.

The others filed through the open gate. Manning headed for the Bell chopper. The Canadian slid under the fuselage of the UD-1, a big chopper, capable of carrying fourteen men. The demolitions expert removed a magnetic limpet mine and clamped it to the steel belly of the copter.

The mine was equipped with a dial for setting the timer to the fuse. Manning used a tiny screwdriver to remove the dial, carefully pressing the detonator to the inside rim of the mine. The Canadian took an aluminum tube from his utility vest and unscrewed the cap. He removed some cotton wadding and gingerly extracted a small capsule.

Slowly and very carefully, Manning inserted the mercury fulminate capsule into the limpet mine near the detonator. Any violent or sudden movement of the UD-1 would cause friction to the limpet and thus heat the mercury. The capsule would explode, setting off the detonator and the plastic explosives within the mine.

Manning crawled out from under the chopper and sighed with relief. The Canadian was accustomed to working with explosives, but he did not like handling anything as sensitive as mercury fulminate or liquid nitro. He gathered up his rifle and got to his feet.

"What did you do?" Savchenko inquired. "You put a booby trap on the helicopter?"

"Just don't lean on it too hard," Manning replied.

Katz, James and McCarter moved to the billet. Alekseyev, Encizo, Savchenko, Manning and Trent headed toward the east wing of the main house. Both groups frequently glanced at the windows of the buildings. None of the structures were especially impressive. The billet was a simple wood-and-plaster building with a tile roof. The main house stood two stories high and filled almost an acre. It was made of stone and mortar with thick wooden doors and narrow windows. The house had been constructed to be functional and endure harsh weather. No money or effort had been spent on frills or ornamentation.

The billet door burst open. Two Asians armed with Type 37 submachine guns—a 9 mm weapon similar to the American M-3A1 greasegun—raised their weapons. McCarter's crossbow fired a bolt. The steel tip pierced the forehead of one of the gunmen. The shaft jutted from the man's skull like the horn of a hideous human unicorn. The Asian's face contorted in horrific agony, an expression that froze on his features in death.

Yakov Katzenelenbogen's Uzi uttered a sputtering cough as the Israeli fired a three-round burst through the silenced weapon. Parabellums crashed into the chest of the second gunman. He fell backward as he triggered his greasegun. The Taiwanese subgun roared and spat orange flame into the morning sky.

Glass shattered from a window, and a gun barrel poked through the frame. Calvin James snap-aimed his M-16 and fired from the hip. A foot-long sound suppressor muffled the report of his assault rifle as a trio of 5.56 mm rounds blasted away the face behind the window.

"What the hell," McCarter muttered as he yanked the pin from a fragmentation grenade. "They know we're here now."

The Briton popped the spoon from the grenade, waited two seconds and hurled it through the open doorway. Excited voices cried out in alarm. The three Phoenix commandos dropped to the ground. The M-26 grenade exploded inside the billet. Windows burst, and the building shook from the violent fury within. At least one victim's scream soared above the roar of the explosion.

"Okay," James rasped as he rose to one knee and readied another grenade. "Have another."

He threw the second M-26 through the ragged remnants of a window. The explosion blasted an entire wall from the billet. Half the roof caved in. No screams of terror or pain occurred as the rest of the structure collapsed, burying the dead beneath the rubble.

20

"We're under attack!" Akira Osato declared as he knotted the obi around his waist. The Japanese gangster charged from his sleeping quarters with a Nambu pistol in one hand and a *katana* samurai sword in the other. "May the gods curse Temujin! This must be that Mongol dog's fault!"

"How did they find out about us?" Chou Minchuan wondered aloud. The Chinese hoodlum was wearing silk pajamas and slippers. He held a fireproof steel strongbox under one arm and carried a German-made Walther P-38 in his fist.

"Temujin!" Osato insisted. His face looked as furious as the anger mask of a samurai warrior. "Khorloin and Yumjaagiyin, his two lieutenants, disappeared last night. Sentries said they took a boat toward Hong Kong. Temujin sent those idiots on a mission of revenge against those commando mercenaries. They must have been captured and forced to tell about the island."

"You may be right," Chou admitted. Voices shouted throughout the house, speaking Mandarin, Cantonese and a smattering of Japanese. "But there is nothing we can do about that now—"

"I can find that dog-eating Mongol son of a whore and cut him in half!" Osato declared, his fist tight around the scabbard of his *katana*.

"What will that gain us?" Chou replied. "First we must deal with the invaders. Then, later, we will settle with Temujin."

"*Hai,*" the yakuza subchief said with a curt nod. "The Mongol can wait, but he shall receive no special mercy because his father is Tosha Khan. We should never have accepted those Mongolian barbarians into the organization."

"We'll try to get our superiors to force out the Mongols in the future," Chou assured him. "For now, we must concentrate on self-preservation and protecting the VL-800 formula—"

"That damnable formula was what caused this mess in the first place," Osato replied. "That was Tosha Khan's insane notion—"

"The formula is valuable," the tong gangster insisted. "It is worth a fortune. It is too valuable to TRIO to allow others to claim it. We have lost too many men, too much merchandise and a base of operations because of the formula. That cost is too high to sacrifice the formula now. If that happens, we will have lost everything and gained nothing from this operation."

"You are right," Osato said, nodding. "We shall lose face if the Occidentals seize the formula."

"Then we are in agreement," Chou declared. "If we cannot defeat the invaders, we will flee with the formula."

"What if that doesn't work?" the yakuza boss inquired.

"Then we will release the VL-800 and all die together," Chou replied. "I'm certain you would favor that to surrender."

"Indeed," Osato confirmed. He thrust the sword into the sash of his kimono. "Death is better than dishonor."

"It is certainly permanent," Chou frowned.

"So is dishonor," Osato told him.

THE SHOTS AND EXPLOSIONS at the billet had alerted the TRIO forces to danger. Asian gunmen appeared from the door of the main house. Others shattered glass to open fire from windows. Yakov Katzenelenbogen, David McCarter and Calvin James bolted to the cover of the warehouse. A volley of automatic fire ripped into the ground, and geysers of dirt spat up from the earth as the Phoenix trio dashed for shelter.

"Well," McCarter muttered as he removed the silencer from his Ingram machine pistol, "this is another fine mess you've gotten us into, Yakov."

"You'd be miserable without Phoenix Force and you know it," Katz replied, also removing the Interarms sound suppressor from his Uzi. Silencers reduced the noise of the report of a firearm, but they also reduced accuracy and velocity of the projectile.

"True," the Briton confessed. "Anybody got any clever ideas about how we're going to handle this?"

"Right now the enemy has to come to us if they want us," James commented as he fed a cartridge-style 40 mm grenade into the breech of the M-203 attached to the barrel of his M-16.

"That's not going to last very long," the Briton replied. "I'm sure they've got grenades. Might even have rocket launchers. Won't take any military genius to realize the easiest way to flush us out will be to blow the hell out of the warehouse we're hiding behind."

"If I hit them with a grenade first," James remarked, "that might make 'em duck long enough for us to move to another position."

A tidal wave of bullets raked the building. Glass burst, and slugs, ricocheting off metal objects whined within the warehouse.

"Don't hit the house," Katz warned James. "An explosion might hit the room where they've got the VL-800 formula."

"I guess they don't keep it in this warehouse," McCarter commented, listening to bullets snarl within the building. A ricochet smashed a windowpane near the commandos' position.

"Christ, I hope not," James muttered.

"TRIO might be a lot of things," Katz remarked. "But they've never struck me as being particularly suicidal. Which means it's unlikely they'll use explosives if we can get closer to the main house."

"That's a nice theory anyway," the Briton muttered.

"Let's see if it works," James remarked, aiming his M-16 carefully and inserting his trigger finger in the M-203 attachment.

The black warrior triggered the grenade launcher. The recoil of the weapon rode into the M-16 it was mounted on. The 40 mm projectile sailed over the roof of the warehouse and descended into the parade field. The grenade exploded near two adventurous TRIO gunmen. The blast shredded the pair and splattered their remains across the front of the house.

The gory debris startled and disoriented other TRIO hoodlums. Katz, James and McCarter suddenly broke cover. The Israeli's Uzi sprayed a salvo of 9 mm rounds at the first-story windows. A gun-wielding TRIO goon dropped his M-3 greasegun and clamped both hands to his bloodied face. Since a parabellum slug had split a cheekbone and drilled upward into his brain, there was only one thing the man could do. He died.

Two more gunmen appeared at the door. McCarter's M-10 snarled, raking the pair with a salvo of Ingram lead. One Asian hit man caught three parabellums in the chest. The guy fell, blood splashing his shirt front while his partner retreated into the house, suddenly less than eager to trade shots with the three commandos.

The Phoenix warriors darted to the side of the main house. An enthusiastic TRIO triggerman leaned over the sill of a second-story window and aimed a Chinese Tokarev pistol at the fleeing figures. Calvin James spotted the gunman. He pointed his M-16 and fired a three-round burst. The 5.56 mm projectiles slammed into the TRIO hoodlum. He screamed as the impact yanked him over the lip of the window ledge. The man broke his right collarbone when he hit the ground. Since both lungs had been punctured by James's bullets, broken bones were the least of his worries.

The three Phoenix commandos reached their objective, although a burst of automatic fire chased the trio and chipped stone from the corner of the building. James opened the breech of his M-203 and inserted a fresh cartridge grenade. Katz removed the magazine from his Uzi. Only two rounds remained. He shoved a fresh mag into the weapon.

"There's another door over here...." McCarter announced, pointing with the muzzle of his M-10.

Suddenly the door opened, and two Chinese killers stepped outside. A small man armed with a Type 68 assault rifle swung his weapon toward McCarter. A large, powerful thug stood behind the rifleman. The big man cursed softly as he tried to clear the jammed breech of a Type 59 pistol—a Red Chinese version of the Soviet Makarov.

McCarter's Ingram nailed the first Chinese with a trio of 9 mm rounds. The Asian's heart exploded when all three slugs burrowed into it. The force of the multiple bullets drove his body back into the big Asian. A parabellum punched through the smaller man's torso and raked the forearm of his muscular companion.

The big man cried out as he dropped his T-59 pistol. However, he reacted swiftly and shoved his slain comrade forward as he charged McCarter. The thug hurled the smaller man's body into the Briton, knocking the Ingram from McCarter's hands. The TRIO goon slashed the side of his hand at McCarter's skull, aiming the stroke at the Phoenix fighter's temple.

McCarter ducked under the hood's whirling arm. The Briton drove a fist into the man's abdomen. He felt as if he had punched a bag of cement. McCarter's other hand thrust a heel-of-the-palm stroke at the Asian's jaw. The big man's head hardly moved.

The Asian hulk slammed the edge of his hand into McCarter's collarbone. The blow drove McCarter to his knees. The TRIO goon prepared to strike again, but he found himself staring into the muzzle of Katzenelenbogen's Uzi. The Chinese froze and started to raise his hands.

Suddenly he uttered a wheezing gasp and doubled up in agony. David McCarter had driven an uppercut between his opponent's legs. The Briton leaped up from the ground and swung a left hook at the side of the Asian's head. The Chinese brute fell against the wall. McCarter swung a boot at the man's lower abdomen and clasped his hands together to slam a powerful blow to the base of the Asian's neck.

The big man fell forward to receive McCarter's knee in his face. The Briton shoved his opponent into the wall again and swung a right cross at the Asian's jaw. The Chinese slumped to the ground, blood oozing from his mouth and nostrils. McCarter hit him again and followed the man to the ground. The Briton raised his fist, but Katz blocked his wrist with the hooks of his prosthesis.

"That's enough," Katz told him. "We don't have time for this."

"He started it," the Briton muttered as he gathered up his Ingram.

The Israeli and McCarter headed for the side door to the main house. Calvin James fired his M-16 at several TRIO hoodlums in the parade field. Two Chinese gunmen collapsed, and the others retreated to the cover of the warehouse.

"No way, fellas," the black warrior growled as he aimed the M-203 grenade launcher and squeezed the trigger.

The 40 mm projectile hurtled into the warehouse and exploded. The building burst apart, and the roof and walls crashed down on the unlucky TRIO henchmen. James jogged to the side door and followed his partners into the main house.

THE OTHER MEMBERS of the assault force were attacked by a group of TRIO killers at the east wing of the main house. Rafael Encizo and John Trent bolted for cover behind a truck parked near the wall. Gary Manning and the two KGB agents were forced to simply drop to the ground and return fire from a prone position.

Automatic fire sizzled above the Canadian and his Russian companions. Manning aimed and fired his FAL, pumping a 7.62 mm round dead center in the heart of the nearest gunman. Vladimir Savchenko triggered his Sterling submachine gun at the enemy, and Rafael Encizo hit them with a volley of Heckler and Koch missiles from his position at the truck. The deadly cross fire cut down three more TRIO thugs.

Two Asian hoodlums dashed to the truck, seeking shelter on the opposite side of the vehicle from Trent and Encizo. Two other thugs chose to stand their ground and fired at Manning and the two Russians. Bullets raked the ground near the three commandos. Dirt splattered Manning as he triggered the FAL to blast a bullet into the forehead of a TRIO goon.

Savchenko cried out when an enemy bullet struck his left shoulder, shattering bone and cartilege at the joint. Major Vikor Alekseyev fired his Sterling and chopped a column of 9 mm rounds across the kneecaps of a TRIO gunman. The man shrieked and fell forward to receive another burst of Sterling slugs through the top of his skull.

Encizo knelt by the truck and peered beneath it. He saw the legs of the two TRIO thugs on the opposite side of the vehicle. The Cuban poked the barrel of his MP-5 under the truck and squeezed the trigger. Parabellums crashed into the ankles and shins of the Asian triggermen. One TRIO flunky screamed and fell to the ground. Encizo nailed him with three bullets in the chest.

The remaining gunman managed to hop to the rear of the vehicle, his right ankle shattered by a 9 mm round. He leaned against the truck and tried to decide what to do next.

The man did not live long enough to make up his mind. John Trent suddenly appeared behind him. The ninja's sword swooped down and sliced the hoodlum's neck from cartoid to windpipe. He tumbled to the ground, blood gushing from his gashed flesh.

Manning and Alekseyev dragged Lieutenant Savchenko to the shelter of the truck. The Canadian ripped open Savchenko's shirt to examine the wound. The depth of the bullet puncture and the bloodied flesh made Manning shudder. Savchenko gasped, his body dripping sweat. Alekseyev took a standard first-aid kit from his belt and placed a field dressing on the wound.

"Oh'edit'ih!" Savchenko ground out through clenched teeth. *"Palzhali'sta, oh'edit'ih!"*

"What's he saying?" Manning asked, checking his own first-aid kit, wishing James was with them.

"He's telling us to leave him," Alekseyev translated.

"Like hell," Manning replied. "If TRIO finds him here, he'll be defenseless."

"I'll stay with him," Alekseyev declared. "The rest of you better go."

"If you have to move him, you'll probably both get killed," Manning told the major. "You think you can hold TRIO off by using this truck for cover? One grenade or a Molotov cocktail will blow this heap to bits."

"Take this," Encizo urged, handing Manning a plastic syringe. "It's morphine."

"Thanks," the Canadian said with a nod. "You and Collins better go. The major and I will look after Vladimir."

"Good luck," the Cuban said as he turned to find that Trent had already left. Encizo shrugged and headed for the rear of the house.

"You don't have to do this," Alekseyev told Manning.

"That's a matter of opinion, Major," the Canadian replied as he injected the morphine into the wounded Russian officer.

21

Rafael Encizo moved along the side of the house toward the rear of the building. He stiffened when he heard movement at the opposite end of the corner. The Cuban held his H&K subgun ready and waited for the enemy to appear.

The sound of something striking a solid object was followed by a soft groan and a startled gasp. A shape fell forward. Encizo stared down at the dead Asian. The shaft of an arrow jutted from the base of his skull.

Think I found Trent, he thought as he stepped around the corner.

Two TRIO henchmen stood at the rear of the house. Their backs were turned to Encizo as they aimed their weapons at the wall surrounding the compound, scanning the area for the archer who had killed their comrade. Encizo stepped behind the closest opponent and slammed the side of his hand at the base of the man's neck. The guy dropped like a stone from a fifth-story window.

The remaining hoodlum started to turn toward Encizo. A blurred missile streaked through the air. The arrow struck the TRIO goon in the neck. The sharp point jutted from one side, and the feathered shaft extended from the other. Blood squirted from both entrance and exit wounds around the arrow. The man dropped his weapon and fell lifeless to the ground.

Trent climbed down from the wall, aluminum bow still in his fist. The American discarded the bow as he jogged toward Encizo. The Cuban noticed a door at the rear of the building. He aimed his MP-5 at the door as Trent approached.

"Is this where they came from?" Encizo asked.

"Yes," Trent confirmed. "I thought it best to take them out silently. They seemed to be exploring the area. Like scouts sent to see about danger."

"So, somebody might get curious," Encizo remarked, moving to the door.

The Cuban and the ninja stood to one side of the door and waited. A few seconds later the door creaked open. Encizo quickly grabbed it and shoved the barrel of his MP-5 through the gap. The muzzle jabbed flesh. A voice grunted, and Encizo squeezed the trigger. Three 9 mm rounds burned into the torso of the unfortunate TRIO flunky at the door.

Encizo shoved the door wide open and jumped back as Trent hurled a *metsubushi* across the threshold. Flash powder ignited and pepper spewed. Voices cried out and coughed, then uttered choking noises.

The Cuban fired a quick volley of 9 mm rounds through the doorway and charged across the threshold, trampling the corpse of the man who had opened the door. He entered a laboratory with two long tables stacked with glass beakers, racks of test tubes and other equipment Encizo did not recognize. An obese Asian clad in a white lab smock stood near a table with a beaker in his trembling hands. Another figure lay on the floor, his clothes stained by bloodied bullet holes in his chest.

"Drop guns!" the frightened lab technician cried in a high-pitched voice. "I have formula here! VL-800! I throw on floor!"

"There's no lid on that beaker, fella," Encizo said, pointing his subgun at the man's face. "I heard VL-800 is lethal when inhaled. I'm calling your bluff, shithead."

The lab tech dropped the flask as he quickly raised his hands in surrender. Trent crossed the room to a closed door, his Colt Commander held ready. Encizo gestured with the barrel of his H&K, urging the lab tech to face a wall.

"Spread-eagle," Encizo ordered, but he realized the Asian did not understand. "Put your hands on the wall and spread your legs. Understand?"

Trent hastily repeated the command in Chinese. The lab tech obeyed. Encizo frisked the guy, found no weapons and used a set of riot cuffs to bind the Asian's wrists together at the small of his back. The Cuban poked the muzzle of his MP-5 behind the lab guy's ear.

"You know about the VL-800 formula, so you know why we're here," Encizo declared. "Where is it? I won't ask twice."

"Chou Minchuan take formula," the chemist replied quickly. "He just here with Akira Osato. They take formula. This is very true."

"Where did Chou and Osato go?" Encizo asked.

"That way," the lab man said, jerking his head toward Trent. "Out the door. Somewhere in house."

"How are they carrying the formula?" the Cuban asked urgently.

"In boxes," the Asian replied. "*Syau-syang'dz.* I do not know the English word—"

"Suitcases," Trent translated. "They're carrying the formula in suitcases."

"Okay, pal," Encizo told the chemist. "If you're lying to us, we'll be back to carve you into fish food. If you're telling the truth, we'll see if we can convince the authorities to go easy on you."

"I tell you very true," the lab man insisted.

"We'll see," the Cuban remarked as he shoved the chemist into a chair. "Just stay put and you'll stay healthy."

Encizo and John Trent opened the door and entered a narrow corridor. Two TRIO thugs, poised in the hall with weapons in hand, turned to face the Phoenix commando and the American ninja. Encizo's MP-5 rattled a violent burst of 9 mm slugs that ripped one hood from breastbone to forehead. The other goon dropped to one knee and raised a Browning automatic. Trent's Colt snarled, and the man's face exploded.

A cluster of fourteen TRIO gangsters had assembled in the main hall. Chou Minchuan and Akira Osato were among the group. Both TRIO subchiefs carried aluminum suitcases; so did their lieutenants. All the tong and yakuza hoodlums held a firearm except Osato, who carried his *katana* in one fist and a suitcase in the other. The yakuza boss was an exceptional kendo expert, and he valued his samurai sword too highly to leave it behind.

Three more tong gunsels were stationed in the upstairs hallway. The TRIO hoods had been concentrating on the outside of the house. They suddenly realized the assault team had managed to enter the building and swung their weapons toward the mouth of the corridor where Encizo and Trent lurked.

Suddenly Katz, McCarter and James emerged from the kitchen and opened fire on the TRIO congregation. The Israeli and British warriors hosed the gangsters in the main hall with 9 mm hail while Calvin James trained his M-16 on the three hoods upstairs. A hoodlum fell against a banister and toppled over the top to crash to the floor below. Another caught a 5.56 mm slug in the bridge of the nose and fell dead in the upstairs hall. The third member of the upstairs reception committee managed to retreat into a bedroom, dragging a bullet-gouged leg.

The gangsters in the main hall did not fare any better. Parabellum projectiles knifed through their torsos and blasted skulls open. Encizo and Trent contributed to the firepower, trapping the enemy in a murderous cross fire. The Cuban drew his 9 mm Model 59 pistol to shoot at the men carrying the suitcases, fearful that the indiscriminate fury of a full-auto weapon might punch rounds through the aluminum containers and release the VL-800 formula.

Chou Minchuan's lieutenant fell against his boss, the side of his head blasted away. The tong subchief cried out in terror when his pet goon's brains splashed across his face. The Chinese gangster dropped his suitcase, grabbed the knob to the front door and yanked it open. Chou bolted outside, followed by two other Black Serpent Tong followers.

Trent pumped a .45 slug into the center of Osato's top henchman's chest. The Japanese thug released his pistol and clutched the suitcase to his breast as if hoping to shield himself from more bullets. As he fell to his knees, the yakuza realized it was already too late. He felt his life rapidly slide from his body. The hoodlum bowed his head and died.

Akira Osato dropped to one knee and fumbled with the combination lock to his suitcase. As bullets continued to scream all around him and his comrades shrieked and fell, the yakuza leader could not remember the code. He had it written on a notepad in the pocket of his kimono. But there wasn't time for that, Osato thought as he pulled his Nambu pistol from shoulder leather. A single 9 mm round through the metal skin of the suitcase would release the formula just as quickly.

The corpse of a TRIO hoodlum toppled into Osato. The impact knocked him to the floor. The suitcase slid away, and the Nambu slipped from his fingers. Osato clutched the scabbard of his samurai sword and sat up.

The shooting had ceased. The bodies of TRIO hoodlums were sprawled across the hall. Katz, McCarter and James advanced from one side of the room while Encizo and Trent approached from the other. Osato slowly rose, holding his head high, determined to die with dignity.

"Put down the sword," Katz ordered. "It's over."

Osato ignored him. The yakuza's attention was fixed on John Trent. The American ninja sighed and handed his Colt Commander to Rafael Encizo. The Cuban shook his head.

"Come on, John," Encizo muttered, but he took the pistol. "You don't have to do it."

"Look at him," Trent replied. "You know what he wants as well as I do."

"You don't have to give it to him," the Cuban stated.

"Anata-wa ninja desuka?" Osato inquired, glaring at Trent.

"Hai," he replied in Japanese. "Yes, I am ninja."

"If you are ninja," Osato said as he smiled, resting his hand on the hilt of his *katana*, "come prove it. I ask you to honor me with battle, so I may die as a samurai."

"I accept," Trent replied with a nod. "Ninja enjoy killing samurai."

Osato's features hardened. He drew the long, curved blade from its scabbard and grasped the hilt in both fists. The yakuza raised the sword overhead and poised the handle at the top of his skull. Trent's right hand rested on the hilt of his *ninja-do*, but he did not draw his sword.

"Calvin," Katz turned to James and McCarter. "Three TRIO bolted out the door. Make sure they don't get away."

"Right," James said with a nod. "Uh...you sure one of us shouldn't shoot the dude with the sword?"

"Trent agreed to fight him," the Israeli replied. "It's his business. John can probably take him, and if he can't, we'll intervene."

"Okay," James agreed with a shrug. He headed for the kitchen to use the side door.

"David, Rafael," Katz continued. "Don't pay too much attention to the sword fight. Some of these bastards might be playing possum. I'm going upstairs to check the rooms. Either of you two want to come with me?''

''I'm coming,'' McCarter replied.

The Israeli and the Briton jogged up the stairs. Trent and Osato hardly noticed. The yakuza was still poised in his aggressive fighting stance, waiting for Trent to draw his sword. The ninja seemed calm as he waited for his opponent to make the first move.

Encizo tried to pay more attention to the surrounding TRIO bodies—none of whom appeared to be alive—than to the duel, but the tension was gnawing at the Cuban's gut. He watched Osato shuffle forward, moving in small, quick steps. Trent shuffled backward, keeping the distance between them roughly eight feet.

Osato jerked his elbows as if to deliver a sword stroke, trying to startle Trent into drawing his weapon. The yakuza realized his opponent was trying to lure him into a trap of some sort and that he was trying to bait Trent into revealing his strategy. The ninja, however, refused to oblige.

''Come, ninja,'' Osato hissed, clearly annoyed. ''Come and fight, you coward.''

Trent did not reply. He moved backward and stepped over a corpse. Osato decided his opponent would be off-balance for a split second and decided to attack. He shouted a *kiai* and charged, slashing the *katana* at Trent's head.

The ninja's sword bolted from the scabbard in a fast, rising stroke. Steel sang against steel as Trent's blade blocked the *katana*. He held the *ninja-do* in his right hand, but stepped to the side with his left foot to keep his distance from the yakuza's blade. His left hand suddenly moved from the small of his back and lashed out with the *manri-kigusari*.

The chain struck Osato. A weighted end whirled around the yakuza's limbs, wrapping steel links around the man's wrists, pinning them to the hilt of his own *katana*. Osato tried to pull away, but Trent's sword struck like razor-sharp lightning. The edge of his *ninja-do* sliced Osato across the throat. Trent's body moved with the cut. He released the *manrikigusari*, pivoted and grabbed the handle of his sword with both hands. He completed the turn to face Osato, his *ninja-do* raised.

Trent struck again. The sword aplit Osato's face open from the crown of his head to his jawbone. The yakuza fell to the floor, crimson jetting from the terrible, deep wounds. His body twitched slightly and lay still.

"Cristo," Encizo whispered. He looked away from the ghastly corpse. "Hey, John? Is it considered fair play to use another weapon during a Japanese sword duel?"

"He wanted to fight a ninja," Trent replied as he snapped his wrist to flick blood from the blade of his sword. "That is how ninja fight."

KATZ AND McCARTER searched the rooms upstairs. They found the man James had shot in the leg. The hood had passed out on a bedroom floor. McCarter knelt by the unconscious thug and cuffed his hands behind his back. Katz watched the doorway while his partner secured the bonds.

"Yaaiii!" Temujin screamed, charging from the hallway with a pistol in his fist.

The Mongol had waited in his quarters, aware the battle was already lost when the raid had reached its zenith. He realized that trying to find the formula would be a waste of time. Chou and Osato would already have it. He knew they would blame him for the failure of the mission and probably shoot him on sight. So Temujin had waited for the opportunity to extract his own private revenge.

There was a major problem with his plan. Temujin ran straight for Yakov Katzenelenbogen, who already had an Uzi held ready. The Israeli triggered his weapon. The last two rounds from the magazine blasted Temujin in the upper chest. The impact spun the Mongol around. His pistol fell, but Temujin immediately reached for his combat dagger.

There was no time to reload the Uzi or even draw the SIG Sauer P-226 from shoulder leather. So Katz charged his opponent, holding the Uzi like a bar in front of his chest. He crashed into Temujin as the Mongol drew his knife. The steel frame of the subgun hit hard, driving the TRIO fanatic into the hall.

Katz stayed with his opponent and swung a boot between Temujin's legs. The Mongol groaned in agony but still struck out with the knife. Sharp steel cut Katz's left forearm. He dropped the empty Uzi and jumped back, blood trickling from the wounded limb.

"I'll get the bastard," McCarter offered, trying to aim his Browning at Temujin.

"Stay out of this!" Katz said crossly as he adopted a T-dachi karata stance, the steel hooks of his prosthesis held at chest level while his left hand was poised at his hip.

Temujin coughed. A glob of blood spilled from his lips. Yet the Mongol's lips twisted into a deranged smile as he lunged with the knife. Katz swung his right arm. The prosthesis struck the knife blade and parried the stroke. Katz's left hand delivered a spearhand thrust. The tips of stiff fingers stabbed into the nerve cluster under Temujin's arm. His fist opened, and the dagger dropped to the floor.

Katz stomped a boot to the side of Temujin's right kneecap. The Mongol cried out and fell on all fours. Katz clamped the tri-hooks of his prosthesis to the nape of his opponent's neck and applied pressure. The steel grip tightened forcibly. Flesh tore, muscles were pulverized and vertebrae crunched. Temujin's body trembled for a moment, then abruptly ceased. Katz released the Mongol and allowed the corpse to fall face down on the floor.

Calvin James and Major Alekseyev carried the senseless figure of Lieutenant Savchenko through the front door. Gary Manning followed. Katz sighed with relief, glad to see all his Phoenix Force team had survived the raid. Then he frowned when he recalled his instructions to James. He moved to the head of the stairs and watched James examine Savchenko.

"What about the three men who ran out of here?" Katz called down to James.

"I was told they're no problem," the black warrior replied. "Vladimir needs help, so we brought him inside—"

"What happened to the TRIO fugitives?" Katz insisted.

"I saw them head toward the helicopter," Gary Manning replied.

The roar of explosion outside startled everyone except the Canadian demolitions expert. Manning could not resist a smile of satisfaction.

"Sounds like they *almost* got it off the ground," he concluded.

22

Phoenix Force, John Trent, the two KGB agents and a handful of disgruntled TRIO hoodlums who had survived the battle, waited by the shore. The conning tower of the *Manta* broke the surface of the South China Sea. The submarine gradually emerged to display the great gray hump of the turtleback. Even the prisoners seemed relieved when the submarine appeared.

"Major," Katz began. "Will you do the honors?"

"Of course," Vikor Alekseyev replied as he aimed his flare gun at the sky and squeezed the trigger.

The projectile shot into the clouds and exploded in a brilliant red glare. A cheer from the crew of the *Manta* reached the men on the island. Alekseyev glanced down at the four metal suitcases containing the VL-800 formula.

"Mission worked out pretty well, Mr. Gray," he commented, "or whatever your name really is. It has been a pleasure and an honor to work with you. It's a pity we have to be enemies."

"Are we enemies, Vikor?" Katz inquired.

"You and I?" Alekseyev smiled. "No, no, we'll never really be enemies. We might have to kill each other in the future, but we'll never be enemies."

"I understand," Katz said, laughing. "Strange business, isn't it? How many other people talk about killing their friends and they don't take it personally?"

"With luck, I'll be assigned to Moscow after this," the KGB officer commented. "They're supposed to promote me to full colonel, you know."

"Congratulations," Katz replied.

"Well, the Kremlin might be a bit upset when they learn Vladimir defected," Alekseyev sighed.

"What?" Katz blinked with surprise.

"I heard him talk about it when he was under the influence of morphine," the KGB agent explained. "Lieutenant Vladimir Savchenko plans to head for the American embassy to seek political asylum."

"Are you going to let him?" the Israeli asked.

"I guess I should shoot him or something," Alekseyev said with a shrug. "But I won't. He'll be going to a hospital when we get back to Hong Kong, and from there he can defect without my knowledge. Best for all of us that way. The Kremlin can't blame me for that. I might not make full colonel, but I'll still get a promotion and a few other considerations."

"I hope so," Katz said sincerely. "You're a good man. I hope things go well for you."

"For you, too, Mr. Gray," the Russian said with a nod. He reached into a pocket and removed an ornate cigarette lighter. "I want you to have this."

"Thank you," Katz replied, accepting the gift.

"There's a miniature camera built into it," Alekseyev admitted. "I took some photographs of you and your men after you removed the masks when we reached Hong Kong. I was going to give them to the KGB Information Section of the Foreign Operations Department, but I'll tell them I lost the camera. The film is still in it."

"I see," Katz said with a nod.

"Nothing personal about taking those pictures—"

"I understand," Katz said, smiling as he offered his own lighter to Alekseyev. "Believe me, I understand."

"You too?" Alekseyev laughed as he took the lighter-camera.

"Film is still in it," the Phoenix Force commander assured him.

Both men smiled. Each closed his fist around a lighter, cocked back his arm and hurled the miniature surveillance devices into the sea.